A WOMAN ALONE

Jeanne watched the passengers returning around departure time. Most of them boarded and went directly to their cabins; a few strolled on deck or waited around, as Jeanne did, to watch the cast-off procedures. Strolling musicians stood on the pier, beautifully singing a lovely but terribly sad song. It was as if the whole island were heartbroken to see the *Liberty* leave its shore. Illogically, Jeanne began to cry. It was too beautiful, too right. It made her believe that no one was to blame for her misfortunes—not her father, Bill, Gordon, not even herself. Above all, not the world. The world was benevolent and lovely, and Jeanne felt all alone in it. She returned to her cabin, sobbing. . . .

(Cover photograph posed by professional model)

Ventures

KATHARINE HOWARD

Book Margins, Inc.

A BMI Edition

Published by special arrangement with Dorchester
Publishing Co., Inc.

Printed in the United States of America.

Ventures

one

Kevin Oliver strained to hear voices coming from the living room. They were familiar voices: the angry bark of his father, the gruff rumble of his grandfather, his grandmother's kindly whine.

"Illegal . . . " was a word Kevin recognized. Grandma had said it. "Mentally unfit," were words that rose above the general whisper. Dad had spit them out.

Everything in his grandparent's apartment was huge, out of scale with Kevin's eight-year-old size. The ceilings were too high, the bedrooms too vast, the furniture too massive. Even the view—looking west across Central Park, across cold lights on paths and walkways to the warm incandescence in old towers of the West Side—seemed larger than life. Like the view from a plane.

The oversized world was amplifying Kevin's anxiety, taking him to the brink of tears. He had a feeling that it was too dark there in the guest room; he slipped off the edge of the king-sized bed and tip-toed to the corner desk to turn on its light. This put him closer to the door.

"She needs help, damn it. You know she won't listen to me, but if all of you will get behind—'' That was Dad.

"Keep your voice lower, Bill," a new voice insisted. Kevin felt sure that this was Uncle Alan. If it was, the situation was improving. Maybe the problem would be solved, now that his mother's wise and kind and funny and loving brother was here to help.

"You're all underestimating her. Jeanne knows what she's doing." Yes, it was Uncle Alan! Kevin listened acutely, scarcely breathing, to hear his mother answer Alan's remark. But she did not answer. She wasn't there.

It was all happening again! The whispered meetings about his mother, meetings he was not allowed to attend. Last time this happened, the police had made it wrong for Kevin to live with his mother. And the time before that, they had made it wrong for Mother and Dad to live together. What could they do to him this time?

It never occurred to Kevin that anyone could want to hurt or frighten him deliberately; yet they did hurt and frighten.

One of Kevin's books was there on the desk, laid open—as he had left it—under the cone of light coming from a desk lamp. A book about exploring outer space. Astronauts. The eerie and enticing surface of the moon. Otherworldliness. Kevin tried to shift his attention from what was going on in the living room to what was going on in outer space. He almost succeeded.

"I could have killed that guy," said Kevin's father.

Then Grandpa grumbled something about " . . . irreparable psychological damage to the child." Whatever that meant.

"I don't think so," said Uncle Alan; "not necessarily."

"Of course not," soothed Grandma. "Everything will be all right. Soon, too. We just need time to—"

"Adele, have you lost all sense of propriety?" Grandpa demanded.

Uncle Alan chuckled. "It's time she did."

Kevin began to feel drawn to the living room as if by a magnet. Hunched up on the desk chair and sitting on his feet, he leaned, his ear leading the way, toward the door. One leg pulled out from under him and the foot touched the floor. Almost without thinking, he found himself in the hall—where bright lights and clear sounds came from the living room beyond the Romanesque archway at the end.

"I wish you wouldn't treat this so lightly, son." Grandpa said earnestly to Uncle Alan.

"I can treat it lightly," Alan answered, "because I'm not worried. Well, not worried about Jeanne. I am a bit afraid that you people will go off half-cocked and make matters worse. I'm sorry, Dad, but that's the way I feel."

Kevin could see them all reflected in the glass of a framed watercolor landscape. He could see the painting, too; and the group in the living room seemed to be combined with it, having a picnic seated under yellow-green willows in a meadow on a bright summer's day.

"I think we ought to call the police," said Grandpa.

"That's what I mean," said Uncle Alan.

"Why do that? Leave the poor girl alone!"

Kevin watched Grandma in the pastoral reflection. She rose from her place and lifted the phone from the corner table. "I thought I'd try once more," she said.

Kevin edged forward. He stopped half-in and half-out of the room, where he could hear, dimly, the sound of the phone's unanswered rings coming from the receiver Grandma held.

"She still doesn't answer," Grandma said.

Alan shook his head and snorted. "Because she isn't there," he said.

"It's Jeanne's confounded irresponsibility that upsets me most," Grandpa said. "She's wandering around in a daze, not realizing that every thing she does, every move she makes, affects lives other than her own."

"Don't you think professional help is what she needs?" Kevin's father asked.

Uncle Alan got angry at that. "What the hell are you up to Bill? What are you trying to prove? I know damn well you'd see her fall completely to pieces before you'd let her go to a psychiatrist! They're all quacks, you told me once. So what do you really mean by 'professional help?'" Alan got to his feet, smoldering. "You've already had her declared incompetant, in effect. What more do you want?"

"Alan," Grandpa said firmly, "sit down. Now Jeanne *has* changed. And it has to be more than her attraction for that Strand person. The court suggested she seek guidance, too. A year ago, she was stable, directed, a competent mother who always thought first of her family, her husband, her child. Now look at her: she's off somewhere without so much as a word, completely unconcerned that she has us all worried sick, oblivious to what her impressionable child might think of her behavior. Clearly she needs *some* kind of help."

Uncle Alan said, as if thinking out loud: "Maybe she told Gordon Strand where she was going."

"I forbid you to call him," said Grandpa.

"You can't believe Jeanne would go back to him!" Kevin's father said, more shocked than angry.

Nothing more was said for awhile. Kevin stood where he felt sure he would not be seen. His mind was whirling, his thoughts tumbling over one another, as he endeavored to understand what he was hearing. Why was everything in there so large? The ceiling was high—like a hotel lobby Kevin had seen once—and the chandelier was like a crystal Christmas tree hanging there upside down. The big black piano was as big as one of Grandpa's cars.

"If she's back with Strand," Kevin's father said, " I will kill him."

Kevin gasped. His father had said that so quietly and matter-of-factly that it had to be believed.

"Kevin?" Grandma called out tentatively.

"Come here, boy." his father demanded roughly. Kevin shuffled into the living room where the lights were bright and there were giant people.

"I told you to stay in your room!" his father

barked.

"It isn't polite to listen to other people's conversations," Grandma said sweetly, so sweetly that it almost went unheard under the blast from his father. But somehow the kindliness came through and reminded Kevin of his mother, triggering the tears he had been holding back.

"Be a big boy," Grandpa said with military authority: "stop that blubbering."

In Kevin's world, he had felt obliged to learn to read subtleties, vibrations, and now he was particularly sensitized. He caught, out of the corner of his eye, the glance Grandpa had given Dad; it was disapproving, as if to say "What kind of sissy are you raising, Bill?" And there was a knowing smile on Dad's lips, and a shrug, as if he were denying responsibility for the unsatisfactory way Kevin was turning out. The shrug also seemed to blame this problem, like everything else, on Mother. All of that went by in a flash in Kevin's mind and made him grit his teeth to stop tearing.

Kevin felt a large hand on the back of his neck; it squeezed affectionately, and Kevin knew it was Uncle Alan without even having to look up. Tears welled up again, and Kevin tipped his head down to hide them.

"Let's go have a talk," Alan suggested to the eight-year-old. He suggested it respectfully, as he'd have spoken to an adult.

Kevin knew that his nod was felt by Alan's hand, that no words had to be said.

"I'm not doing any good here," Alan said to his mother, Kevin's Grandma. "Don't let 'em do anything we'll all regret," he requested. It was obvious to Kevin that Alan trusted her judgement more than anyone else's in the room. Kevin smiled: he felt that way about *his* mother, too.

* * *

Grandpa, Gilbert Mason, watched disapprovingly as his son carried his grandson from the room. Alan had tossed Kevin over his shoulder like a sack of potatoes. "An awesome, awesome thing," Mason muttered, "guiding a growing mind." He shook his head. "Perhaps it's as well that Alan hasn't a family. He would spoil them unforgivably. I don't understand how he managed to turn out as he has. He's nothing like either of us, Adele. Neither is Jeanne."

Adele Mason smiled a trifle sadly. "They seem to have preferred to raise themselves. Or raise each other, I've never known which." She added, trying to up her husband's spirits a bit, "I agree they're not very much like us Gilbert, but they're good people, and not so very mysterious."

"I used to assume they were good people," Gilbert muttered. "When I think of Alan and Jeanne, the image I have is of two gawky teenagers riding bicycles, going to school, learning to dance, being normal kids. I never think of the woman who's left her family in disgrace, or the famous man who's living in an openly illicit affair with that actress. They just can't be the same individuals."

13

Adele prodded gently. "Think of those gawky teenagers cooking up elaborate schemes to play hookey from church, smuggling questionable literature to each other, and flirting with the, well, the wrong political ideas. Remember the time Alan got stuck in the mountains where he'd gone fossil hunting alone. We thought for sure he was dead, but he came bounding in a day later with some exciting discovery that outweighed the danger he'd been in. You may not know this, Gilbert, but our daughter lost her virginity with her cousin, Tommy, when she was fourteen. That young. When I found out, she said she wished she had done it sooner."

Gilbert was about to express alarm when he remembered: "Alan learned about sex with a high-school girl—when he was twelve."

"See," Adele suggested, "they're not so inconsistent." She stepped to the telephone again. "Perhaps Philip Pomeranz knows where she's gone. . . . " Adele dialed a number and waited. "He doesn't answer." She dialed Jeanne's number again, waited a longtime, then replaced the receiver.

"Why would she tell Philip anything?" Bill Oliver asked. "He's just the family lawyer, right?"

"Oh, that, and a very old family friend." Adele said, a shade cryptically as if there were other reasons she would rather not mention—even to her husband and son-in–law.

"What do you suppose Alan is telling Kevin?" Bill wondered aloud.

"Too much, undoubtedly," Gilbert said.

14

"Well, it's time somebody told the boy *something*," Adele said, expressing indignation politely.

There was nothing more that needed to be said. They waited for the phone to ring and listened to the faint sounds of traffic on Fifth Avenue twenty-five floors below them, and to the occasional remote whine of the jetliners that bisected Manhattan on their approach to LaGuardia Airport.

Music erupted from the guest room.

"Good God," Gilbert Mason complained; "they're playing records."

Adele smiled abstractedly; Bill continued to stare blankly at the phone.

* * *

Kevin had placed the needle with unerring accuracy on the lead groove, and his narrated version of *The Nutcracker* had begun its familiar music. He was still standing on the chair he had needed to reach the phonograph atop the high chest of drawers; his head was almost level with his uncle's. "Turn it down?"

"I think it's a bit loud, yes. We don't want to have to yell at each other."

The picture of the two of them shouting amused Kevin; he chuckled as he turned the sound lower.

"You know what arithmetic is?" Alan asked him.

"Sure. Two plus two equals four."

"Do you know what algebra is?"

15

"It's something else you do with numbers, isn't it?" He jumped to the floor. Kevin had never wondered why, but he knew Uncle Alan was the only adult—counting his father, his grandparents, his teachers, everyone he knew—besides his mother, with whom he could speak without fear of disapproval. Even when Alan was angry at him, it was clear that Kevin had merely done something wrong, and not that something was wrong with him. Kevin plopped onto the bed and faced his uncle, who was sitting comfortably at the desk chair. "I think they study algebra in junior high."

"Does this make sense to you?" Alan asked, tossing a sheet of paper on which he had scribbled: "$a + b = c$."

"Does that mean that d plus e equals f, and g plus h equals i?"

Alan shook his head. "The letters stand for numbers, just about any numbers you want them to. Algebra is a kind of short cut you can learn to use only after you know all there is to know about arithmetic." Alan smiled. "It's that way with understanding people, too. First you learn the basics, then you can go on to the more complicated things. Can you guess what I'm going to say next?"

Kevin groaned. "Yeah. That I'm too young to understand about what happened with Mom and Dad and Mr. Strand and everything, and I'll understand when I grow up." Alan laughed delightedly. "If I'd been as smart as you are when I was your age—"

"Mother told me you didn't want to have any

16

children. Is that true?"

"Oh, I'm not sure I *never* want kids. Not for a while anyway. But back to arithmetic. I tricked you a bit; I wasn't going to say, 'Wait till you grow up,' I was going to say, 'You can't handle the algebra of the situation now, but the basics, the arithmetic, ought to be easy enough. I'll tell you whatever I can."

"Can't you teach me the algebra about understanding people?"

"Not really. That's one of the things people have to teach themselves as they go along. Get me going, Kevin; tell me what you know about the court trials and everything."

Alan Mason stretched, crossed his ankles, and listened to the boy's simplified, but essentially accurate, rendition of a sequence of events that included infidelity, discovery, an unfriendly divorce proceeding, a custody hearing, and now this new trouble. Alan watched and listened with total sympathy but no pity—as if he were saying to the boy: "Yes this is bad, but you can get through it just fine, because you're strong enough." Alan was struck, as he often was, by the similarities between himself and his nephew. Not only did the child remind Alan of himself at the same age—brainy, a bit fragile, vulnerable—they even looked alike; but both had the Mason dark hair, olive skin, and blue eyes . . . from a real American-melting-pot hodgepodge of ethnic stocks.

Kevin ended with the question Alan expected: "Where is my mother?"

"I honestly don't know, but I'm not worried

17

like the others are. Look at it from her point of view, Kevin. If you had discovered that you didn't really like the person you'd been married to for ten years, that there was someone you liked much better, that there were reasons why you could never love that new someone, that the whole world seemed to disapprove of everything you were doing, that the courts were keeping you from ever living with your own child—whom you loved more than anyone on Earth, that it wasn't even certain that your parents loved you anymore . . . well, where would you be?"

Kevin was thoughtful, wide-eyed, but not ready with an answer.

"I believe," Alan said, "that if I were your mother, I'd just go away—leave all of those problems behind and just go off somewhere to be alone and have time to think it out, time to understand it all."

"You mean she doesn't understand it either?"

"I seriously doubt it."

"Uncle Alan, is Mr. Strand a criminal?"

"No. Did anyone tell you he was?"

"It's the way everybody acts. But I always liked him."

"I sort of like him, too, kid; and I know he thinks the world of you."

"Can courts be wrong?"

"You mean, can they make mistakes in their judgment? Oh indeed they can, Kevin. They're just there to enforce the laws, and they can be wrong about how to inforce them; or the laws

18

themselves can be wrong. I think they're wrong about a lot of all this.''

''It must be horrible to learn that you've married the wrong person. Is that why you and Margaret won't get married?''

''Uh—probably partly that. We know we care for each other, but we're not quite sure we want to . . . hey, what subject are we talking about, anyway? Save that for some other time, when you're about thirty years older.''

Kevin giggled knowingly.

The first side of the record ended, the arm rejected, and the room was quieter.

''The court said I have to live with my Dad. Were they wrong about that?'' Kevin had begun his question easily enough, but during the short time of it tears had polished his eyes. Alan knew the boy had tried to sound off-hand about something of crucial importance.

''I think they were wrong, Kevin. You and your Dad don't get along very well, do you?'' Kevin shook his head timidly.

''Would you . . . would you like to come and visit me and Margaret for a while? Nothing permanent, but—''

''Yes! At your penthouse? I'd love to!''

''Uh—don't say anything to your father or grandparents yet. I'll have to handle this thing very diplomatically.''

''Diplomatically?''

''Without hurting anybody's feelings—if I can.'' Alan spied the children's book on space exploration beside him on the desk; he tossed it onto the bed by Kevin. ''Here, dream up a plan for your poor mother; imagine she's off to Mars where a great oracle at a relaxation spa can help her learn how to start life all over again without changing any of the good things. I've got to get back to that gang of misguided loved ones in the parlor—to make sure they haven't brought in the FBI, the CIA and Mr. Keen, tracer of lost persons. Don't worry, Kevin, things will begin to look up pretty soon.''

* * *

Philip Pomeranz found a parking place rather easily on Bleecker, around the corner from the studio-gallery of Gordon Strand. His sleek gray Chrysler looked too elegant for the block of weatherbeaten older cars and an occasional new VW. And he—dressed in a gray business suit, his tie loosened but still in place—looked incongruous walking the famous Greenwich Village street among the casually and skimpily clad NYU students, hippies, obvious gays, and tourists.

Philip hesitated at the door to Gordon's studio. The place looked straightforward and more respectable than most such shops and galleries along this stretch of ancient brownstone buildings in the Village. There was a single display window in which were hung several appealing pen-and-ink sketches of New York streets and a large oil canvas showing a piece of an old rotten pier, probably in the Hudson River somewhere, with the glistening spires of Manhattan piercing a background fog. All of these framed items were signed "Strand" and were marked "For Sale." The door sign said "Closed," but there was light coming from somewhere in the back of the store, and a radio playing.

Philip hesitated once more, then rang the doorbell.

More lights came on. The locks on the door were unbolted one at a time.

"Come in, Philip," Gordon said, opening the door.

"Good of you to see me so late," Philip said, entering.

"Us free-lance people have no 'late,' Philip. That's for you lawyer and banker types. May I get you a drink, some coffee, a joint?"

"Scotch?"

"Coming up."

"Soda and ice." Philip watched the tall blond—handsome enough to be an actor or model—deftly mix their drinks. What Philip knew about the man never gibed with what he saw. Worst of all, Philip found that he not only liked but trusted Gordon Strand . . . and that went against all reason. "Gordon, before we talk business, would you mind if I used your phone? I have—"

"Certainly. It's right behind you; second shelf of the bookcase. Want privacy?"

"No. In fact, you should hear this, too." He dialed the Mason residence.

"Is anything wrong? Something about Jeanne?"

Philip nodded. "I'm not sure I'd say 'wrong,'

Gordon, but . . . hello, Adele; this is Philip . . . yes, I know . . . yes, I *have* heard from her. I found a note slipped under my office door when I was leaving this evening. I guess she or a messenger left it, oh, between five and seven . . . the note said that she has moved out of her apartment and is going on a trip, alone. We're not to worry. . . . a week or two, apparently . . . no, she didn't say. That's . . . that's really all I know . . . of course, of course, and you let me know if *you* hear . . . what? . . . hello, Gilbert . . . well, I don't think you ought to try, Gilbert. If she wants to get away for a while, I think you ought to . . . the airlines? Well, unless we bring the police into it, I don't think we could do more than have her paged at the airport and hope she's . . . but she's *not* a missing person, Gilbert . . . all right, I'll see what I can do and call you back.''

"Good for her," Gordon said, when Philip had hung up. "May I see the note?"

"I . . . suppose so," Philip removed it from his breast pocket.

It was scrawled hastily and said:

"This time, Philip, I am writing to my lawyer, not to my old friend. I don't feel that I have friends anymore. Everyone who comes to mind seems either to be someone who has betrayed me, or someone I feel I have betrayed in some way. But my intellect knows better and assumes some might worry. Please be the one to know that I have given up my apartment—it's where Gordon and I were together, and it no longer seems right for me to stay there. My things

22

—what little I have bothered to keep—are in storage. My mind is scrambled, and I no longer know what I want or what is right. I have to get away somewhere alone. I know this makes it sound as if I'm leaving for good, but I suspect that you, or someone, will hear from me within a couple of weeks. If you don't, please don't worry. I'm living with a kind of perpetual anger that keeps me from being too depressed. Jeanne.''

Gordon said haltingly, ''It's nothing I did. It's what I *am* that's hurting her so.''

''I don't think that's true,'' said Philip. ''But of course you have to be the judge of that.''

Gordon seemed to be battling something in his mind. When he next spoke, his manner was confidential but assured. ''Philip, I used to consider myself remarkably well adjusted. I was a homosexual; I knew it; I was content to be something of a loner, never to have a family; and I behaved accordingly. I never expected to hurt anybody, influence anybody.''

Philip interrupted: ''Gordon, you don't need to go into all this with me. I don't blame you for the mess Jeanne got into. I don't think she does either. And my own attitude is pretty much one of live and let live.''

Gordon laughed—at an absurdity not a delight. ''I guess that's why I wanted to tell you. Because I sensed you'd offer a sympathetic ear.'' Gordon saw that Philip was uneasy with the subject. ''One more thing. I want you to know that Jeanne was not just . . . just an experiment for me. We met at a time when she needed someone new and I was disgusted by gay life and thought she was charming and very appealing. I really do care for her . . . quite a lot. I had made up my mind to tell you that even before you got here, because I can think of only one reason why you'd want to see me. You want to buy the portrait, don't you?''

Philip smiled and nodded.

''Why?''

''First of all, it's good art. It's one of the finest examples of portraiture I've ever seen. A good investment. It shows so many aspects of Jeanne Oliver . . . Jeanne Mason, that is. It's almost more like Jeanne than Jeanne is.''

''You're in love with her, aren't you, Philip?''

''No!'' he answered abruptly. He seemed astonished both at the audacity of the question and his own reaction to it. ''I'm practically old enough to be her father! I watched her graduate, marry, give birth to Kevin, live with Bill happily and then not so happily . . . and all the recent unhappiness . . . she's like a member of my own family. I love her, Gordon, but I'm not *romantically* drawn to her. Certainly not.''

Gordon laughed; it was a friendly gesture. ''Whatever you say. Have I the option to cross-examine, Counsellor?''

Philip said weakly, ''I'd rather you didn't.'' He added lightly, both by way of confession and to change the subject. ''What would that do to the price of the portrait—make it higher or lower?''

''I think our haggling will have a certain bibli-

24

cal quality to it, Philip. You know, like the child and the two women claiming to be its mother." He lifted the framed portrait from a slot in the wall-storage rack. "Am I willing to give it up for nothing? Are you willing to squander your whole fortune to have it?"

Philip chuckled. "I suppose that, within reason, you could name your price, Gordon. I'm very eager to have it—even more so now that I've seen it again."

"I honestly don't know how to name a price, Philip. Why don't you just take it for now, on semi-permanent loan. You can . . . well, sometime soon you can make me an offer. I'll tell you in fairness that on the open market, a portrait—even though it's considerably more difficult and time consuming to paint—won't fetch as good a price as, say, a landscape, something more universal. That landscape in the window is currently marked to sell at twelve hundred. And that's a mite high. Also . . . this will give you time to be really sure you want Jeanne's portrait handing on . . . your wife's living room wall."

"No comment on that last notion, But fine, if that's the way you want to handle the sale."

The two men—whom the world would consider very different souls indeed—sat comfortably in each other's presence. When he had finished his drink, Philip declined the offer of a second.

"No thanks. Got to go on home and start phoning airlines offices. I didn't want Gilbert and Adele to get their hopes up, but I probably

25

can find out if she's ticketed on any departing flight.''

"Good luck—"

"Thanks."

"On *not* locating her. She can take care of herself. She's not about to jump off the Brooklyn Bridge."

* * *

The 35,000-ton cruise ship *City of Liberty* quivered gently in her berth at Pier 88 on the Hudson River. The sleek new ocean liner—spotless white with swept-back lines and myriad multi-colored flags—was disembarking the last of its visitors preparatory to early morning departure. "All visitors must go ashore at this time," came the announcement, reverberating through the ship's corridors and out into the blimp-hangar of a terminal building.

A woman ran, struggling with three suitcases, to the terminal ticket desk.

"You just made it," said the agent with an engaging British accent; "but you've no need to rush now. Plenty of time, really."

He tore a leaf from her ticket book and peered over the counter at her suitcases. "Luggage tagged?" He saw that each bore the ship line's tag with her name and cabin number. "We'll take your bags for you. Board by way of gangway two, and have a pleasant voyage, Miss Mason."

As her foot touched the deck of *City of Liberty*, the ship's low, powerful whistle sounded a

26

single long bleat.

A rain of paper streamers exploded in the morning sunlight. The lines of wind-curled paper caught on the gangways that were being swung back into the terminal.

People on land below caught the streamers and held fast to them, as if they might keep the ship from carrying a loved one away.

Choruses of goodbyes burst like the clouds of confetti from decks and from the mobs below on the pier: and a great cheer rose as the faintest movement indicated that the ship was about to pull out.

Jeanne Mason watched impassively for a moment and then walked slowly around to the other side of the ship where there was no such blatant sign of happy life and good cheer. On the other side she found only a few white–uniformed members of the ship's staff.

She leaned against the faintly vibrating rail and watched the stubby hard-working tugs guide the great floating hotel out into the center of the Hudson channel.

While other passengers watched the world-famous Manhattan skyline travel majestically by, Jeanne idly observed the passage of the rusty industrial piers of New Jersey.

As the ship navigated New York Harbor, the crowd moved to Jeanne's side of the ship in anticipation of a near brush with the Statue of Liberty. Jeanne had to move on to find another spot of solitude.

She stopped on a little balcony outside the forward bar, called The Sea Turtle. Ahead the

27

sun was actually rising, but with the forward motion of the ship it seemed to be falling beneath the black silhouette of the towering Verrazano Narrows Bridge.

"You've sailed many times before, I take it," said someone who had approached beside her.

She turned and vaguely noticed a man, a stranger. "No, I—"

"Then the sea itself appeals to you more than the sights connected with the famous city behind us?"

"I—I just came here to get away from the crowds."

"My name is Mark Harris."

"Jeanne turned to face him. She noted, but ignored the fact, that he was an unusually handsome man. "I'm Jeanne Mason. I'm sorry. I'm not very good company right now. Please excuse me."

She left him there, without glancing his way again, and made her way down to her cabin.

A paper caught her eye: a telegram.

Puzzled, she opened it slowly. Jeanne felt sure that no one knew where she was or where she was going. Even if she had known about last night's search in which her parents, her ex-husband, her ex-lover, and her lawyer had participated, she would not have expected a telegram. It said:

"Don't try to forgive yourself. Try to see that there is nothing to forgive. I'll always love you."

It was not signed.

two

Jeanne had meant it precisely, in her note to Philip, when she'd said her mind was scrambled. Ideas, people, events, things—all of it was tumbling around in her head like clothes in a dryer. First one thing would surface then another, then an earlier item would pop up again looking entirely different. A hurricane her mother had barely lived through in Florida. Humiliation by a third-grade teacher. Bill Oliver's naked body. The first time, with Tommy. Kevin's loose tooth. Alan's old shell collection . . . where could it be today? Jeanne opened her eyes and looked ahead:

The sun was high above, its light flashing through cables and booms and machinery on tall masts as the ship lunged gently up one wave and down another. A hint of a rainbow appeared in each fan of sea-water spray that was tossed into the air when the ship's bow cleaved a wave. The sun was hot. The wind was cold. The air smelled uncommonly sweet and fresh.

Already, within hours of departure this first day out, people had shed their day-to-day clothes and donned shorts and tank-tops and deck shoes. Jeanne could hear them laughing and shouting as they threw themselves into shuffleboard, deck tennis, and the like. But here on her little balcony there was no one to disturb her or demand her attention, nothing to disturb her chaotic reminiscence. . . .

Sharon Henson invited Jeanne and Alan to visit her big country house above Westchester. Alan was off horseback riding with some local boys, and Jeanne and Sharon were running and shrieking and playing Indians—down by the stream, out of sight of civilization. . . .

"Indians are supposed to be bare-breasted," Sharon insisted, pulling off her little tee-shirt. She, as yet, had no reason to be self-conscious. Jeanne removed hers, too, and tied it around her waist.

At age nine Jeanne had no breasts either, but she was on the chubby side and could imagine that she had. It was a decadent and exciting thing to imagine.

The girls did their war dance around the stake to which Jeanne's Cindy Doll had been tied. Cindy was the privileged white lass, the daughter of a regimental captain, an unadulterated villainess who wanted to capture Indian braves to make them her slaves.

While Sharon wasn't looking, Jeanne took from her shorts the two matches she had snitched from the kitchen.

"Jeanne! What are you doing?" Sharon yelled, seeing the smoke rising from the make-believe stake that wasn't so make believe any more. Cindy was going up in flames.

Jeanne was amused, delighted at the practical

joke, indifferent to losing her doll, which she was tired of anyway, and a trifle intrigued by the symbolism of destroying the manipulating, helpless, hostile, pampered female she and Sharon had believed Cindy to be.

Sharon, on the other hand, screamed in geniune terror, as if she were witnessing the ritual murder of a living soul.

Sharon and Jeanne were never quite able to be friends after that.

What do you suppose happened to Sharon, Jeanne wondered: did she grow up to be a Cindy Doll?

"Hey, cut that out! It's *my* serve!" someone yelled from a deck court nearby.

"I'm ready to quit for lunch anyway."

Tommy McCall poked Jeanne playfully in the stomach, "The world would never let us get away with it," he said to her dramatically. "Not first cousins. Never first cousins. . . ."

That was probably what had made him seem so exciting, the fact that he was out of reach. And most of what Jeanne had learned of life had come from historical romances . . . at least she fully assumed *they* were truer than Sunday School and more meaningful than tenth-grade biology.

"Why would the world have to know?" she asked, succeeding at sounding as dramatic as he. She rolled slightly in the grass to face him, to be closer. His hand landed, as if by accident, on her thigh. She noticed his mouth fall open in surprise at his own action and her acquiescence and saw his Adam's apple work as he tried to

31

swallow.

"I do like you, Tommy," she said, and she really did. Although she nearly called him Heathcliff. His hand moved up her leg, and she laid her hand on his thigh. And moved it. . . .

Jeanne knew what had become of Tommy McCall. He went to M.I.T. to study physics and married a computer specialist named Judy something.

Tommy was gentle. They made love right there on the back lawn on a summery afternoon. He touched her gently, as if afraid she might break. She explored his body, his shamelessly volunteered sex organs, as timidly. He pushed easily, undemandingly, until her childhood gave way and her woman's body was all his . . . and his body was paradoxically there for no reason but to give her pleasure.

This was Tommy's first time, too. But these were modern youngsters who had read books. And somehow—for those precious moments—they both were fearless. They talked as they explored, and they learned. Her orgasm astounded, alarmed, and amazed them both. They laughed and snuggled close.

Tommy's parents soon took him back to Florida. There were a few scorching letters, then a few friendly ones . . .

I don't think, Jeanne mused, that I'd ever have felt a moment's guilt if that orgasm had not felt so fantastic! Why did sex have to be such an important part of life? Jeanne wondered. It seemed against all sensibility. Maybe the need for it was just an old wives' tale.

Alan always accepted sexuality so matter-of-factly.

"Mr. Pickins," he said, "we're all nearly adults here. You can say what you really mean. You're trying to tell us that masturbation isn't a good idea. But you've surely read the surveys, the psychological reports. You must know that there's not a kid in this Bible class who hasn't masturbated, and that some of us do it rather regularly. So be frank with us. If you think we shouldn't do it, tell us why it's unhealthy. Most experts nowadays think it's a necessary step in one's sexual education, and harmless, generally speaking. . . . "

Alan had been asked to leave the class.

As far as Jeanne could remember, that was the last time he had gone to church—for any reason whatsoever. Not even for weddings and funerals. Funny. Much as she and Alan could talk about practically anything, God was one subject that had never come up between them. She felt sure he no longer believed in a diety—not in any conventional sense at least.

What do I believe? Jeanne wondered.

"That God hath joined together . . . " said her wedding vow.

"So help you, God?" they asked her in court.

" So help me, God," she answered, in something of a daze.

"This is an informal hearing, Mrs. Oliver," the magistrate droned, "yet you must be conscious of being under oath. In this petition for divorce, brought before me by your husband and his attorney, we find convincing evidence in your denial of Mr. Oliver's conjugal rights for extended periods, your first-clandestine and then open affair with an admitted homosexual, Gordon Strand—''

Jeanne interrupted, ''He hadn't admitted that until this proceeding forced him to.''

''Don't interrupt, Mrs. Oliver. We also face your abject abandonment of your husband and child. It is only fair that you be offered a chance—here in court, under oath—to present material in your own defense. Before you speak, I must advise you that you have so far provided Mr. Pomeranz with arguments insufficient, in the Court's opinion, to allow him to conduct a proper defense for you. I'm hoping you can be more persuasive in person than your words seem when presented to the Court by your lawyer. Suppose you begin with your chance meeting with Mr. Strand . . . and let us see the events through *your* eyes. . . .''

The feelings all came back. Standing there on the balcony overlooking the forward deck of the ship, with the water glistening under a cloudless sky, with no land in sight, with her mind and heart away on some alien world and her body here utterly alone . . . still she felt all those powerful emotions that had overwhelmed her in that moment in the courtroom.

How dare you! she wanted to scream. How dare any of you interfere with my life, tell me what to do, threaten to take my boy away!

She wanted to scream. Just stand up and scream. She couldn't see; the profound anger was monopolizing her brain, threatening to ren-

34

der her unconscious. How dare you! she thought obsessively.

"Mrs. Oliver? Do you feel all right?"

Eventually words came. "Your honor," Jeanne said, her voice shaking, "The facts are in the briefs."

That was all she had said, all she *could* say.

The next day, Jeanne Oliver was Jeanne Mason again.

She signed her name that way when she applied for a new Bloomingdale's credit card. It was rejected—Jeanne had no credit established as Miss Mason, only as Mrs. Oliver—until her father co-signed an application. Jeanne concluded, and said to her mother, "Jeanne Mason is a fairly worthless person, isn't she?"

"Don't be ridiculous!" Adele replied, missing the point. "All this will be over soon, and life will go on, you'll see!"

It was that enormous yellow and white Cadillac. Jeanne, dressed in a lacey Easter frock, sat in the back seat with Alan, who looked like a miniature man in his pale beige vested suit. Around them were huge plastic dishes covered with wax paper, sealed with string. One of the parcels was a large open basket of oranges.

"That keeps 'em from getting scurvy," Alan explained softly.

Somehow, this was not a gala occassion—though it ought to have been. They were driving along the beach road, back when the Masons lived for a short time in New Bedford, Connecticut. The surroundings were going from meagre to shabby to positively dangerous looking. They were in the slums.

The Cadillac pulled up in front of a dilapidated frame house in the driveway of which squatted what was left of a 1940 Ford.

"All right, children," Adele Mason said sweetly.

Something in her voice lent great importance to the event to come. Jeanne and Alan were learning about charity.

It was a terrible hassle getting out of the car carrying such unwieldy parcels, but Jeanne had the easier time of it: Alan was struggling with the 20-pound turkey.

The father of the house was drunk; he grabbed the turkey almost angrily. Jeanne saw anguish in his eyes—the first spiritual pain she had ever seen—and never forgot it. The mother wept and said "Thank you . . . thank you . . . thank you. . . ." over and over again. One of the dozen or so dirty children spat on Alan's beautiful brand new suit,

Alan was startled but not really offended. The pity with which he smiled at the filthy youngster hurt the kid more than a sock in the jaw would have. The little boy punched Alan in the stomach and then doubled over, fell on the ground, and cried as silently as he could.

Jeanne was frightened; she dropped both of her containers, spilling their contents on the broken sidewalk, and ran back to the car.

"May'nt I get you something from the bar, Miss? You've been out here for such a long time you're bound to be parched."

"What? Oh, no thank you. I'm just . . . think-

36

ing.''

"That's apparent enough, and you couldn't pick a better spot for it than mid-ocean. Sorry. I didn't mean to disturb you.''

The waiter was about to return to The Sea Turtle, but Jeanne stopped him. "I *will* have something—a tall glass of white wine and soda with lots of ice.''

He nodded approvingly and ambled off to get it.

Jeanne glanced down at her bare forearm and noticed it was decidedly pink. Could she have been standing here long enough to pick up a sunburn? Jeanne wondered if she'd remembered to pack suntan lotion. At that moment, she could not recall packing at all. Surely the ship's gift store carried such sundries.

Reminded of it by nothing, Jeanne suddenly thought of the mysterious telegram . . . sent by whom? Someone who had discovered her plan and had not attempted to stop her. Someone who approved. Gordon? Philip? Mother might have wished her well; but she hadn't the imagination to do it this way. Alan?

When the waiter returned with Jeanne's drink, he found her laughing aloud.

"And here I thought you were in a sad mood,'' he said, courteously disappearing before Jeanne had time to worry about a tip.

The telegram had done its work: being unsigned it forced Jeanne to consider all possible senders—and realize that she had numerous supporters. But there was an inevitable counterpart to that line of thought: there were so many who could not have sent it, who did not approve of her activities.

Jeanne walked through the bar and out onto a long port-side deck; it faced northward and was completely in shade. Breezy and cool.

A dolphin arched playfully out of the water not far from the ship. Farther out, another leapt up, and another and another. The nearest dolphin was quite an exhibitionist. It zoomed up high, did a full roll mid-air, and hit the water with an exaggerated splash.

"Horace, look!" exclaimed a dumpy, cheerful old girl in bulging trousers. "Bring your camera! Dolphins!"

Jeanne watched the man addressed as Horace. He cautiously fitted a telephoto lens to his camera and gamefully allowed his wife to act as his director. They looked perfectly happy, Jeanne thought. They were people to whom life was not a mystery, to whom happiness was taken for granted. They ought to have reminded Jeanne of her parents, but they didn't.

A steward made himself heard before he came into view: "Last call for luncheon," he was announcing. He rang a bell between each pronouncement of it.

Jeanne was not hungry, but her drink was empty. Why not? she thought. Why not get good and plastered and go to bed right after dark?

This plan she carried out to the simple letter of it—allowing her mind to carry her wherever it seemed bent, to force her to consider bad times and allow her to experience some of the good. Her emotions moved backwards—like negatives and saved when all the photographic positives had been lost: she faced her bad memories with equanimity; she faced her memories of good times, good people, and good promises. But she felt the pain, none the less.

Private investigator Carl Bitlinger yawned. He wasn't used to appointments in the line of duty taking place at 7:45 a.m. Luckily the Mason building wasn't far from his West Eighteenth Street flat—a few blocks up and a few blocks over, on Fifth Avenue. The building was respectably tall and old enough, built in the 40's from sturdy masonry; it looked dignified. Art-deco bold capitals were carved over the door: MASON FURNITURE EXCHANGE. Carpeted halls, heavy oak door outside the executive suite. Plush waiting room. Pretty receptionist. Bitlinger yawned again—just as the man he presumed was Mason opened his inner-chamber door and said, "Come in, Mr. Bitlinger." He said pointedly to his receptionist: "Perhaps our guest would like coffee."

"Black," Bitlinger told her.

The old man's own office wasn't nearly as impressive as the rest of his building. Obviously this man *worked*. He wasn't just for show. "What can I do for you, Mr. Mason?"

"Find my daughter."

Mason handed him a scrap of paper. "She left this with her lawyer, who . . . reluctantly forwarded it to me. The lawyer is Philip Pomeranz, whom I think you know."

"I believe he recommended me to you."

"Philip said he checked the airlines and learned that she booked no passage, not under

39

her own name, anyway. But as you can see from the note, Jeanne *has* left town."

Bitlinger scanned the message. "When?"

"The note arrived last evening, between five and seven."

"How old is she, sir?"

"Thirty-two. Legally at liberty to do whatever she pleases. I do not want her . . . *apprehended*. Merely located. I want to be assured she is safe, and I want to be able to communicate with her."

"It looks as if she's not all that eager to be found."

"Do you only look for people who want to be found, Mr. Bitlinger?" He handed over an envelope. "Your retainer. Do you want operating expenses in advance?"

"No, I'll bill you. Do you have a picture? Sample of handwriting? List of vacation spots she's enjoyed before? Things of that nature?"

"Some of what you want is there in the envelope. You'll also find my home address and phone number. Call my wife if you wish."

"Is Jeanne married?"

"No."

"Is she mentally stable? At the present time, I mean."

"I doubt it."

"I'll be in touch. Thank you. I don't think I'll hang around for coffee. Better get right on this."

The investigator hurried to the elevator, to street level, out of the building. Not that it mattered, but he didn't much like millionaire Gilbert Mason.

three

Jeanne was up and out ahead of the sun the next morning. The pre-dawn sky was hazy, the wind was steady and damp, and the sea was like glass, hardly moving. The earth seemed to be awaiting some momentous event. Jeanne felt some of that anticipation, but with no hope of anything actually happening.

"*Hut* two three four. . . . " Sound preceded sight, but soon a tribe of joggers emerged on the vast deck where Jeanne stood near the larger of two swimming pools. Jeanne wondered when such a team could have been organized among passengers who were strangers to one another. How, in fact, did strangers *ever* meet? Further: why did they ever bother? What conceivable value could one human being be to another? Of what value was anything? All those stories about troubled young men searching for the meaning of life, Jeanne mused; why bother? Why search for anything? Whatever you find . . . will turn out to be something else.

Jeanne wandered to the fantail, the semicircular tail end of the ship, below which the ocean roared and boiled from the violence of the propellers and e gines. Certain and instant death for anyone who cared to leap into the churning wake. And so easy to do. Just climb up the railing—which seemed obligingly to have rungs like a little aluminum step ladder—and walk off into the air.

Jeanne had read a statistic once about the numbers of people who leap or fall overboard from ocean liners. The number was not as low as she had imagined it would be. People actually did it. Could it be, she wondered, that they booked passage intending to do away with themselves? Could such a motive have been hidden at the back of *my* mind? Jeanne pondered.

She noticed that she had rested one foot idly on the bottom rung of the railing. No, no—she said to herself rather theatrically—that way lies madness.

She heard the joggers approaching again. They had made it all around the ship on this deck and were starting another lap. "*Hut* two three four. . . . " Huffing and puffing and chatting among themselves and laughing.

"Look there, Alice—low over the water, near the ship's wake. Isn't that a frigate of some kind?"

Jeanne noted, mainly with indifference, that the dumpy lady—evidently named Alice—and her husband, Horace, were at it again with their cameras and binoculars. This time it was birdwatching, not dolphin study. Near where the middle-aged couple were propped against the ship's rail, someone, or something, stirred under a blanket on a deck chair.

The something-under-the-blanket laughed, sputtered, and went into a coughing fit. It emerged as a rather pretty young woman who had apparently been sleeping there. From the cross-hatched pattern on her cheek, made by the deck chair's plastic fabric, she looked as if she might have been there all night. Her long blonde hair was in thorough disarray. The blanketed young woman seemed unable to stop coughing. She pulled the cover back over her head and lay there convulsing, causing the deck chair to creak and hop with each lurch.

She wasn't far away, so Jeanne asked her: "Can I do anything to help?"

She tossed the cover away and jumped to her feet. She held onto the railing at the fantail and gasped for breath. Her brightly-colored blanket was caught by a gust of wind and tossed overboard. Its reds and oranges and whites flickered gaily against the persistant gray of the sea.

"I'm okay, she said, finally. Her breathing was almost normal. "My name's Donna," the girl said. "Have some coffee with me."

Jeanne felt she had been placed in an awkward position. "No, I—no thank you, I—"

"You vant to be alone," Donna said in Garbo seductive. "I can take a hint." She grabbed her large canvas bag from the deck chair and walked—haughtily, Jeanne thought—toward the enclosed bar/coffee-shop on the opposite side of the pool. Jeanne felt sure that the girl, a perfect stranger, had been hurt by Jeanne's rejection.

She was probably in her mid-twenties, very

skinny and very pretty—maybe she was a model—yet she wore faded jeans and a wrinkled man's white shirt, which looked as if it had been slept in and probably had. Her canvas bag was far larger than what would be needed for cash and cosmetics, especially with a cabin always nearby. Perhaps she shared a cabin with someone she didn't like, and/or didn't trust.

She's in trouble, Jeanne thought, like I am.

It's because we're trapped together on the open sea, Jeanne reasoned—trying to explain to herself why the girl interested her so. It's because we mean nothing to each other, and there is no future to such a friendship—she thought, wondering why she felt that this strange girl, alone in all the world, was the person she might talk things out with. None of it made much sense, except: I think she's a lot like me.

"Donna," Jeanne called out.

The girl stopped just before opening the door leading inside. She waited, stressing that now it was Jeanne's move.

"Where can we get coffee at six in the morning?" Jeanne asked her as she approached.

"They serve emergency rations for early risers here at the game deck bar. What's your name?"

"Jeanne."

They skipped the preliminaries of talking about the weather, the beauty of the sea and sky, the virtues and shortcomings of the *Liberty*. Donna's first words were:

"Well, what are *you* running away from?"

Jeanne surprised herself by answering: "I need to find out whether I *am* running away."

"I'm running away from nothing. Lots of nothings. I'm looking for something, anything. So far I haven't found too many good reasons for bothering to stay alive. A man?"

Jeanne smiled. "Several. How about you?"

"Mankind, I guess."

By the second cup of coffee, and the second English scone, Jeanne was talking to Donna as easily as she'd have talked to an old friend. More easily. She had never told anyone:

"I married far too young. I was twenty-one. And very very stupid. And Bill was very very handsome. Or so I thought, anyway. Oh, that wasn't all there was to it. He was warm and witty and practical—or so I thought. And so masculine. At least he seemed the epitome of what I *thought* masculine ought to be."

"Big cock?"

Jeanne was determined not to appear rattled by Donna's deliberate shock tactic. "Average, I guess," Jeanne answered as evenly as possible.

"Go on," Donna urged sincerely, as if appologizing for being crude. "Why did he seem so masculine? I mean, what *is* masculinity to you?"

"Self-assertiveness, confidence, strength—"

Donna nodded. "Big cock."

Jeanne ate the last of her buttered scone. "What is it you're not taking seriously, Donna—me, our conversation, masculinity? What is it?"

"Maybe it's your seriousness. Maybe . . . no,

45

I'll tell you what it is; it's the whole idea that *ideas* like masculinity—matter one hoot in hell. It's just a label, that's all. There's no such thing as masculinity. Or femininity. Or confidence. Or any of that bullshit.''

"Then what does exist?"

" Coffee. Want another cup?"

"Do you want to talk about coffee beans and plastic cups and wrought-iron tables and chairs?" This was ridiculous! Jeanne was angry at Donna for disappointing her as a conversationalist. The kind of anger reserved for long-time acquaintances. "Listen," Donna snarled, apparently as angry as Jeanne.

"We don't have to talk about anything. Certainly not about—" Donna cut herself off sharply.

Jeanne was quickly sympathetic, no longer angry. "Okay, whatever it is, we won't talk about it, I promise." Jeanne picked a usually safe subject: "Where did you go to college?"

Donna laughed. "Try something else."

"Uh . . . Where'd you grow up? I hear New England in your voice, don't I? I'm from up and downstate New York."

"Bully for you."

"That was my last attempt," Jeanne said as she picked up the check and got to her feet. Donna did not look up and did not try to stop her. She didn't even thank Jeanne for the coffee.

Jeanne walked over to the starboard rail. There we were, she mused, two women about to have nervous breakdowns. Jeanne had about decided to go back in and apologize when

Donna appeared and took up residence a foot away, against the same trailing.

"So," Donna said, "you married this big hunk of man who had a—let's say he had a man's athletic body, and not a grain of sensitivity. Right? Then what happened?"

Jeanne smiled. Donna was right; an apology by either of them would have been a waste of time. "A year later we had a son, Kevin. Then I was so busy raising and getting to know the child, watching his personality develop, that I still hadn't the sense to take a good look at the man I'd married. I was getting to know myself, too, during those years, I guess. I found that I wasn't quite the person I used to think I was. I remember deciding once that I was getting to be more logical. Certainly more independent. All that time, Bill was just Bill to me.

"He wasn't getting much of anywhere in business. He had tried all sorts of sales jobs, administrative jobs; nothing was working. It occurred to me that as long as the only thing he liked was cars, he ought to sell cars. Don't ask me why, but that had never occurred to him. Am I babbling? Does any of this make sense?"

"Yeah, well, go on. I'm following you."

They found a couple of deck chairs near the pool and continued their talk, listening to the water slosh with the gentle rising and falling of the ship.

"My father lent him the money, quite a lot of money, to open a showroom," Jeanne continued. "The one thing I still admire about Bill is his determination. He made it work. He sells

47

those esoteric foreign sports cars."

"Where?"

"Manhattan."

"His name's not Bill Oliver, is it? Oliver's Showrooms at Broadway and Fifty-something?"

Jeanne cringed. This girl, this fellow-traveler, like another lost soul crossing the River Styx, suddenly became real. There was a connection to Jeanne's own life, to her past. Perhaps Jeanne had said too much, confided too much. "That's right," Jeanne said, the animation gone from her voice.

"Well, he may be a drip to you, sugar, but I think he's gorgeous!" Donna giggled. "He sold me my *512*. Don't tell him it's mangled under a hundred feet of salt water at the base of a New Hampshire cliff. It would break his heart!" With a shrug, Donna added, "If he remembers who I am—which I doubt."

Jeanne laughed. "Knowing *anyone's* Ferrari—that's what a *512* is, isn't it—is under a hundred feet of salt water would break his heart. They're *people* to him."

"Does he race them?"

"He's done a little racing." Much as she wanted to open up completely to this girl, Jeanne found herself holding back, trusting her a little less, now that Donna knew who Bill was.

"So then what happened," Donna prodded, "in the life and times of Jeanne Oliver? Have an affair with a much younger man?"

Donna sensed the barrier Jeanne had erected

between them. When Jeanne hesitated, Donna interjected pointedly: "Come on, Jeanne. Just because you had a little stumble there . . . you can't back out now. We're committed, you and I. The game must be played. To the end, if necessary. It won't work if we don't go all the way. So I knew Bill Oliver slightly. Big deal. Out with it, Jeanne. This is your life." She waited for Jeanne's reply.

There was an odd sort of logic to it. Somehow they *were* committed, Jeanne realized. Either that, or they had to revert to being just acquaintances who would pass on the decks or see each other casually at ports of call and smile, nod, and say, "Nice day. . . ."

"A year younger than Bill and me," Jeanne answered.

"And?"

"And what?"

"He was very different from Bill?"

"Yes, very different."

"He was sensitive, gentle, had a soul?"

"He was a painter."

"Was? Then it's over?"

"It's over."

Donna said, without a trace of mockery, "Was it beautiful, even for a little while?"

Jeanne smiled. "It was beautiful for about three months."

"Then you can die fulfilled," Donna said. There was a tinge of irony or humor in her voice, but Jeanne felt sure the girl was merely hiding the fact that she really meant what she was saying. "If you've had your three months,"

Donna went on, "you can say 'fuck you' to the world and look all the nasties right in the eye. You have nothing to run away from. Nothing at all."

How incredibly simple that sounds coming from Donna, Jeanne thought. Yet there's so much the girl couldn't possibly comprehend. How young her notions are! And what an unhappy life she's led, if just three months of happiness would be worth dying for!

"That man over there," Donna said conspiratorially, "he's incredible!"

Jeanne followed Donna's unadulterated stare and saw a remotely familiar face. "Oh yes," Jeanne said, "he is good looking. His name is . . . Mark something-or-other. He's British, I think."

Donna looked at Jeanne wide-eyed. "How do you know?"

"He spoke to me for a minute when we were pulling out of New York."

" Damn! You saw him first."

Jeanne laughed. "He's all yours."

"Really?" Donna said it so loudly that everyone near them on the pool deck heard her—including Mark something-or-other, who looked her way and smiled.

She smiled back seductively and said to Jeanne under her breath: "Sweet Jesus!"

Jeanne got to her feet, dusting a few scone crumbs from her lap. "Let's meet later, Donna. What's your cabin number?"

"Tell you what, let's have a cocktail before dinner tonight. Six-thirty. Here."

"It's a deal," Jeanne said.

Donna watched until Jeanne was out of sight, briefly reflected upon the warmth she felt she had received from the lonely lady, the unexpected kindred spirit, and then sprinted to the public bath house on the deck above.

You'd hardly call this a powder room, Donna mused, almost giggling to herself, as she yanked a bikini out of her purse and hastily changed into it. The women's room here was strictly utilitarian, with metal walls, tiled floors, porcelain fixtures, and a row of frosted round portholes. Very nautical. Just a "head," as the sailors would say, with a few benches upholstered in awning-stripe deck canvas. Donna was all alone there. Presumably, most preferred to return to their cabins for their needs.

The hunky young Britisher was nowhere in sight when Donna returned to the pool, but— with a confidence born of experience—she felt sure he would return. She lay fetchingly on the blue tiles at the pool's edge and pretended to sunbathe, oblivious to anything around her.

After a while she began to feel thoroughly baked, and tried to turn for basting without seeming less than glamorous, or tangling her carefully draped hair. One of the people in the pool, which she had so pointedly ignored, was *him*. He was right there at the pool's edge, and when she turned she ended up practically nose to nose with him.

"Has anyone ever told you that you have marvelous hair?" he said softly.

"I hear it every day," she said, with a smug

51

but vulnerable smile. She looked down into the water and tried to gain some impression of his body. It was definitely trim and athletic, a good sign. At a glance he seemed to be stark naked, but after briefly having the thought, Donna realized that it *had* to be that his suit was of a tan that roughly matched his skin.

"Come in. The water's warm."

" I think I'd feel safer out here."

"I shouldn't have thought you'd give a damn about feeling safe."

Donna smiled knowingly, enigmatically, hoping it covered for the lack of a clever retort.

He pulled himself easily out of the water and sat with a wet plop beside her head.

Yep, great body, Donna appraised as she pushed herself to a sitting position, letting her eyes climb up to his face. Her hot arm brushed past his cold thigh. His trunks *were* tan,

The sun was fairly high and had burned off all traces of morning mist. The only wind was that created by the ship's own passage through the air, and the sea was still calm.

"You body is positively picturesque," Donna said, casually, as if there were nothing odd in her saying it. "Lift weights?"

"Moderately. I'm an actor, so I have to be prepared for the flesh to show. But that's unfair. I was about to say something similar to you, and now you've spoiled my originality."

"Sorry." She might have said: that's why I said it. But she felt she had made her point. "I'm not an actor, or anything else in particular. But you're right, my hair and my body are satisfactory. Do you think I'm being too forward?''

''You're being too something, but I'm not sure if it's forward.''

Well, thought Donna, he hasn't run away so far; and I've got him intrigued anyway. ''How's your mind?'' she asked.

'' Fine. How's yours?''

''Wise beyond my years.''

''You Americans can be disarmingly candid.''

''You Englishmen speak so beautifully that I can't tell a thing about you. You *sound* like a bloomin' genius. You know who you sound like? Richard Burton.''

''It's a cross I have to bear.''

''Have you ever acted in America—in the States, I mean?''

''Only on the telly. I was in several episodes of the BBC production of *Crime and Punishment*. You fellows showed it on your public broadcasting channels.''

''I didn't see it.''

''My agent's trying to get me a Broadway show for the fall. Do you live in New York?''

''Uh—near it.''

''You'll have to come see me in the show.''

''If.''

''All right. If.'' He added: ''I'm told I really do have a good crack at this part. They've asked me to audition.''

Dandy, Donna thought; he feels he has to justify himself to me. Good start. Damn good start.

''What's an English actor of *Crime and*

Punishment calibre doing on a leisurely ocean cruise? Aren't you supposed to be too busy haunting agents' offices for this sort of vacation? Let's have it—are you traveling alone?''

"All alone, pretty lass. Actually, I *work* on this prison barge. I'm senior entertainment officer. One must eat, mustn't one?''

Donna briefly looked disgusted.

"Did I say something to offend you?''

"Oh no. I just should have figured out that you worked here. It explains a lot. I have only one more serious, *really* serious question to ask you—''

"Your cabin or mine?'' Noting her surprised expression he explained. "I thought I should be the first to bring *that* up, anyway. You've beat me to everything else.''

She ignored him. "The serious question is: what is your name?''

"Mark Harris. Yours is Donna something.''

"How did you know that?''

"I caught a snatch of conversation between you and Jeanne.'' Again he was defensive. "Couldn't help hearing, honest.''

"Donna Andersen.''

He lifted her hand and lightly kissed her fingertips. "Delighted, Lady Andersen. Your cabin or mine?''

"*Now?*'' Donna had decided, deep down, that she would go now if he insisted, rather than risk losing him. But she hoped he'd say later. Perhaps her tone of voice conveyed her preference to him.

"We'd have to be awfully quick about it, just

54

now. I have a rehearsal that should last most of the afternoon—we have some new talent premiering this evening—and I have to get a bite first. Join me for lunch? We can go to the games-deck buffet without even having to dress."

"Sure. And you can tell me all about what it was like to grow up . . . where?"

"Torquay—in the South of England, Devonshire."

"Can I come to rehearsal?"

"Come see me tonight. I'm emcee for the variety show at the Club Tropicale." An inflection demeaned the Club's name as pretentious. "Afterwards we might even swing and sway to the anachronisms of Dicky Hendron's band."

" I'll be in the front row."

"Front *table*. I'll reserve one for you and Jeanne."

Donna roved her eyes again over his muscular torso, his tight stomach muscles, and convinced herself: I've got him right where I want him. She couldn't wait to tell Jeanne.

* * *

"Care to order, Miss?" a waiter asked Jeanne.

"I'll wait till my friend arrives," she said pleasantly. It was past six, and Donna had not yet appeared at the pool bar, where the two were to meet.

Jeanne had spent a tense and depressing afernoon reliving the early years of her marriage to

55

Bill, searching for truths, turning points, changes in the relationship. She had tried to take her mind away by attending the afternoon feature at the ship's cinema. It was something about NASA's faking a trip to Mars, and it made very little sense to her. Leaving in the middle, she had picked up an Agatha Christie paperback from the gift shop—but it turned out to be one she had read under a different title; this was a British edition. She considered reading it again, but after page seven the twist ending came back to her in a flash, and she tossed the book away. She thought of going for a swim, donned her suit, thought it over, changed back into her slacks and sleeveless blouse, and walked the decks. Endlessly walked the decks. Thinking. Or was it thinking at all, or just wallowing in images and ideas and remembered feelings?

She was facing aft, looking through the wall of glass that overlooked the sun deck. Beyond the pool (where a few well-broiled passengers still floated leisurely) there was the rounded stern of the ship, and beyond that the boiling aquamarine wake stretching back to the sharp line of the horizon which rose and fell gently with the pitching of the ship. The sky was royal blue, and a few gathering clouds caught traces of amber from a sun not far from setting.

Donna ambled in, pulled out the wrought-iron chair that was waiting for her, and slouched into it. "I've decided I can't figure him out," she said.

"Who? What would you like to drink?" Jeanne asked.

"Vodka and tonic and lots of peanuts. Mark Harris, that's who. *The* Mark Harris."

"He certainly works fast. Or you do."

"We both do. But I don't know whether I *like* him or not. All I know is that he's incredibly handsome, that he's probably going to try to seduce me tonight, and that I'll probably let him do it."

Jeanne flagged the waiter and ordered a pair of vodka and tonics. Jeanne was smiling, offering Donna friendly support, but inwardly she was doubting that her first impression of Donna had been valid; at the moment she and Donna seemed miles apart. Jeanne would never have behaved this way toward a man she hardly knew—didn't know at all, really. She couldn't resist challenging: "But shouldn't you wait until you know him a *little* better?"

"I figured I'd better hop in the hay with him before I get to know him. Just in case."

"In case what?"

"In case he turns out to be a drip. That would turn me off, and then it would be too late. Speaking of being turned off, I'm going to make him leave the lights *on* —so I can watch every one of those muscles ripple!"

Jeanne laughed. "Have you been going through life acting like this, or is this a new approach?"

"I figure you've got to grab whatever's available, when you've got the chance. That's what you did isn't it, with—what was his name?"

"Gordon."

"Gordon. There you were with a happy

home, lovely kid, and a clod of a husband. Along comes Gordon. You can't let it go by, and you take him when you've got the chance. Same thing. How can you get anything out of life any other way?''

Jeanne felt a flush of guilt and embarrassment; but she could not have said what specifically caused them. She stared disbelievingly at Donna while her mind flashed random pictures at computer-like speed: Gordon's smiling face, his honesty, his sadness; Bill's brutal handling of the affair, his cruelty to Kevin; Kevin's bewildered, loving eyes; Jeanne's own feeling that, with Gordon, the world was for once a kind, gentle, and intelligent place. No—it had not been an impulsive romp for the hell of it.

''But what goes through your head,'' Jeanne asked, remembering Donna's aversion to serious conversation and trying to keep her voice light, ''when you're having sex with just a body? Is it all a fantasy?''

The question obviously hit Donna hard; but she recovered and answered flippantly, ''I'll let you know tomorrow.''

Donna had been eating peanuts ravenously. The bowl was empty now, and she held it high above her head until a waiter, with a sense of humor, replaced it up there with a full one. Donna shot an affectionate grin to him, then cautiously lowered the brimming bowl to the tabletop.

''Care for another?'' the waiter asked, indicating their nearly empty glasses.

Jeanne answered yes for both of them, thereby establishing that the drinks were on her.

"Listen, Jeanne, I appreciate your generosity. As the English say, I'm on my beam ends. I really can't reciprocate."

Jeanne smiled. "Don't worry about it. I'm one of those wealthy divorcees . . . at least until Father disowns me, which he might do any day now."

"And all that alimony?" Donna chomped on a handful of nuts.

"I Wasn't granted any alimony. *He* sued for divorce, and custody; and I was considered well-off on my own."

"Well," Donna lifted her glass cheerfully, "here's to Father."

Donna excused herself as Jeanne joined the ambling groups responding to the first dinner bell.

* * *

It seemed the right thing to do, the expected thing to do, the sane thing to do . . . Jeanne took out a few minutes to write some post cards. She was acting like a normal traveler, she thought. Her little stack of cards—purchased from the gift shop in the afternoon—was at her left along with several Haitian stamps (the cards would be mailed from their first port stop); and her pen was poised. The cards all showed her ship, *City of Liberty* on the high sea at night with all lights ablazing. An awesome, romantic, far-away-places type of image.

Jeanne was at a desk in the little study provided for passengers, on B deck. There were a couple of others there, too, catching up on correspondence while gazing out to sea through the wide windows that opened onto a view that was itself like a postcard picture: a just-risen nearly full moon cast its long kite tail of light out across the black ocean and lightened the edges of numerous fleecy clouds. It occurred to Jeanne that a cameraman about a hundred yards away out there could take a picture of *City of Liberty* exactly like the one on her cards.

It was a thought impersonal enough to write about and yet personal enough to reflect her ocean-going experience. But whom should she write it to? Undecided, she wrote that image on one of the cards.

Reading it over, it seemed a rather pointless thing to communicate to anybody.

In her present state of mind, it would have been all right to send it to her mother, or to Alan, she supposed. And they'd be delighted to receive it.

She wanted to send it to Kevin, but she doubted it would mean much to him.

Gordon would understand her intent exactly. But it would not be appropriate to send Gordon the only card. He would misunderstand it. So would anybody else who found out she had sent it. It would seem to all that he was foremost in her mind—which was not true.

Jeanne smiled, laughing at herself inwardly. The person foremost in my mind at the moment, she reasoned, is *me*.

She had a fleeting urge to send a card to Marjery Cirino, who had been her best friend in college. But she hadn't kept up with Marjery during the past few years, probably no longer had her address. That's what she needed, though, a friend, a confidante. Marjery and Donna weren't all that different, really. Apparently. Donna was younger.

Send the card to Donna and save the stamp, Jeanne whimsically proposed to herself.

She scooped up her things, the problem solved by virtue of being evaded, and headed toward Club Tropicale—for a raucous evening of entertainment she didn't relish, and a chance to get to know enigmatic Donna a bit better.

* * *

Donna wasn't in much of a mood to talk. She was studying The Englishman as he directed the events of the evening.

Jeanne watched the Club Tropicale variety show with very little interest. There was an adagio dance team who did the tango rather spectacularly and who sweated a lot, a magician who caught bullets in his teeth, a rock singer no one had ever heard of who was billed as the rage of three continents, a chanteuse named Diedre Dawn who cried real tears singing "My Man," and interspersed throughout was the repartee of Mark Harris (who had been introduced as a prominent English actor).

Jeanne studied Mark keenly, mostly for Donna's sake—trying to see Mark through Donna's eyes. Curious how she felt so close to Donna at

61

this moment. It's being trapped together in an isolated world, Jeanne insisted to herself again. New York is on some altogether different planet. But this was an insufficient answer, and Jeanne knew it. Was it jealousy? Did she envy Donna's easy notions about men and her success with handsome Mark Harris? No—that wasn't it, either, Jeanne felt sure.

Mark certainly was good looking, and he had an arrestingly suave manner. His humor— which seemed ad-libbed but might not have been—was innocent enough, but there were incongruous little cynicisms. He made a daring reference to the *Titanic*, ending it with, "Today the women and children would have to organize and fend for themselves!"

The audience loved Mark Harris, though, and Jeanne watched Donna drinking him in. Or was it his evident popularity she was drinking in? That, Jeanne chastised herself, was an insulting idea, and she had no real reason to believe it described Donna's motives.

Feeling that Donna wouldn't miss her under the circumstances, Jeanne slipped away from the frantic floor show and loud music and stepped out into the star-bright night of the promenade deck. Trying to get it all out of her system, Jeanne simplified:

I like Donna; I don't like Mark. But Donna *isn't* my little sister and has to live her own life . . . make her own mistakes. I mustn't get mixed up in this.

But what if Donna's right, Jeanne speculated, and I'm wrong . . . wrong about Mark, wrong about men, wrong about what's most important in life?

Oh, no, Jeanne retreated—as she had when the notion of suicide had passed through her mind—that way lies madness. This is no time to begin to doubt my whole outlook on life.

She stopped stolling at a giant glassed-in map illuminated by a ghostly-white fluorescent tube. The map showed North and South America and was headlined, "Daily Run of *City of Liberty*." For the first time since leaving home, leaving everything behind, Jeanne took an interest in where the ship was going. The dotted line left New York Harbor and headed south toward the Caribbean. According to the map pin at the end of the line, at sundown tonight the ship had passed roughly between Florida and the Bahamas and would reach their first port stop, Port-au-Prince, Haiti, sometime tomorrow.

Unexpectedly, Jeanne felt some excitement at the prospect of visiting a strange new place. She noticed her feeling and realized this meant she was beginning to wind down, to be herself again.

She wandered up to the promenade deck.

The high moon. The subtle roll of the ship. A life preserver proudly lettered *City of Liberty*. It all reminded her of a 1920's Noel Coward play her college club had done. In it a young man and woman on their honeymoon stand against a ship's rail with a full moon reflected in the water behind them. They vow to try desperately to continue loving each other as intensely as they do at that moment. She tells him she could die

63

that very night, perfectly happy. The couple walk on, and the audience sees the life preserver they've been standing in front of; it is lettered S.S. TITANIC.

Jeanne said aloud: "Definitely in bad taste." She had recalled Mark Harris' joke about the Titanic's women and children.

That brought Donna back to mind. Other pieces fell into place, and Jeanne finally discovered the truth:

It's not that Donna and I are alike—it's that we're so different. Donna clearly has nothing to tie her down, no cares about what tomorrow might hold, no worry over the "right" thing to do, no hangups about men and sex and responsibility. Yet she seems to be happier than I! She seems to be better equipped for living! Much as I disapprove of her actions, I *feel* that I ought to be more like her. Well . . . true or false? Does that wild child possess some secret of life up to now denied the heiress of the Masons?

Sun-bathing chairs folded and stacked for the night . . . white horn-shaped loudspeakers . . . mysterious superstructures of metal beams and buttresses . . . rows of canvas-covered lifeboats . . . lovers strolling along the rubber-matted promenades . . . the faint salty smell of sea air .. the cool wind . . . the perpetual surf sound made by the ship's passage through wave after wave after wave. . . .

" I'm on an ocean liner!" Jeanne said aloud, delightedly. Her delight delighted her, and she laughed, believing that for a little while at least, all was right with the world.

four

"I need some friendly advice," said Alan Mason.

"You know I'll help if I can," Philip Pomeranz said sincerely.

They had met early evening in the Cracker Barrel, a restaurant-bar on Thirty-fourth Street, near Philip's office in the Empire State Building. They were at a booth in a quiet dark corner nursing oversized martinis.

Alan laughed. "I feel like I've come to ask a favor of the God Father. I really do feel sneaky about this, and I hope you'll keep this confidential."

"That's easy," said Philip, in a playful mood. "Give me a dollar."

Alan forked over, quizzically.

"Now you've retained me professionally, and I'm bound to respect my client's request for confidentiality. You're planning to rob Chase Manhattan Bank? What is it?"

"I want to get Kevin away from his father."

"I'm with you. How?"

"That's the advice I need. I guess there's nothing much we could do legally—right?"

"Not unless you know things about the situation I don't know."

"I doubt that I do. All I know—*believe*, really—is that Bill Oliver is a brute who might harm Kevin spiritually, psychologically. I don't think Bill has an iota of an idea how to raise an unusually bright, unusually vulnerable, unusually delicate young man. I also believe, from things Kevin himself has either told me or itimated, that poor little Kevin is terribly afraid of his father—without quite understanding why. I *think* I understand why. I think it's because Bill is uncommunicative and tends to try to influence the boy by insult and innuendo—"

"You're touching on something I've wondered about. Elaborate a bit, Alan."

"Kevin does a drawing. Bill says, 'That's nice, meaning that it may be nice but it's unsatisfactory, improper, *unmanly* for the boy to be drawing at all. Kevin brings home a straight-A report card and a note saying he's not doing too well in athletics. Bill ignores the intellectual accomplishment and actually punishes the boy for falling down in sports. Punishes him! Kevin told me his allowance had been cut in half and he'd been promised a whipping if his sportsmanship did not improve. Kevin told me about it not because he believed his father was wrong, but because he thought maybe I could help him understand his father's reasoning."

"What did you tell Kevin?"

"I told him I thought his father was dead wrong, and I tried to prove it by telling him how much I'd needed my academic pursuits and how useless I had found that dumb year I spent trying

66

to make the basketball team—because *my* father wanted me to play.''

''Did he understand?''

''Completely. Of course that wedged open even farther the gulf developing between him and his father. That's another thing: Kevin has become somewhat courageous in talking back to his dear old dad, and I'm afraid it might make Bill so angry he might seriously hurt the boy some day. That's the way Bill is. He hits anybody he can't reason with.''

Philip smiled. That side of Bill's nature was well known.

''You've got me concerned, or should I say, more concerned. But what can I do?''

Alan scratched his head, grimaced a bit, and ventured: ''I got carried away and suggested to Kevin that he might be able to come to my place to visit for a while—a month or so, I implied.''

''Ouch.''

''Yeah, you see the problem. Besides having to battle Bill, there's my fundamentalist father in the way—who wouldn't hear of polluting his only grandson's moral education by letting him live in an apartment of fornicating sin. Never mind that Margaret and I have a happier home than any *married* couple he knows. So I have to back down, since I see very little chance of success in the venture.''

''Spoken like a corporate lawyer. You do all right for a beatnik playright.'' He thought it over and realized: ''I know what you're asking me. You want me to invite Kevin to stay at the Pomeranz house for a while—until Jeanne gets back at least—"

"Or longer. Jeanne's fairly powerless to help, thanks to—"

"Thanks to me," Philip finished.

"No, thanks to the court."

"Thanks to me," Philip repeated more softly. Alan reflected upon Philip's downcast eyes. Handsome face, Alan thought, not like an actor's or model's but like a benevolent and successful lawyer's—angular, a little wrinkled, shopworn, temples grayed more by effort and tension than by years. Eyes that are honest, perhaps even naive in some ways, eyes that reveal the very inner turmoil they're being asked to conceal.

Alan said, "No one blames you, Philip, except yourself."

Philip looked surprised that his soul had been read, but he trusted Alan enough to acknowledge the accuracy of the reading. "You're a playright, Alan," he said: "would you write a play in which common sense was inoperative in the world, in which on one had the power to reach other minds through reasoned arguments, in which the more logical one became the less he was understood? Wouldn't you rather picture the human race as potentially open to truth? Wouldn't you create a hero who was able to persuade even the most recalcitrant bigots to see the truth eventually?"

"You expected to be that kind of hero?"

"I always expect it, every time I go into court." He smiled a trifle self-deprecatingly. "It's the swashbuckler in me, I guess. And I usually find that the court is after the same thing I want—the truth. They don't always see it right away, and occasionally they don't see it at all. But it's up to me, it's my *job* to be sure of my truth and to make them see it, too. This time, *this* time I wasn't worthy of what was required of me. I can't very well blame the mores and moralities of the times, now can I? I can't very well blame the law itself.''

Alan twirled his martini glass by the stem. ''Maybe I'll write a play someday about unearned guilt and how it eats away at a man. I suspect you'd figure into my thinking rather heavily.''

Philip smiled gratefully. ''I hope I come to see it that way.'' He thought for a moment, his eyes revealing to Alan that he had left his morbid self-contempt for another time, then said, ''Yes, I'd love to have Kevin come live with us, for as long as we can have him. I've thought of it before, actually, but couldn't think of how to broach the subject . . . with my wife. Now I can—''

''Blame the idea on me,'' Alan suggested, laughing.

''I'll do just that.''

''I'd think Hilda would enjoy having Kevin around—''

''Oh, she would, she would,'' Philip agreed enthusiastically.

Alan frowned. There' was something going on in Philip's head that Alan could not decipher. He assumed that this was yet another expression of the guilt Philip felt over losing Jeanne's case. "Can I help you communicate the request to Father?" Alan asked. "It occurs to me that it would help to have him supporting us in this. Don't ask me why, but Bill tends to do whatever Dad wants him to do."

Philip shook his head in wonderment. "Amazing isn't it? I've noticed that, or thought I had. Yes, there is something you can do, Alan, indirectly. But it's Kevin I think you ought to have a talk with. Try to keep him from mentioning that the first thought was to ship him off to you and Margaret, and now there's been a change of plans. We don't want Bill to get the idea that you and I are conspiring to take his son away. He does love the boy, you know."

"Does he? Perhaps. Sure I'll talk to the kid. He's smart; he'll play along with us—gleefully, I imagine."

Philip subtly motioned for the waiter to bring another round. "How goes the play?" he asked, pointedly changing the subject.

Alan took a deep breath and let it out, smiling as he did so. "We're at the apoplexy stage. I'm a bundle of nerves over it. It goes into production in about six weeks, and it still hasn't been cast yet—except for Margaret, of course. I wrote it with her in mind, you know, and luckily the producers and the director agree she's perfect for the part. But we're stumped for a leading man."

"A name or a newcomer?"

"It doesn't matter to me. *They* want a name, naturally, but they're considering two Britishers I've never heard of—Leslie Neal and

Mark Harris. Names ring a bell?''

'' 'Fraid not, but I don't follow show business all that closely. Tell you what, some night when you're up to here with the play and need to get completely away for a spell, drop by and we'll get quietly stinking drunk.''

"That's a deal." Alan leaned forward and conspiratorialy raised an eyebrow. "You haven't asked me if I've found Jeanne. Does that mean you know where she is?''

"I'm not telling. She slipped me a dollar, too, in spirit.''

"Good for you.''

* * *

Jeanne felt like she was being followed. It was a silly notion, she convinced hereself, but there it was. . . .

She was wandering interestedly through an open air art market, where rows of paintings and tables of statuettes were being offered for sale. She was in Port-au-Prince, the colorful capital of the fantasy-like island called Haiti. The hues were intoxicating: no two buildings, flowers, people, cars, fruit, or above all pieces of cloth, seemed out of the same dye vat. Jeanne kept being reminded of all those brightly colored bits of glass in kaleidoscopes.

Gordon had been especially fond of Haitian art, and Jeanne had seen his several canvases of it. Now, for the first time, she understood something Gordon had tried to convince her of: The colors the native artists used in such profusion were not an exaggeration! They merely painted life as they saw it.

Gordon had once talked of bringing Jeanne here. Maybe that's why she had this feeling that hidden eyes were watching her. It could also have been the simple eerie association with Voodoo. Its artifacts were all around. Odd designs scratched on pieces of tree bark. Little dolls for sale—presumably for sticking pins into. Small clusters of drums made of gourds covered with skin held tight with plastic clips, which had signs over them like: Genuine Mystic Drums of the Voodoo. For tourists, obviously.

The native inhabitants were beautiful people, Jeanne thought. Somehow their racial mixture had been an ideal one and yielded an island of dark-eyed, delicate-featured mulattoes. Skin the color of *cafe-au-lait*. They seemed friendly enough, too. And their smiles struck Jeanne as proud, not in the least subservient. Here, she ventured, the customer might not always be right. It was an admirable trait, but somehow it seemed a shade ominous in the context of Voodoo art and artifacts.

Jeanne paused at a table of carvings—ranging in style from ugly primitive to sleek and simplified modern. There was one, in mahogany, of a regal native woman lightly balancing a huge basket of fruit and flowers on her head. The detail work was exquisite. So was the price: $550.

"Madam?" A man who evidently was the proprietor accosted her.

"This is beautiful," Jeanne said, "but very

72

expensive.''

"I have others less expensive," he said, his accent tinged with French, "and less beautiful." Jeanne smiled and put back the museum piece on the table. She wondered about the wisdom of displaying such a valuable item in an outdoor show, until she saw the brawny guard eyeing her—not suspiciously but steadily.

"Nice, aren't they?" a man said to Jeanne. She hadn't noticed him before, but evidently he also had been perusing the statuettes.

"They are," she agreed. She moved on to avoid conversation with the stranger. But she felt that his eyes were still on her. He had looked like a typical tourist, down to the flowery shirt and camera around his neck. He had short hair, almost a crew cut.

When Jeanne stopped to admire the paintings of a famous native artist, René Exumé, the floral-printed tourist again appeared beside her. "Are you from *City of Liberty*?" he asked pleasantly.

Jeanne was annoyed. "I'm sorry, I really don't feel like having company," she said, moving on again. It occurred to her that she had not seen him aboard ship; but then it was a big ship.

Someone yelled, "Jeanne!" And she easily recognized Donna's voice. Donna and Mark were strolling arm in arm across the marketplace in Jeanne's direction.

"You must join us for late lunch," Mark insisted.

Jeanne didn't particularly want to, but it was a sure-fire way to elude the annoying man. Besides, Jeanne thought, I really ought not be alone all the time. She looked to Donna for some sort of clue whether she was really wanted, or Mark was merely being polite. Donna smiled cheerily and shrugged, as if to say, "Why not?"

"Come along," Mark prodded; "I'll take you to an out-of-the-way cafe where we can have some really genuine Creole food. A step or two off the tourist paths."

It turned out to be three or four steps off. Mark had to do all the ordering and negotiating because only he knew sufficient French to converse with the Creole-speaking natives. As foreign as the luncheon turned out to be— guinea hen with sour orange sauce, and rice with black mushrooms—it was apple pie Americana compared to the treat Mark had in store for later. Jeanne was reticent—for one thing, she continued to feel like an unwanted relation who was being tolerated out of kindness; but Mark convinced her by recommending they split up for a while and meet after dinner in front of the *Centre d'Art*. Mark and Donna promised to pick her up there, promptly at eight, in a rented car that would bring them into the mountains to an authentic Saturday night Voodoo ritual. "This won't be the watered-down version the cults in Port-au-Prince perform for the tourist trade," Mark insisted.

Jeanne felt another wave of doubt, later in the day. Her imagination fed her a headline: MASON HEIRESS FOUND SLAIN AT VOODOO ALTAR! What a silly way to die, she thought. More likely, she mused, a headline

74

might read: UNIDENTIFIED TOURISTS FOUND IN WRECKAGE AT BOTTOM OF REMOTE MOUNTAIN PASS. Or: TRAVELERS SUCCUMB TO VOODOO TRANCE AND MISS THEIR BOAT. *City of Liberty* was sure to pull out at midnight, on schedule, whether all were aboard or not. Could she trust Donna to be punctual? Highly doubtful. Mark? Well, probably, since not only his passage but his job was at stake.

It hadn't occurred to Jeanne to sign up for any of the guided tours offered to her on the ship before arrival at Haiti. With the afternoon to kill, she wished she had. *Time to kill*, she reflected; what a depressing attitude! She consequently bolstered her will, pushed re-runs of her troubles out of her brain, and decided to take a local tour bus she found available outside the Rent-a-Car place.

Jeanne's main thoughts, while she waited for the bus, were of her father. She was beginning to see his actions clearly for the first time. He *had no right* was the idea that kept recurring to her. He had no right to interfere, no right to influence Bill or Mother or me! His insufferable old-fashioned ideas of right and wrong . . . were at the root of so much of the problem.

Jeanne wondered: what does he see in Bill? Why does he like him so much? It occurred to Jeanne that her father—from his actions at least—cared for Bill like a favored son. Why? she wondered.

"Jeanne!" Donna yelled, just as their bright red Ford pulled up. Jeanne went with them.

The drive into the mountains was breathtaking, but more than that, it was unusual. There seemed to be not a square inch of even the most precipitous terrain that was not occupied. Farms and orchards were at times almost vertical. Along the roadside, women—dressed like gypsy queens—carried massive loads in baskets on their heads, like the mahagony statuette Jeanne had admired so much. And the colors! Even past sunset, with the twilight lavender turning to black with alarming speed, the reds, ochres, greens, chartreuses, and violets . . . remained bright and intense. The coloration—on the natives and in the foliage—was like a New England autumn gone berserk.

The meeting house looked for all the world like a structure Jeanne had seen once in Florida—a large white frame structure, its paint peeling, with peach-frosted windows and a green lawn dotted with weeds—very much like the old Baptist church her mother had once shown her, the church Adele Mason had attended as a small child. The congregation arriving on foot was different, though, in several ways. The dark-skinned believers were dressed in carnival motley and draped with jewelry and charms, and they lacked the euphoric seriousness of the American Protestants—instead they looked a little drunk and a little frightened.

Mark pulled the car into a parking area in some tall grasses—between an old jeep and a dilapidated pick-up.

"Won't they resent our being here?" Jeanne asked.

"Not a bit of it. They're friendly peasants who expect us to make a modest contribution on our way out. We're off the tourist thoroughfare, but if there's a place where there aren't any tourists, I haven't found it."

Inside the walls around the big open expanse of hard-wood floor were draped with rugs, fabrics of all colors, and snake skins; from the open rafters hung myriad objects Jeanne guessed were fetishes of some significance: gourds, dead flowers in bunches, bottles, likenesses of human figures, paper streamers and—stretched across several beams—an enormous stuffed snake; upon inspection, it seemed to be fabricated of numerous snake skins spiraled around it. One of a group of drummers was thumping a steady rhythm, slow, anticipatory, as the participants filed in and took their places on folding chairs and standing at a railing that three-quarters circled the open floor. In the center of the floor stood a tall pole painted in swirling black and red.

Thump . . . thump . . . thump . . . thump . . . went the drum, with no accent beat to break the monotony of it.

"That's the *houngan*," Mark whispered to his ladyfriends. "The sorcerer of this temple."

The *houngan* stood proudly, in a dimly lighted corner well away from the enclosed fire that gave the temple its only illumination. Several long black snakes wound lethargically around his arms and neck.

"The snake," Mark narrated, "represents *Damballa Wedo*—their rain god. These people

77

are largely farmers, so *Damballa* is their chief deity." He gestured toward the corps of drummers who were evidently preparing to attack their instruments in concert. "The *rada*— sacred Voodoo drums." Thereafter a word would have to be shouted to be heard. The drums had started.

The effect of the drums was startling, alarming, Jeanne thought. The hair on her neck and arms tingled. The congregation began to sing a song of worship, sexuality, and—to Jeanne's sensibilities—insanity. There were words in some strange language, but they were irrelevant to her.

The *houngan* inched forward into the light; as he did so, a tribe of half-naked dancers filed slowly toward the floor and circled the pole. On a thousand-year-old cue, they burst into a dance of such incredible frenzy that Jeanne worried about their own safety. Nothing could have been more intense, Jeanne thought. By now, she was enrapt, fascinated. The *houngan* joined the dancers, carrying a gourd of white paint and a brush made of mysterious black fibers. Human hair? Jeanne wondered. The *houngan*—who no longer carried his snakes—began to write on the floor with the milky substance. Jeanne looked to Mark; she wanted to ask him what the designs meant.

He caught her intent, smiled, and said nothing.

Could it be, Jeanne wondered, that these people were worshipping symbols the meanings of which had long been lost to racial memory?

78

Repeating the actions because their predecessors had repeated the actions? The notion was so barbaric Jeanne suspected she had misinterpreted Mark's meaning. He leaned over and said loudly, directly into her ear, "Not even the worshippers can tell you the meaning of those symbols—or of the ceremony as a whole, for that matter. They accept it all utterly on faith—because sometimes after one of these rituals, it rains." He added, "Predictably, of course, only during the rainy season."

Mark had slipped his arm around Jeanne's waist as he spoke. Reasonable enough. But he had left it there. Even with the ritual consuming her thoughts, Jeanne was more aware of Mark's forwardness; she found it presumptuous and inappropriate. She was about to squirm loose—speaking to him would have been futile—when she saw a face that made her forget even Mark. It was the man with the crew cut, the tourist who seemed intent on making her acquaintance. It seemed an absurd coincidence that Jeanne should find him here—standing ten feet away, smiling at her. He was following her! He shrugged, as if to apologize for something, then turned his attention to the dancers on the floor.

The drumming had suddenly accelerated—as if the men pounding their skin-covered gourds had been joined by another corps of drummers. Gasps and sighs rose irresistibly from the dancers and the gaping congregation. Jeanne didn't blame them; she felt like moaning herself. A woman dancer began to shout on every fourth beat of the rhythm; her shouts became screams. Suddenly, she froze as if ossified, her mouth open, her eyes bugging out. No one expressed concern; on the contrary, they seemed to pour out even more energy. They danced around two objects now—the pole and the possessed woman.

Suddenly there was an ear-splitting scream. It was Donna! She screamed again and again, at the top of her lungs, with tears flooding down her cheeks.

When Mark made a move to comfort her, Donna fainted, sinking into his arms.

The toss of his head was Mark's only way of saying to Jeanne, "Let's get out of here!"

The natives would say you were possessed by a *loa*—a divinity, a great ancestor or something," Mark said to Donna.

They were returning to the ship by taxi. Donna did not reply. Her crying had stopped, though, and her puffy eyes were blinking and looking around naturally enough.

"Feel better?" Jeanne asked.

Donna nodded and blubbered, "I'm sorry. It . . . it reminded me of . . . something."

"Really?" Mark challenged; "how could *that* remind one of anything, except maybe another Voodoo ceremony?"

For the first time it occurred to Jeanne that Donna was a mysterious girl indeed. Though they had talked often, and intimately, Jeanne knew hardly more about her than her name.

80

five

At sea, on another gorgeous Caribbean day, Jeanne was sunning by the pool, remembering the happy time she and Alan had had as teenagers on a cruise rather like this one to Bermuda. Running wild on the ocean liner, imagining all sorts of adventures—piracy on the open sea, a Jules-Verne-like trip around the world. Uninvited, Mark slipped into a deck chair beside her. "Hello, Mark," Jeanne said without much enthusiasm. She didn't know why, but the man's sincerity still seemed suspect to her. Maybe it was his polished English; she hoped that wasn't it.

"I can't seem to break through some sort of wall you've set up," he said.

"Walls are put there to keep people out," Jeanne said sardonically, not meaning to be unkind.

"Touché." He stood up grandly. "In fact, that wounds me to the heart." Before rolling off into the pool he said simply, "Ciao, Jeanne, lovely Jeanne."

What the heck is he after? she wondered. Jeanne would have made small talk—asked him how Donna was, for instance—if he hadn't so hastily departed. The Voodoo incident was two days ago, and Jeanne hadn't seen Donna but once or twice since—then only to speak in passing. At those times Donna had seemed bubblingly happy, as if nothing unusual had happened to her.

Odd, Jeanne thought, how a stranger can become a best friend and then suddenly a casual acquaintance . . . but really not so odd, since something like it happens everytime a woman falls in love. Donna was definitely in love. Or insane. Or both.

When Jeanne had found herself magnetically drawn to Gordon, so that thoughts of him constantly dominated her idle thinking, she too had let friendships . . . not slip exactly, but sit on a shelf. Jeanne was getting a glimpse of that action from the other side now: *her* friend had found a man, a man Jeanne approved of no more than her own friends had approved of Gordon. It tends, Jeanne mused, to limit the things we can talk about.

The subject of love stayed with Jeanne for a time; she did not disembark at Curacao, and instead remained aboard the nearly deserted *City of Liberty*. She looked out at the colorful, red-roofed homes and buildings of the quaint Dutch community, so clean and untroubled-looking.

She wondered about things philosophers shunned as not open to reason. Why do people fall in love? What is love? What happens *inside*? Which was true—that people were drawn to opposites, or to others like themselves? Bill, it would seem, was an opposite—physical, unintellectual, unartistic, uncommunicative—while Gordon was more a soulmate. Both loves had been disasters eventually. Did that mean that Jeanne had somehow failed to prepare herself for successful love? Was she doomed to either spinsterhood or a string of casual affairs—like Donna? Which, she wondered, would make her happier, if it turned out those were her only choices? What ever happened to prince charming . . . till death do us part . . . *Father Knows Best*? Was life really to be nothing more than *Alice Doesn't Live Here Anymore*?

Something, Jeanne reasoned, was killing the idea of *romance*.

But there was modern Donna—head over heels, in the best tradition of all those legends and fairy tales and historical romances.

Jeanne frowned at her heavy thoughts; she frowned at Donna's apparent good fortune: she frowned at the incomprehensibility of it all.

She spoke aloud: "It just isn't *real*."

She meant love.

* * *

"Did the board meeting go well today?"

"I think we got what we wanted. The decline of the relationship of the dollar to the yen has made us reconsider our imports from Japan; but we found other European sources."

Jeanne's parents lived their lives in a businesslike manner, never expressing affection for each other directly, deducing each other's deeper feelings out of the casual talk that interrupted their long stretches of silence.

"I have some news, Adele."

"So have I, Gilbert."

They sat at the small table situated in the bow window of their lofty apartment, and sipped tea. This had become a ritual born of Gilbert's habit of working until seven in the evening. A pot of tea, unimportant conversation, or just a time of sharing space while looking out at the lights of the city, served as his way of winding down prior to a light supper.

By convention, Adele shared her news first:

"Philip called today."

"Pomeranz?"

"He's going to ask Bill to let Kevin stay with him and Hilda for a time, to give Bill a better chance to get himself settled."

Gilbert shook his head. "Bill shouldn't let Kevin go. I'm thinking of Kevin, of course, who needs the guidance of his own father; but also Bill needs the companionship of his son at a time like this. Bill has suffered a tremendous betrayal, you know. Though we both love our daughter, surely you can see where justice lies in this situation."

Adele poured herself another half cup of tea. "I told Philip I thought it a very kind gesture."

Gilbert shrugged, as if to say: "It's up to Bill."

Adele let sufficient time pass to be sure Gilbert had no more to say on the subject, knowing he was extending the same courtesy to her. Then she asked him, "What do you have to tell me?''

"I've found Jeanne.''

Adele knew from his off-hand inflections and lack of stress placed on his words that Jeanne was safe and sound. Her query was therefore almost disinterested. "Where is she?''

"On a cruise ship in the Caribbean. I must say, Philip was no help to us on this. I had to hire a detective.''

Adele smiled and muttered, "That's resourceful of her.''

"It's cowardly,'' Gilbert asserted.

"When does she return?''

"Next Sunday morning. I'm going to meet her, of course. Will you go with me?''

"I'm not sure that's wise. Shouldn't we wait for her to come to us, when she's ready?''You overwhelm me, Adele. After all she's done!''

"Forgive me . . . but what has she done?'' she reflected. "Apart from leaving without much notice.''

Gilbert attacked his faithful wife with a look of profound accusation, as if Adele had finally revealed some congenital stupidity. "She's embarrassed every member of this family — except you, for some reason.''

"Oh . . . she has embarrassed me, Gilbert. I never know how to take it when a friend asks me how she is. I'm always afraid they're hoping I'll say she's miserable and hopelessly destroyed. My second feeling, in such cases, is always pity and sympathy for Jeanne.''

Gilbert's next expression was one of resignation, one Adele knew might be accompanied by something like "Women!" said with condescension and disbelief.

"I think I should tell you that I'm planning to take a firm hand in Jeanne's rehabilitation. You might assume that we failed her in some way as parents. I don't subscribe to that hogwash, not a bit of it. We offered that child and her brother not only every material comfort and advantage; we offered them affection and firm guidance. You know we did—or you would know it if you saw the issues unsentimentally. She chose to reject that guidance, to be less than appreciative of the advantages. It may seem cruel to you, but if she intends to remain part of this family—an active part of this family—she will have to be treated firmly once more. Like a child who has insufficiently matured . . . until she grows into life's responsibilities as an adult.

"She will live here with us so that we may oversee her activities. And her allowance will be stopped until she can prove herself worthy of it."

Adele's mouth was slightly agape, and tears were clouding the azure eyes behind her spectacles. "That seems too harsh," she said shakily.

"Are you challenging my judgement?"

"No; I know you will do whatever you think is best."

* * *

French Martinique—the glorious "Pearl of the Antilles." If it weren't in the wrong ocean, it

86

would have had to be the inspiration for the mythical Bali Hai. It was a turning point in the cruise; it meant that the return leg to New York had begun.

Jeanne was uncommonly euphoric watching the island draw nearer as the *Liberty* approached the French Line pier at Fort de France, the island's capital. She wanted to reach out and embrace the whole island, throw her arms around the mist-enshrouded volcanic peak—feel it and see it all at once. Jeanne found herself in her most positive mood in many a month. She felt girlish, adventurous for a change. Although life seemed as confusing as ever, it was beginning to promise excitement and interest . . . above all, *interest*.

Jeanne had read of notorious Mount Pelée—a volcano which had erupted with such force in 1902 that a cloud of incandescent smoke had descended with the power of a red-hot hurricane, and buried the town of Saint-Pierre, killing thirty thousand inhabitants. A modern Vesuvius and Pompeii. Still, the island had survived, rebuilt, and fluorished. Jeanne wanted to see it. She suspected in advance that this would be the high-point of her trip. It was at last occurring to her that she was on vacation!

Boarding the tour bus, she felt sudden regret at being alone. She wanted Alan with her, so they could pretend, as they had when they were teenagers. They would be explorers, daring the violence and unpredictability of a hungry volcano. But Jeanne was alone, and she'd make the best of it.

Through the charming, bustling town, the tour guide talked of trade items—of perfumes, china, porcelain, silver, and rum—while Jeanne idealized the simple small-town life of the enviable natives. He talked about agriculture, gross national product, and political allegiance to France—while Jeanne looked out at slopes of pineapple, forests of banana trees, the edges of the lush tropical rain forests . . . and dreamed of chivalry among the plantation owners. Somehow, a picture came to her that mingled images from her past fantasies: a palace in a tropical jungle with Arabian horses in the stables, and the music of Chopin rising from a grand piano inside.

When the guide told of the disaster of Pelée, Jeanne thought of the phoenix spirit in man — the will to rise again from the ashes, to rebuild, to fly once more . . . as she intended to do with her own life. She felt, somehow, that she had begun the reconstruction already.

At a rest stop Jeanne's bus met another filled with passengers from the *Liberty*. She noted the familiar faces—Alice and Horace were among them, cameras a-clicking—and there was Donna. Alone.

Donna waved and smiled with an eager expression that had some hint of embarrassment in it.

Jeanne laughed; she understood that expression. "I've never known anyone more transparent," she said. "I suppose it means you have an honest soul. Want to tell me about it . . . him?"

Jeanne arranged an exchange of tour seats,

and joined Donna on the way up the slopes to the volcanic come of sleeping Pelée.

"It's the first time in my life I've ever felt this," Donna said. He put me on a damn leash and pulled me around like a puppy dog. It wasn't a fantasy, like you said; it was real. It was him, really him. He said what you said, too—that I'm as transparent as glass, that he could see everything in me there was to see. All that liberation stuff, all that tough woman-of-the-world stuff I've been laying on you . . . it's all a pile of crap. I'm *his* . . . and he knows it, and I know he knows it, and he knows I know he knows it. And it's all right!"

Jeanne laughed. "Slow down. It's hard to follow all that. I certainly get the drift, though. I . . . and I think it's wonderful, really."

Donna frowned and asked, oddly, "Do you know how I feel?"

Jeanne hesitated. "I think so."

Donna considered Jeanne's hesitation and at last concluded, "Of course, you understand! Anybody would, because it's the same everywhere and with everybody; it always has been and always will be. I'm in love, that's all. I'm in love."

At another stop, they wandered away from the bus crowd to a spot where they felt greater privacy. It was deep within the rain forest, among giant ferns, lush tropical trees, and moving shafts of sunlight cutting through the haze.

"He caught me being defensive," Donna continued, "and trying to make him prove himself. He made me trust him. I don't know how; he never came out and said, 'Trust me,' but it felt like that anyway. We've been together every night since we met. It's like I've come home, somehow. Every time I look into those eyes of his I feel like I've died and gone to heaven!''

Jeanne listened with only part of her mind, the other part was thinking that *those eyes of his always seemed a bit lethargic to me, perhaps even deceitful. Ah, well, beauty is in the eye of the beholder.*

''He'll be in New York this fall, at least he probably will, and we're planning. . . . ''

I ought to try to bring her back to earth, Jeanne thought; *but if I'm wrong, if this affair is honest and really good, then I mustn't dampen it for the world! Maybe I'm just guilty of seeing this through my own eyes, rather than trying to see it through hers.*

Mark was on deck when they returned. He slipped an arm around each of the ladies and escorted them to the poolside bar. The sun had just set and, in the manner of near-equatorial sunsets, twilight was very rapidly turning to night. The music coming from somewhere was ''Begin the Beguine.'' Mark picked up where the tour guides left off:

''Cole Porter didn't really begin the beguine, you know,'' he said suggestively; ''it's native to Martinique, and it's the sexiest, most sultry dance you'll ever see. Sure you two don't want to go back ashore, to one of the gambling casinos to see a floorshow? I feel you're cheating yourselves returning so early to the ship. We don't sail until midnight.''

"Will you go with us?" Donna asked, feeling he had just been hinting for an invitation.

"Can't, he replied. "Got work to do. Tomorrow night's our shipboard Calypso Ball, and there are preparations to be made. Uh . . . incidentally, he said to Donna; "I think you'd better make other sleeping arrangements for tonight. I'll need my beauty rest." He turned to Jeanne and said, laughing, "The little lady has been taking up most of my time lately."

Donna took that to mean: There's no one I'd rather have spent the time with.

Jeanne thought: He wants to get rid of her. Jeanne also considered it impolite of him to say such a thing to Donna in her presence. But Donna was from a generation that "let it all hang out," and she didn't seem to mind.

For passengers who had elected to spend the evening aboard, the kitchen had arranged a games-deck barbecue—chicken served with an Indonesian rice dish, and all the salad one could eat. Jeanne, Mark, and Donna enjoyed it, carrying on small talk—mostly hearing Mark's "little known" facts about the Caribbean—drinking in the incredible array of stars in a moonless evening and the hibiscus-scented tropical breeze.

Mark wasn't the only one who had been missing sleep; Donna yawned frequently and, minutes after Mark excused himself to go to work, she curled up in a deck chair and went to sleep.

Jeanne roused her once to suggest that she return to her cabin, rather than sleep in the damp outdoor air. "I'm fine," Donna assured her.

Jeanne watched the passengers returning around departure time. There were Horace and Alice. She seemed tipsy, and he steadied her with one arm and carried a mound of wild orchids in the other. Most of them boarded and went directly to their cabins; a few strolled on deck or waited around, as Jeanne did, to watch the cast-off procedures. Strolling musicians stood on the pier, beautifully singing a lovely but terribly sad song. It was as if the whole island were heartbroken to see the *Liberty* leave its shore. Illogically, Jeanne began to cry. It was too beautiful, too right. It made her believe that no one was to blame for her misfortunes—not her father, Bill, Gordon, not even herself. Above all, not the world. The world was benevolent and lovely, and Jeanne felt all alone in it. She returned to her cabin, sobbing.

She felt the ship quivver with the first vibrations of power. A vessel the size of *Liberty* did not lurch, did not seem to move at all, in fact; but she knew that they had to be leaving Martinique behind.

Unable to sleep, she returned to the deck some time later and found no island in sight. A crescent moon was rising off to starboard— warm, golden.

"Mystical, isn't it?"

She turned, startled, to face Mark Harris. "It's beautiful," she agreed unenthusiastically. Wasn't he supposed to be working late, then sleeping soundly?

"I thought you might come up. I've been waiting for you."

92

"Why?"

"I know you often roam the decks alone at night."

"No, why have you been waiting for me?"

"To speak with you. To get to know you better."

"Why?" He offered Jeanne a cigarette, which she declined, then prolonged the lighting of his own. "Something to do with desiring the unattainable, I suspect," he said with a shrug.

Jeanne was taken off guard completely. *This* had never occurred to her. She was infuriated on Donna's behalf and felt flattered simultaneously. She thought in a flash: *It's all just a line!* He had been using Donna, using them *both* merely for diversion.

"Would you," she asked hesitantly, "spell that out for me?"

"You prefer the direct approach?" he asked, in his sexiest voice. "I'd have thought you'd rather have had a courtship dance . . . at least three times around the maypole, as it were."

"I prefer an honest approach. Donna—"

"Donna is an intelligent, delightful girl. She'll make some man very happy some day, but she's lacking in the more mature emotions. You're—"

"About ten years older than she. I'm probably older than you are."

"We're not talking about chronological age, are we?"

"I'm not sure what we are talking about."

"I'm fond of Donna, but I mainly cultivated her friendship in order to get to know you better.

I've had my eye on you, and only you, really, since that first day out of New York. But I'm at a loss. How does one approach you?"

Jeanne was so indignant and disgusted that she couldn't reply at all. She turned away from him and walked some distance down the railing. When she stopped, her fingernails dug into the wood of the top rail as she composed her thoughts, preparing to tell Mark in very precise English what she thought of him. He might suspect the worst, but he could in no way be prepared for the torrent of contempt waiting on the tip of Jeanne's tongue. Ready, her eyes narrowed in fury, she turned. Sure enough, Mark was walking toward her.

But beyond Mark stood Donna, her hands on her glistening cheeks, watching in horror. She had to have been lying there in the dark, under an overhanging deck, on a sun lounge.

"Donna!" Jeanne blurted out.

Mark whirled to see Donna behind him . . . just as she vaulted up the railing and launched herself out into the blackness of space, a good forty feet above the churning sea.

six

Jeanne screamed, but before her scream ended she had moved into action. She struggled with a life preserver, trying to loosen it from its brackets. Without looking, she flung it overboard.

Mark stood there dumbfounded.

"More life preservers!" Jeanne yelled.

That jolted Mark out of his mementary stupor and he sprinted toward a glassed-in lever on the nearby bulkhead. "Don't bother!" Mark shouted as she was hurling another overboard. "Try to keep your eye on where she fell!" He broke the glass and grabbed the lever that was marked: MAN OVERBOARD ALARM.

A whooping alarm sounded its mournful, terrifying howl.

Though the decks had been virtually deserted moments before, suddenly there was a swarm of white-uniformed crewmen running toward the spot where Jeanne and Mark stood straining to see Donna in the ship's lights and trying to determine how far back along the wake she must have struck the waves. Not only could they not see Donna, but they couldn't even see the bright white life preservers Jeanne had tossed over.

There was a percussive *thoooop*! as life preservers were shot from some sort of catapult back along the wake.

"Did she go over the stern?" an officer demanded of Jeanne; "or here over the side?"

"Over the side. She jumped way out!"

"Good," he said as he signaled the emergency crew to prepare the nearest rescue boat for lowering.

The man-overboard alarm had been shut off, but the main rumbling whistle was now bleating periodically.

Jeanne could see by lights on the stern that the wake was starting to curve; the ship was turning. Passengers were coming on deck, many of them in house robes or with hastily donned trousers, shirts, and bare feet. They quickly learned what had happened.

Jeanne studied the curving wake. It would take *ages* to make a full return. She suspected that the distance to be covered could be measured in miles.

"The water's too deep for anchors," someone close by said.

"Why do they even bother?" said a companion. "I don't see how they could find anybody—even in daylight!"

As if in partial answer to the passenger, a string of search lights flashed into life and began to scan the black waves.

Jeanne saw that the wake was now such a wide curve that she could no longer see a straight stretch of it.

Captain Martinson's voice came over the

loudspeaker to say: "Will all passengers please stand clear of the starboard side of the ship— that's the side on your right as you face forward—and clear of the stern. It's been noted that some of you are carrying cameras. Please do not use your flash! You could mementarily blind a rescuer and hamper the operations. I repeat, please do not use flash!"

The massive *City of Liberty* shuddered as the propellers began to act as brakes, slowing the ship as it coasted toward where Donna might still be afloat.

"There are sharks throughout these Caribbean waters," Jeanne heard someone say.

"You've been seeing too many *Jaws* movies," someone else quipped.

"The coffee shop's closed; do any of the bars have coffee this time of night?" another asked.

"I don't know. Let's go see; we'll have plenty of time."

"It was a woman who fell."

"Fell or jumped?"

Jeanne looked over at Mark. To his credit, he seemed petrified. He said, "Tell me this isn't happening."

Jeanne was too distressed to tell him anything.

"Look! Isn't that somebody?"

"No, just a shadow on a wave."

"Mommy, what's happening? Are we sinking?"

"No dear; of course not."

"Honey, I'm going back to bed. You can tell me what happened."

Alice—of Horace and Alice—rested a hand on Jeanne's arm. She said, "We haven't met, dear. I'm Alice Tinling. But we've smiled at each other as our paths have crossed, and I've learned that the young woman overboard is your very attractive young friend. If there's anything at all I can do to help, please tell me. I thought you should know that. Horace and I are in D25."

Jeanne smiled gratefully. "I can't imagine—"

"Well, for example, we have immersion heaters and a little hot plate. If you or the young lady should want something hot to drink, come to us. Anytime, anytime at all."

Perhaps the most comforting thing about Alice was her assumption that Donna would be picked up safely, that it was only a matter of time, and that the worst that might have happened to her would be a slight chill.

The wake ironed out into a straight line again as the ship continued to slow . . . moving into water too deep for the use of anchors, with no landmarks, and no certainty that there was anything for the blackness to be found.

"Where's her cabin?" Jeanne asked Mark. "She'll need dry clothes."

Mark's mouth was white, almost blue in the moonlight. "She doesn't have a cabin," he said.

"What do you mean?"

"She's a stowaway." Mark mumbled, as if he were unaware that Jeanne was listening: "Wouldn't you know . . . the first time I've ever shielded a stowaway, and she makes herself conspicuous—in the worst possible way.'' He recovered enough to hide his concern for his own hide and tried to instill a note of realism. He told Jeanne, ''Even if she survived the fall, they'll never find her in the dark. She's miles away.''

Jeanne had not struck another human being since early childhood. If she had stopped to think, she would have had to wonder how to go about it. Her arm just swung out, as if of its own accord, and slammed a fist into Mark Harris' jaw.

He stumbled and sat with violent suddenness on the hard steel deck.

He sat there immobile, speechless, like a criminal who knows the jig is up, until everyone heard an officer say into a bullhorn: ''Train your torch over there, Sid; isn't that something?''

Another officer came by and ordered Jeanne and Mark away from the descending lifeboat, but not before the two of them glimpsed something white on the black water.

''Just a life preserver,'' a man shouted back.

The great ship was motionless in the water.

''Please be perfectly quiet on the deck,'' said a voice over the loudspeaker. ''Listen very carefully.''

There was only a whisper of wind and the sound of gears churning as cranes lowered the boat, stopping it just above the water.

''There's another life preserver,'' said the man with the bullhorn.

Silence.

''Lights slightly to port. That's it. A little

99

more."

Silence

"There she is. Lower the boat."

A loud cheer broke from passengers and crew members alike. Jeanne felt her knees buckle and grabbed the nearest railing for support. The captain's amplified voice insisted: "Quiet on the deck! And stand well back from the operations of the rescuers and the boat!"

Jeanne heard a feeble voice out there somewhere crying, "Here . . . here . . . hurry."

seven

City of Liberty's hospital was on E-Deck, right at the waterline and just above the engine rooms. It was quiet there except for the eerie periodic sloshing of the sea outside and a steady, almost inaudible rumble from the engines below.

Captain Martinson, white hair over a stern face, wearing a white uniform and leaning against a white metal bulkhead, was the blinding sight Donna saw as she blinked open her eyes. She had been only remotely aware of the procedure of hoisting her stretcher aboard ship, and she had slipped into an uneasy sleep for an hour or so. Coming awake now, she began to shiver.

"What do you suggest I do with you, Miss Andersen?" the Captain asked in a voice that revealed great self-possession, and with that British pronunciation that seemed the epitome of discipline and efficiency.

Donna licked her dry lips; she could still taste salt. "T-t-toss me back in and wait for me to grow up?"

"This isn't as funny as you might imagine." Captain Martinson rubbed the side of his nose delicately, studying Donna. "The water was warmer than the air. Why are you trembling?"

"I d-d-d-don't know."

"May I take it that you are no longer anxious to die?"

Donna was grateful that the man was not going to play games with her, but she began to fear he might embarrass or humiliate her. She also felt that if he did, she would deserve it. "No, I no longer want t-t-t-to do that."

The Captain waited, his arms folded, his head tilted back expectantly. He was frowning, but his expression was not altogether unkind.

Because she felt like an infant being chastized, Donna readily understood what he was waiting for. She gulped, cleared her throat, licked her lips, and said, in a small voice, "Thank you . . . for saving me."

He nodded, thought that over, and said, "Sincerity seems to come hard for you, Miss Anderson. I'm grateful that you managed it for me just now." He looked away and let his arms fall slack at his sides. "I apologize for that remark."

" Oh, you have a right to be angry."

"Indeed I have, but not to be caustic. Forgive that, please. It gets us nowhere."

His fairness brought tears to Donna's eyes. "What are you going to do?" she asked him, biting her lower lip.

"I've not decided. I've never had a stowaway jump—let's say fall—overboard before." He took a chair and pivoted it on one leg so he could sit facing Donna. "There was a woman once, a passenger I rescued twice. The third time she jumped—on a night much like tonight, with

102

choppy seas and very little moonlight—I wished my conscience would let me leave her out there. She clearly didn't care to be rescued. But I felt I had no choice. We made our circle, strained our generators flooding the area with light, searched for six hours . . . and never found her. I wanted to be hard and conclude good riddance, but I could not do that, not even with that woman. We were almost two days late returning to port because of her. So far you've delayed us only four or five hours—at operating costs of around $7,000 per hour. Call it $30,000.''

Donna chuckled inanely. She was contrite, but, simultaneously she was thinking: What can they do, shoot me? Some part of her felt as if she'd pulled off the perfect robbery—or piracy, maybe.

The Captain seemed to be reading her mind, and understanding her, to an extent. "I'll tell you who pays, Miss Anderson—two thousand passengers who will lose port time in St. Thomas because of the time we must make up returning to New York.''

One part of Donna was so sorry she thought she'd die; the other part was shrugging and saying: big deal.

The Captain said, "I have a daughter a bit older than you. She was involved in all the anti-Establishment brouhaha some years ago. Took drugs in the name of open-mindedness and rebellion. Lost all semblance of a moral code while trying to insist that her code was superior to any she found in the world around her.'' He stopped and regarded Donna with an affection that seemed unwillingly granted. "You're like her. She was never as pretty or as . . . innocent, I think.'

"Did she die?" Donna had been puzzled by his use of past tense.

"She's in an institution. Too many overdoses, too much depression, too little professional help in time."

Donna was jolted by the story and felt she had to get off that subject at once. "I really am sorry about all this," she said.

"How do you suppose you could apologize to two thousand passengers?"

"You're really rubbing it in, aren't you?"

He nodded. "I suppose you haven't the price of a ticket—$945?" Donna laughed. "No," she sputtered out.

"I figured. Normally, then, you would be dropped off at the next port and left there to fend for yourself."

"Lucky for me we aren't at the N-n-north Pole."

"I said, 'normally'. In your case, the fare has been paid by a passenger, Jeanne Mason."

Through tears that were bubbling up again, Donna said, "I w-want to see her."

"She'll be down sometime today. Right now, you need rest and sleep. You're in shock, you know. Scared to death out there, weren't you?" For the first time, he smiled at her.

She nodded, trying to hold her lower jaw steady.

"I must have a bite of breakfast, then get

some sleep myself.''

"Who'll be running the sh-sh-ship?''

"A qualified officer who's to take command while I'm on holiday. Thanks to you, he will see us into port without my help. His first solo with *Liberty*.''

He stopped at the door, his hand on the knob. The expression on his face changed; it put a gulf of distance between himself and the troubled girl he had felt warmth toward. He said, "I don't know and don't care to know the nature of your problems, Miss Andersen, but, with your apparent mental capabilities, it can't be the end of the world for you. I assume you did a lot of thinking as you floated around in your life preserver out there. That ring, incidentally, was probably the one tossed you by Miss Mason; it would have been the closest to you. In any case, I want you to realize fully that what you did was thoughtless,utterly reprehensible.'' He was not smiling as he left.

* * *

Philip Pomeranz stood outside a familiar walnut-paneled door. It led to the apartment where Jeanne and Bill Oliver had lived so happily together—or so Philip had once assumed; and where Kevin had started life with all the advantages one could have wished for a child—or so it had once seemed.

Philip's errand now was to rescue Kevin from his father before Bill could make life intolerable for the son he did not understand. Philip did not know quite what he was in for.

A role would have to be played. The real Philip Pomeranz had no business entering that door. It was the role Philip had played with Bill Oliver for years—pretending to like him, to share his interests, to understand his goals. This had been a necessity; otherside Philip would have admitted to everyone his real motive for maintaining this relationship: that he loved Jeanne. He had played the role for Hilda, his wife, too. If she ever wondered what Philip and Bill saw in each other, she never mentioned the curiosity. The role had gone all the way; he even played it for Jeanne. She saw through it to some core underneath, but even she had not guessed the whole truth. She once asked Philip, ''How do you two manage to find so much to talk about?''

It takes superhuman effort sometimes, he thought with mirthless amusement as he stood there preparing to ring Bill's bell.

Another herculean effort was required—like the alchemist's scheme for turning lead into gold—for Philip to convert his hatred and jealousy into friendly behavior. The role had not been a totally dishonest one; Philip was in part bending over backward to be fair to a man whose life he envied.

This time there would have to be an additional act of subterfuge. Bill must not guess Philip's real reason for wanting to take Kevin. As Jeanne's lawyer, Philip had tried every legal means he knew to keep Kevin and his mother together. Now he was going about it in an underhanded way and without Jeanne's knowledge and approval.

Just one more time, Philip convinced himself as he raised his finger toward the bell. He rubbed his clammy right hand against his pinstriped trouser leg at the same time. Like an actor rehearsing his part, Philip reminded himself: This just a casual offer out of friendship, my way of easing Bill's transition into the life of a bachelor father.

"Philip!" Bill exclaimed as he pulled open the door. "Walk right in and take a seat, any seat. What can I get you? The usual?" Bill clearly had a head start on the alcohol.

"The usual will be fine, old buddy," Philip said, pressing Bill's hand in a warm greeting. It could be worse, Philip reflected; he could be harboring a grudge because I defended Jeanne. But of course, we did lose. Maybe it's some kind of twisted generosity on his part. Maybe he's just drunk.

"How you been keeping yourself?" Bill asked as he dropped ice cubes noisily into a highball glass.

"Can't complain. And yourself?"

"Fine and dandy," Bill said, not bothering to hide a sarcasm that reversed the meaning of his answer. "Having a rip-roaring, wild old time." He handed Philip the drink, scooped his from the bar, and toasted: "To the life of a bachelor!"

Philip laughed uneasily. "Not sure Hilda'd approve of that."

"What the hell, drink anyway." Bill downed half his drink in one gulp.

Philip sipped his Scotch and water. He said, knowing he treaded on thin ice, "Hoped I'd find you in better spirits."

Bill pushed his palm against his forehead, as if he had a splitting headache. "You came here with something on your mind, didn't you, chum?" He said it hostilely, and Philip was reminded of Bill's way of taking his aches and pains out on others.

"I have . . . Hilda and I have an idea, Bill." He took on something of the manner of a salesman, a bantering technique he and Bill had engaged in on occasion. "Tell you what I'm goin' to do, my friend. At absolutely no cost to yourself, I offer you, absolutely free, the chance to get used to this new bachelor life of yours. How would it be," Philip wound down and spoke more seriously, "if Hilda and I took Kevin off your hands for a while, until you get things sorted out?"

Kevin, who must have been listening, walked solemnly into the room and stood near the end of the couch beside Philip.

Bill surveyed the two of them with a puzzled smile. "You're such a phoney son of a bitch, Philip," he said, still smiling. "I've never been able to figure out *how* phoney."

"I—I'm completely serious, Bill. We really would enjoy having Kevin for a while, and I think it would do you lots of—"

"This not a court of law!" Bill roared suddenly, slamming his open hand against the bar top.

Philip could feel sweat breaking out on his

108

forehead, but he answered calmly enough, "I don't need a legal right to make a friendly gesture, Bill." He watched every visible muscle of Bill's grow tense and then slowly relax. Bill broke his own spell and stepped behind the bar to refill his glass.

Kevin readied his mouth to say please; but Philip signaled and shook his head subtly.

"Want a refill, Philip?" Bill asked in an almost normal tone of voice.

"No thanks; I'm still nursing this one."

Bill pulled a smouldering cigarette butt from an ash tray, looked at it as if there were something odd about it, snuffed it out, and lighted another one. He said, letting out the first long cloud of smoke, "He'd have to pack a few things."

Philip heard Kevin gasp, and he assumed Bill also heard it. "He could go with me now, if you don't mind." Philip suggested.

"Sure," Bill said, "why not." He said to his son impersonally, "Need help packing?"

"No, I can do it!" Kevin said as he ran from the room.

Bill grabbed his forehead again and muttered, "He doesn't like me very much, I guess." He moved his hand, leaving a reddish imprint of fingers on his head. He said coldly, "If you turn this kid over to his bitch of a mother, I'll have you practicing without a license so fast you'll have to hire another lawyer to keep you out of jail."

"I know the law, Bill," Philip said. "Are you all right?"

He grumbled, "Can't get rid of this damned headache. Nerves, I suppose." He conceded, "Maybe this is best for the kid."

Philip nodded. They listened to banging sounds coming from Kevin's room—drawers and closet doors opening and shutting. Kevin returned, carrying two small suitcases.

Damn, thought Philip, he didn't take quite long enough; he obviously already had them packed.

"Will he need any money?" Bill asked, apparently oblivious to the evidence of a put-up job.

Philip laughed awkwardly. "Hell no, Bill. This isn't a permanent arrangement, you know." He was trying to ignore the sickening knot in his stomach.

Kevin stood anxiously by the front door, watching the two men who were in some way deciding his fate.

Philip downed the last of his drink, left the glass on the bar, and said, "Take care, Bill. Call if you need anything."

He said, "I'll do that," as if he didn't mean it.

"Bye, Dad," Kevin said meekly.

"Bye, Son," Bill said unhappily.

Outside, Philip walked rapidly, carrying Kevin's bags, with the boy running along behind.

"Did I do it all right?" Kevin asked. "Uncle Alan said I wasn't supposed to say anything about—"

"You did fine, Kevin," Philip said perfunctorily.

Before hailing a cab, at the corner of York and Sixty-third, Philip steered Kevin inside the door of a neighborhood bar. It was early, and the bar was virtually deserted.

"Help you, sir?" the bartender asked.

"Would you mind keeping an eye on the boy for a minute?" Philip asked.

"What's wrong?" Kevin asked.

"I don't feel so hot. I'll be right back." Philip's insides felt as if they were being kneaded by rough hands. He threw open the men's-room door and prepared to vomit. But the sensation began to pass. He splashed water on his face and stood still while his turmoil subsided and his breathing and heartbeat returned almost to normal.

He hoped he'd never have to see Bill Oliver again, for any reason. He doubted he'd be so lucky.

* * *

Gilbert Mason's receptionist rang in on his intercom to announce Mr. Bitlinger.

"Send him right in."

The short-haired man—devoid of his flashy shirt and tourist's cameras—entered smiling. "You got my cablegram?"

"Yes. Let's see the pictures."

Bitlinger reached into a manila envelope, extracted a stack of black and white prints, and fanned them out. "I don't think there's any doubt," he said. "She matched the photos you and your wife gave me, and she was traveling under her real name. Here. . . ."

"Yes, that's Jeanne. Who's the man with her?"

"I didn't get his name, he—"

" Why not?"

"I believe he was with the other woman, whose name I learned was Donna Andersen. She and your daughter seemed particularly friendly, as if they might have been traveling together. Do you recognize her?"

"No. I'm sure she's just an acquaintance from the ship." He quickly flipped through the stack and reached the bottom one—in which Donna was being led to the door of the Voodoo temple by Jeanne and the man. "What's happening here?" Mason demanded.

"The girl was upset by the ceremony. Not surprising. It was an upsetting ceremony."

"And then?"

" I followed them back to the ship, left them, and took a plane back."

"Did you find the storage company for me?"

"I did. Five Boroughs Transfer and Storage in Queens. They knew your name."

"They should; I've dealt with them for years. How many cubic feet?"

"It's all here; I got a copy of her inventory sheet."

Mason accepted it without gratitude. "Good work, Mr. Bitlinger. I may use your firm again. You'll bill me?"

"First of the month."

Mason was on the phone even before Bitlinger was out of his office. "Get me Fred Hensel at Five Boroughs Transfer," he ordered his receptionist. "Fred? Gilbert Mason. I understand you're storing a few things for my daughter . . . Jeanne Mason, yes . . . I'd like you to have them sent to my home . . . no, that won't be necessary in this case; I'll sign for them . . . tomorrow will be fine; thanks, Fred. "

* * *

As she tried to sleep, Donna's mind was like a time-lapse motion picture of the sky—haziness, then racing clouds, darkness, stormy flashes, a blank. . .

She saw the white walls of the hospital, then an image of the tossing black sea. A remembrance of the stunning blow when she hit the water, the cold, the utter darkness, the panic.

Then she saw the hands of the hospital clock, the spastic ticking of the hands, the unfamiliar markings on the face of it, the maritime numbering of the hours. "What time is it?" she once asked aloud; then her mind wandered away again. . . .

The empty chair where the Captain had sat, the sensation of Mark's hands on her body, his body against and within hers. His laughter, his teasing, his kisses, his mouth on her breasts.

The empty chair again, and the white walls; but Jeanne was sitting there now . . . Jeanne *was* sitting there!

"What is it? Don't be frightened; it's over," Jeanne whispered.

Donna sat bolt upright in bed. "Jeanne—I'm

so sorry, so embarrassed.'' Tears began to flood down her face.

Jeanne reached out and hugged her. ''Donna—you misunderstood what I was—''

''I know that, damn it. I'm so sorry!''

''When Mark made that pass at me I was was so infuriated I nearly threw *him* overboard! I was afraid you thought—''

''I did. That's why I jumped; but I think I knew the truth even before I hit the water. I did a lot of thinking out there! It's just that it was bad enough when I heard Mark betraying me, and when you didn't say anything to him, or hit him or anything, I thought you had betrayed me, too! I couldn't take it. I just—I don't know, I just jumped.''

''I *did* hit him,'' Jeanne said, crying in spite of her resolve not to and laughing at the same time. '' Hit him so hard he fell on the deck.''

''You decked the bastard! I wouldn't have guessed you had it in you!''

''Know where he is now? In the brig.''

Donna pulled up the sheet and wiped tears from her face. ''What do you know; there is some justice in the world, after all. Solitary confinement, I hope.''

''Well, actually, I don't think they have a brig. Confined to quarters, I think they said. He's been fired, permanently relieved of duty.''

''I guess the—what is it?—the Calypso Ball will survive without him.''

''It did survive without him; it was last night. You've been asleep quite a while.''

Donna glanced up at the wall clock; she still

couldn't read it. She stared for a minute at the mound made by her raised knees under the sheet. "Thanks for paying my fare," she said timidly. "I don't know what I'd have—"

"You'd have managed," Jeanne said, smiling.

"I'm not so sure. I'll pay you back somehow, someday."

"If you want to."

"No, honest, I really will."

"If it's any consolation, I was probably as terrified here, as you were out there."

"I've never been so scared," Donna said frankly. "You know, there were two things that brought me to my senses: the thought that if I didn't straighten up, my hair would turn white—I even laughed at that one—and the sight of the *Liberty* circling around. I only lost sight of the ship when I was at the bottom of a wave. I knew you were coming for me."

"It's over now." Jeanne smiled.

"In a way," Donna said cryptically.

This was something of a new Donna, Jeanne thought. She wasn't so eager to ridicule serious matters anymore—not at the moment, anyway. It's a horrible thought, Jeanne realized, but I think the awful experience did her some good.

"Can I tell you what I learned out there?" Donna queried.

"Yes—please do."

"I'm not sure I can make anybody understand this, but here goes. There's something I've been doing wrong all my life. I don't know whether it's from social influences, rotten parents, or my own stupidity. It's the way I've tried

115

to be independent. I swallowed all the women's lib stuff whole, of course; most of the girls I know did; and maybe it's all to the good. But it didn't mix well with the previous attitudes I had. Wait, that's getting off the subject. The point is that I thought I was being independent as long as I . . . carefully chose the people I wanted to run my life for me. Get it?''

Jeanne tilted her head and frowned. ''Not yet; keep going.''

''I mean—that feeling of being betrayed by you and Mark; it was much more than that. It was *doom*! I thought of my self as a living puppet, and I had handed my strings to you and Mark.''

Jeanne was still confused. ''Buy why?''

'' Why? Uh, Mark because he was a prize catch, and you because you're the kind of woman I've always wanted to be—confident, capable, realistic. More than anything, it's that you're realistic—able to look life in the eye and take things as they come. I figured you would know what was good for me, if anybody would.''

All Jeanne could say was, ''For heaven's sake.''

''See, I *trusted* you and Mark. The kiss of death, right? When I trust somebody, I give them the wheel, put them in my driver's seat. I mean—there are lots of people in this world I just couldn't go along with, right? So I try to pick people who'll make me do things I approve of. Perverted, isn't it?''

Jeanne laughed lightly. ''Probably, but I don't

think it's all that unusual.''

"And here I was—broke, running away, a stowaway with nowhere to go and no one to turn to, except that I had these two super-wonderful people who were holding my strings.''

Jeanne commented, ''That's an incredible burden to place on anyone's shoulders. I wouldn't have let you—''

"Of course not. Nobody would! At least, not if they knew about it.''

''I—I want to tell you two things Donna. I felt some of that toward you—not the puppet bit, I think, but the feeling that maybe you were the kind of woman *I* ought to be.''

''You're kidding.'' ''The other thing is, I think you're being too hard on yourself. Aren't you exaggerating all this a bit?''

Donna was slightly annoyed. ''Listen, if you're not going to believe me, I won't tell you things.''

The rumble of the engine stopped suddenly, and the sloshing of the sea outside was barely audible. It was quiet enough for Jeanne and Donna to hear the insect-like buzz of the fluorescent light above Donna's bed.

''Are we in port?'' Donna asked.

''We're just coming in. I caught a glimpse of the island before I came down to see you.''

There was an unexpected clunk from somewhere below, as if the vessel had lowered its landing gear. Then a rasping hiss came quietly from down there somewhere.

''Altering the engines,'' Jeanne hazarded.

The hiss became a grinding sound, and suddenly the *Liberty* pitched forward, then it lurched back again. Everything was dead silent.

"Bumpy landing," Donna remarked. "That wasn't Captain Martinson bringing us in; it was an assistant learning how to do it. Hey, is the floor slanting?"

"I think it is a little."

"Sweet Jesus," Donna gasped, we've run aground!"

* * *

"New York's most attention-getting subculture," Alan Mason wrote in an article for the Entertainment section of the New York Times, "is its theater world. Most of its members—the producers, writers, directors, actors, singers, dancers, designers—live somewhat oblivious to the reality ordinary people inhabit. The majority of them are not avid newspaper readers, sports fans, churchgoers, political activists (except insofar as political machinations affect the arts). Having nothing but their values and passions to unite them, they are more magnetized to one another, more set apart from other social groups, than any ethnic neighborhood or special interest groups."

Alan was re-reading the carbon copy of his handiwork as he ascended to the twenty-third floor of the old Thespis Building in Times Square. The original copy of the article had just been dropped off in person by the author at the Times office. Now that it was too late, Alan wished he had exempted two professions from his thesis: the producers and writers who were generally less drawn into the subculture than the others. Oh, well.

It was one of those very show-biz groups, those pools of togetherness that Alan's elevator was taking him toward—a production meeting for his new play.

While by no means a Neil Simon, Alan Mason was fairly well established. His Off-Broadway hit *Dirty Dealing* was still running after three years, and last year's Broadway mystery-comedy *Night of the Bats* had enjoyed a respectable nearly-year-long run. Now a Mason play was "about to take off for outer space," as his producer had put it—meaning that *Conquerors and Candlelight* was to be a huge production with an inordinately large cast and an astronomical budget. An enormous risk, in other words—time for Russian Roulette and, as Alan had put it to his producer, Wif Kist, "time for taking bold steps, not tip-toeing through all the hits of the past!" Wif was still insisting that Alan change the name of his play to the less intriguing *Champagne and Caviar*—because it seemed safer.

Thoughts of Jeanne were at the moment farthest from Alan's mind.

It had been thundering for the past hour and, as Alan looked out the big window at the end of the twenty-third floor, he saw it begin to rain.

He opened the door to 2303

"Allah be praised! It's the author!" said a towering wild-looking woman with a breathy voice. Her thin tent-like dress ballooned behind her as she loped forward and extended a hand. "I'm Jo Savalon. I'm going to turn your dreary characters into real people." She laughed huskily and then said, apparently in dead earnest, "Seriously, I love your play, and I'm thrilled to be costuming it."

Alan smiled. "Thank you. I've seen many of the shows you've done, and I'm pleased you're with us."

"How refreshing; you didn't make a joke. Come, let me show you some designs. I've taken a liberty or two that I'd like to explain—"

"It always rains on the damndest days," said director Andrew Holloway as he barged into the room. "Alan, I think I've solved the action problem in the second act."

"What problem?" Alan asked timorously.

"Didn't I tell you? It'll require just a little rearranging of entrances and exits."

Jo Savalon realized she had missed her chance to have Alan to herself; she reached over to a desk and picked up a copy of the script and handed it to him.

"Page sixty—"

The phone rang.

"I got it!" someone yelled from an inner office. Alan recognized the voice of Wilfred (Wif) Kist.

The play's business manager, Chuck Willis, just said, "Uh . . ." but the six in the room got the idea; he wanted them to be quiet. They shamelessly eavesdropped on their leader's phone call:

" '. . . Virgin Islands? Are you serious? It's

not a collect call is it, operator? Okay, put him on . . . Mark Harris? Yes I remember your name. What can I do for . . . I suppose that can be arranged; is something wrong . . . your ship did what? How can an ocean liner run aground? Where? Hold on a minute. . . . " He called out to his secretary, who was evesdropping along with everyone else, "Jan, what auditions do we have on for tomorrow? Open calls, isn't it?"

"Yes," she confirmed, "all day."

"Pencil in an appointment for Mark Harris at two in the afternoon. We'll read him for the role of Steve during our lunch break." He turned his attention back to the phone. "Fine, Mark . . . no you won't need anything; we'll have a script for you . . . right. Thank you for calling." Knowing his conversation was being overheard by all, Wif yelled in a last bit of information. "He's coming in two days early, that's all. Get back to work!"

"Now about the costumes," said Jo.

"Now about the second act," said Andy.

Wif interrupted them both again by shouting, "We can't open. We're out of money!"

He entered the main office into the shocked silence he obviously expected.

"Because," he continued sweetly, "I've decided we either go all the way with *Champagne and Caviar*, or we don't do it at all. So, early this morning, kiddies, I booked us into the new Manhattan theater, the 'Hippodrome of the Twenty-First Century,' itself. *C&C* will inaugurate it."

To the shocked silence was added the sight of

six wide-open mouths.

"So," Wif went on, " we need another hundred thou. From somewhere."

"But that's a house for musicals!" Jo interjected. "Not that I'm complaining, but you *aren't* —"

"No, we're not turning *C&C* into a musical, but now we'll be able to do those ten set changes in the wink of an eye. People will leave thinking they *have* seen a musical!"

"Where's the money coming from?"

Wif Kist, producer of more hits than flops, had their undivided attention. He was an impish and flashy little man who thought it shocking to wear casual clothes to work; today he wore an Hawaiian print shirt and rainbow-striped trousers. He said slyly, "I think I know where I can get it." His eyes were on Alan.

They waited.

"From an interested party who has four times more money than all of us put together twice. One Mr. Gilbert A. Mason, Esquire."

Alan smiled and shook his head. "Dad wouldn't gamble a dime in show business. Besides that, he expects me to make it on my own—and he seriously doubts I can do it as a playwright. You know—if the old man can do it, so can the sprout. Not a chance."

Wif scratched his left ear. "For a writer, you lack imagination. You know the old guy; surely you can find a way to get around him. How about if we give a part to your wayward sister, keep her off the streets for him. Pretend she's an actress. . . ."

122

Alan wasn't in the least offended by Wif's reference to Jeanne; no disrespect was meant by it. "That won't do it. But I'd love to offer her an office job with us when she gets back—this weekend, I think. How about it?"

Wif narrowed his eyes and waited. He was only interested in a deal. "You keep thinking about it," he admonished. "And I'll make you one deal right now. You get me one hundred thousand dollars—and I don't care how you get it—and I'll let you keep your original title. We'll forget *Champagne and Caviar* was ever mentioned."

Alan grinned. "I'll give it some thought," Alan said with a shrug.

"There, that's settled," said Jo Savalon. "Now, about this dressing gown for Marabella in scene one-six. . ."

* * *

Jeanne and Donna watched jets take off and land at the airport of St. Thomas in the Virgin Islands. They were at a small table in an outdoor cafe adjoining the main terminal building. The shipping line had provided air fare back to New York for passengers not eager to wait for the *Liberty* to be put afloat again.

They were superficially relaxed. Donna smoked a cigarette and blew smoke upwards in lazy clouds that dissipated in the sunlight.

A waiter brought their drinks: two exotic things served in coconut shells with a gardenia floating on top.

Donna lifted her coconut for a toast. "Repeat after me," she urged Jeanne. "I solemnly swear. . . . "

"I solemnly swear," Jeanne repeated smiling.

"To strive above all. . . . "

"To strive above all."

"For independence of spirit. . . ."

"For independence of spirit."

"Whatever that turns out to be."

Jeanne laughed. "Whatever that turns out to be."

A loudspeaker squawked, "Flight 922 for New York is now ready for boarding. Passengers should proceed to the boarding gate." And the message was repeated in Spanish and French.

The two women looked at each other and then quickly glanced away. "Let's wait just a few minutes and finish our drinks," Donna suggested.

Jeanne nodded.

"I wasn't scared to go back. I really wasn't—until just now," Donna confessed.

"Me, too," said Jeanne.

Jeanne took a sip of the cold, luscious elixir, and somehow the very luxuriance of it—the assault of all those sweet flavors—helped her to gain perspective. "Name it, Donna," she insisted.

"Name what?"

"The fear. Let's make real animals of the bug-eyed monsters. What are you afraid of?"

"Life."

"Too vague. What's frightening about life?"

"Hmmm—planning it, I suppose. Deciding how to live. I've just been running and drifting, waiting for some plan to fall into place—for somebody to *give* me a plan. Now I've got to be the one to make things happen."

"You're afraid you can't do it?"

"Uh—I think I can do it. But what if I do it wrong?"

"We both seem to have done it wrong the first time. What do we do about that?"

Donna raised her eyebrows and smiled a silly grin. "Try, try again. Oh, I see what you're getting at. That all I really need is the confidence that I've got the nerve to keep trying." She was pensive a few moments, then laughed. "I'm still terrified."

"Well, at least now you're laughing about it."

Donna said, in the manner of a psychiatrist, "And now, Miss Mason, what seems to be *your* problem?"

Jeanne took a deep breath and focussed inward. "I'm afraid . . . to say to people . . . that's the way I am, take it or leave it." She took a sip. "Oh, that's not quite it. I'm afraid I won't like it if they leave it."

"Too vague. Run that through once more." "Everyone . . . wants me to mend my ways and do things their way. They want me to be a good girl . . . and I've discovered that lots of very good people have very different notions of what *good* is. Everyone wants me to. . . ." Jeanne interrupted herself. "Well, not everyone." Smiling, she took a folded paper from her purse and handed it to Donna.

Donna read the telegram aloud. "Don't try to forgive yourself. Try to see that there is nothing to forgive. I'll always love you." She scanned the rest of the page and flipped it over to look at the back. "It isn't signed!"

Jeanne nodded. "Someone wanted me to realize that I wasn't doomed after all, and that I wasn't alone." Suddenly Jeanne let her drink clunk to the tabletop as her eyes grew hazy. "I just realized who had to have sent it!"

Donna suddenly grabbed Jeanne's wrist. "Look," she hissed through clinched teeth.

Mark Harris stood no more than ten feet away. He saw them and seemed momentarily startled.

He had the grace not to greet them as old friends, but not the sense to keep his mouth shut. He smiled in an almost comradely fashion as he stepped toward them. "I take it you're both flying back to New York."

They didn't answer him.

"There's one of those little cocktail lounges in the back of our plane. I'd like to buy you a drink and try to apologize, if you'll join me when we're airborne."

Donna smiled and shook her head. She said very politely, "No, I'm sorry; I forgot to bring my arsenic." Her fingernails were digging into the skin of Jeanne's wrist.

They rose and left him standing there as they hurried to the departure gate.

eight

Stewardesses had just distributed stereo ear-phones and were hurrying to strap themselves down as the jets of the mammoth Eastern airliner rose to a whining roar.

They were next in line for takeoff.

Jeanne and Donna hooked up their earphones and scanned the available channels of sound. Jeanne could hear Donna's selection faintly; it was something with a frenetic disco beat, played as loudly as Donna could stand it. Jeanne stopped her search on one of the classical channels that was offering a Rachmaninoff symphony. For Jeanne, this was a perfect underscoring for takeoff.

Whatever happened, Jeanne wondered, to that dream—my dream of flying?

All through childhood, she and Alan had sworn to each other that one day they'd have pilot's licenses. They both loved taking to the air. Yet neither of them had gone on with it. In college, Alan had taken a couple of flying lessons and that had been it. Maybe, Jeanne thought, it's kids planning to be firemen when they grow up, or movie stars.Something you dream about only until something more practical takes over.

But she still loved the thrill of flying. As the symphony climbed in power and pitch, as its interlaced melodies began to drive and drive and drive, she felt herself being shoved back in her seat, like an astronaut in a blasting rocket ship.

During these moments Jeanne could feel that her head was utterly empty. She could watch the runway drop away, then the treetops, the town, the bay, the island—and soar up into the clouds without a care. At that precise moment she felt no apprehension concerning what she might find at home, and no worry for tomorrow.

Donna's presence had so vanished from Jeanne's awareness that she was startled when she felt her right earphone being lifted away and a damp finger touching her cheek.

"Who was he?" Donna asked nervously. "Who sent the mysterious telegram?"

Jeanne smiled warmly. "My brother, Alan." It occurred to Jeanne that of all the people she knew, Alan would be the only one who could share the excitement she felt.

"Some brother," Donna commented. "You're very close?"

Jeanne perceived Donna's simple need to talk, and surmised: "Flying scares you?"

"Terrifies me. Funny thing, though, I *like* it. Masochist, I guess," she reflected. "The only thing I can remember my brother doing for me is putting bugs in my bed."

"A younger brother?"

"Two younger brothers. Terrors. Is Alan older than you?"

"Just a year. We're practically twins."

128

They chatted until the plane burst out the top of a blinding mountain of peach-colored cotton. By then, Donna was calm and listening to her music.

I wonder, Jeanne thought, while she listened to quieter stereo, if Alan could be behind some of my problems. Just because he was always *there*—and I always loved and admired him so. Much more than my father or any other adult, Alan represented *men* to me; he must have. If I'd had only Father to, well, study, I probably would not have grown up expecting to find such an ideal man. A man like Alan. I might never have become so frustrated with poor Bill, might never have longed for more. Gordon was a lot like Alan—well, except the sexual thing. Gordon was gentle, rational, and creative. Gordon was, or seemed to be, everything Bill wasn't, everything I felt I'd die without. But there was something awfully wrong about all that, about the way I went about it. I hope I didn't hurt Gordon too much. We never should have tried to have an affair. I know what people would tell me; they'd say I need to see Alan is just a man, a man with human failings just like any other. But that's not the answer. It can't be.

A stewardess hovered over Jeanne and caught her attention, knowing better than to try to shout so a passenger under earphones could hear. She smiled and made sign language that offered cocktails or coffee or tea.

Jeanne removed her headset. "Coffee, please."

Donna mumbled, "Make it two."

Donna had been thinking, too. Jeanne saw an expression on her face that looked like the reflection of some unendurable horror—as if in her mind Donna had stumbled over a dead body.

Jeanne laid her hand over her friend's. "Donna, what is it?"

Donna's expression dissolved, like a movie cross-fade, into a look of mere worry. "I just . . . I was remembering . . . nothing. It was nothing."

Jeanne left Donna alone again and tried to turn to her own problems, but for a time the dark worries simply refused to return. There was a break in the clouds below, and far away on the aquamarine Caribbean there was a tiny ocean liner taking another boatload of escapees, vacationers who were leaving their troubles behind them. You're going to have a wonderful time, Jeanne thought, sending her good wishes to the ship of strangers. Near the horizon where the layer of clouds met the royal blue of the sky, another jet streaked along in the opposite direction, leaving its pencil line of vapor behind.

In her mood of surrender to the spectacle outside, Jeanne could let random thoughts flit past, make their points, and then be forgotten.

I won't call Gordon, she thought. Then her mind centered on the faint colors of the approaching sunset. I'll have to work through Philip to see what can be done to get Kevin out of Bill's clutches. Looking up, Jeanne discovered that an evening star could already be seen even though the sum was still a round ball in the western sky. Surely, she thought, Father has cooled off by now. I wish Mother would stand up for what she truly believes is right. I'll stay at a hotel until I can find a place; I don't want to impose on Alan and Margaret. My things are safe in storage for as long as I want to leave them there. I want a job. Just anything to start with. With what Father gives me, I guess I don't need to work, but I think it would do me good. Independence of spirit, Donna said. And she's right.

The bright orange ball of the sun suddenly splayed a fan of heat into the purple shadows among the clouds. It was an abrupt, upside-down sunset.

On an inspiration, Jeanne turned to Donna. "Let's open a shop together."

Donna grinned. Apparently her thinking had been leading her to the same intersection. "Of course," she said.

"Well, we've got to start somewhere," Jeanne continued, reasoning out loud. "I'm not nuts about becoming a secretary, and what else is there?"

Donna nervously lit a cigarette. "I've been thinking about . . . not about some Fifth Avenue boutique, but some little Greenwich Village hole in the wall. We could sell little art objects and small antiques. Some imported things. Maybe some exclusive lines of funky clothes and jewelry."

Jeanne laughed. "It sounds mind-boggling! We can't just—"

"We won't rush into it, but we shouldn't take our time about it, either. I need some project like this—*now*. The first thing to do is work up some idea of cost and operating budget, and then figure out where the money—''

"My father might," Jeanne finished. "Father hasn't advanced me any great sums since college; maybe his arm could be twisted. Of course, he always thought college for a woman was a waste of time and money. So far, in my case, he hasn't proved far wrong."

"What did you major in?"

"Nothing. Liberal arts."

"Me, too. And it broke my father; he hasn't got a red cent anymore."

"Was it college or the Ferrari?"

"No," said Donna hesitantly, "the Ferrari was a gift. From somebody else." She hastened to add, "Nobody I can go to for a loan, not anymore." She dropped that subject like a hot coal. "Let's get an apartment together. Scrimp and save money and plot and plan."

This was a new idea to Jeanne. She had assumed she'd get a small place for herself and, if things could be worked out, for Kevin. She had previously been looking forward to having a place alone, expecting to need privacy for quite a while longer.

"I'm not sure," she said to Donna. "There's my son to consider, and—"

"I'll get by," Donna said curtly.

Jeanne was on the verge of changing her mind, since obviously Donna had been hurt by what must have seemed rejection. But she stopped herself. We have to quit playing games, she realized, and treating each other like helpless children, especially if we're to go into busi-

132

ness together. We mustn't allow each other to be so fragile!

"I'm being silly," Donna said of her own accord, "I'm sorry. And I *will* get by." She squeezed Jeanne's hand. "Besides, I have some unfinished business to take care of. I won't see you for a day or two."

Jeanne was feeling unusually good about herself. As if to test her self-esteem, she turned and looked back toward the cocktail lounge. There was Mark Harris, leaning on the bar, looking directly at Jeanne and Donna. He wasn't smiling this time.

At first, Jeanne felt nothing but satisfaction over the fact that she felt nothing. Then came a fury of emotion; she felt unaccountably pleased by Mark's contriteness and attention, and at the same time disgusted with herself for feeling it. In another split second the full reality of what he had done came back to her, and the look she gave him shrank to withering contempt.

She turned back to say something to Donna about it, but Jeanne was stopped by what she saw.

Donna wore her look of inwardly directed horror again; and this time the muscles of her face were squeezing tears from her eyes. She caught Jeanne staring at her, and quickly turned away.

* * *

Adele Mason watched her husband.
She had developed a new caution, an aloof-

ness that allowed her to watch Gilbert, even watch herself, with a continuing sense of curiosity. She had no answers, not even any clear questions; but she felt an impending calamity in her family that had to be prevented somehow. It's a tribute to our closeness, she thought, that the members of this family still speak to one another.

It bothered her that Gilbert had chosen a chair he seldom relaxed in to read his paper. It put him right next to the phone, as if he waited to pounce on it should it ring. That kind of obsession was not like Gilbert—not like he used to be.

Emotionally she sided with her children in their estrangement from their father; but who was right and who was wrong? Adele hadn't a clue. Did it matter? Yes, morality mattered to Adele McLyndon Mason. It always had. She knew it mattered to Gilbert, too, and she sensed that it was his very notion of morality that was about to cause him to commit unkind, uncomprehensible, and perhaps terrible acts. And there seemed to be nothing Adele could do about it.

What would her mother have done? Adele knew the answer: nothing. Adele's mother had lived in comparative luxury until marrying Mr. McLyndon back in the high-flying 1920's. Adele's father, a gambler at heart, lost everything in '29, but did Adele's mother complain? Never. The breadwinner's wishes and habits and capacities were not open to scrutiny. You loved him; he owned you.

"A woman's lot," her mother told Adele, "is

to ease a man's lot. He, in turn, provides." It was as simple as that; and, Adele felt sure, it had worked with the certainty of a science for her mother. Though she died almost in poverty, when Adele was in her late teens. Mama died knowing she had lived the life expected of her. Not, perhaps, happy—but content.

Adele noticed that Gilbert had rested his paper in his lap and was staring off abstractedly. She said to him, apropos of nothing he could have been aware of, "Did I ever tell you that my mother opposed women's suffrage?"

"No," Gilbert said. "But that would have been like her. A gentle soul."

Mama was definitely, Adele thought, not a boat-rocker.

Mama's one avocation was playing the organ at church, and during one very lean year, she had taken a few piano pupils. Adele remembered the result (she had been around eight at the time). Papa had been so mortified at the public evidence of his inability to support his family that he had taken to drink. Mama would thereafter have preferred to see her whole family die of starvation rather than lift a finger to earn a penny. With Papa's drinking they had come close a few times, but they hadn't starved.

Adele sat at the baby grand piano Gilbert had bought her years ago. "Would you mind?" she asked him, her fingers about to touch the keys.

"I'd rather you didn't," he said.

She silently closed the lid.

The phone rang.

As if stressing his lack of eagerness, Gilbert

let it ring twice before picking it up. "Hello. . . .
" He said to Adele: "It's Alan."

Her watchfulness had been triggered.

Gilbert continued to speak to his son. "Called
you from where? You mean Jeanne's back in
New York?"

Adele noted that he seemed neither relieved
nor worried. He seemed angry.

" Why did she call *you*?" Gilbert continued.

Meaning, Adele saw, that she ought to have
called here first.

"To thank you for what? A telegram you sent
. . . when did you send . . . then you've known
where she was all along?"

Anger again, but there was pain now, too,
pain that betrayed how much Gilbert cared for
his children. Cared improperly, perhaps, but
cared deeply, nevertheless.

"She asked you to call . . . why didn't she call
us herself? . . . Don't get sharp with me, young
man . . . Tomorrow? She'll call us at her *leisure*,
you mean!

Like a hurt little child, Adele thought. She
marveled at her perceptiveness and wondered
why she had never noticed these things about
Gilbert before. Or had she noticed them and
worked hard to keep them meaningless?

"Where is she now? . . . What do you mean,
you don't know?"

Adele smiled. She knew her son; he probably
hedged by claiming not to know the precise
geographical location of the cab that was carrying her.

"Call me when you find out!" Gilbert insisted, then rang off.

But that's obvious, Adele thought. She's on her way to see her little boy—as I would do under the circumstances. She's on her way to Philip's.

But Adele was not about to say anything. Let him guess, she resolved. She smiled smugly to herself and thought Mama would never approve!

* * *

Hilda Pomeranz opened the door, cocked her head, and smiled. "Jeanne," she said warmly, opening her arms for a hug.

" Hello, Hilda," Jeanne said, returning the warmth and the hug.

Hilda called out, "Kevin!"

But the boy was already there two feet behind Hilda's ample shape, ready to leap into his mother's arms.

Jeanne squeezed him so tightly he coughed, and that made them both laugh. "Well," he said with mock displeasure, "I'm glad to see you, too!"

"Then squeeze harder!" Jeanne begged. She had promised herself she wouldn't, but she was crying.

Kevin said, "I'm okay, honest." "Hey, you got a suntan!" he added.

"I've been to the tropics," she said gaily, wiping tears away.

Hilda remarked, "You do look wonderful. How . . ." She seemed to think better of asking

137

how Jeanne was.

"I'm fine," Jeanne answered anyway. "Much better, really." She laughed and confessed, "Running off like that might have been the sanest thing I've done in the last couple of years. How are you? How is Philip? *Where* is Philip?"

"Here," he said. He had come in from the rear of the house and was standing in the archway to the dining room. "I told everybody I wasn't in the least worried about you," he said, his voice not quite steady. "I wonder if I fooled anybody?"

He stepped to meet Jeanne and took both her hands—even though a friendly hug would have been quite appropriate.

"You were right," Jeanne confirmed. "There *wasn't* anything to worry about."

They stood there looking into each other's eyes, smiling, hands still clasped, until Hilda said, "You didn't bring your luggage. We'd like you to stay here, you know."

Philip seemed suddenly apprehensive; he dropped Jeanne's hands.

Jeanne understood at once that such a move might jeopardize Kevin's stay with the Pomeranzes; she had considered the fact before. "I've decided it would be better all around, Hilda, if I stay in a hotel for a while, till I can get settled again."

Hilda started to protest.

" I know you'd like to have me, but . . . not right now, at least. Thank you, though; I'm extremely grateful for the offer."

"Why not, Mommy?" Kevin wanted to know.

Hilda seemed to catch on (Jeanne was surprised that it took her so long), and started to explain things to the little boy, using a near-babytalk Jeanne detested: "Now, Kevin, if that's what Mommy thinks is best—"

"It's not that, Kevin," Jeanne explained, perhaps overcompensating for the babytalk by being too adult; "it's that all the problems with your father and my parents, all the legal complications, are still not quite ironed out. You and I are not supposed to live together at the moment, remember?"

Kevin just said, glumly, "Yes, I remember." He added a futile argument: "It's very nice here."

Hilda asked Kevin, her voice five notes too high, "How about a nice glass of milk and some cookies?"

"I'd like that," he replied politely. He looked to his mother almost pleadingly, hoping he would not have to go out to the kitchen with Hilda to get his refreshment.

Jeanne put her arm around her son possessively. She noticed that both Philip and Hilda seemed unaccountably uneasy; and they were uneasy in different ways. Hilda *usually* seemed uneasy, in her general manner, and this was just more so.

Hilda was short and chubby. She dressed and groomed in a manner befitting a spinster librarian, or perhaps the secretary of some character out of Dickens. Jeanne rather liked Hilda, or felt sorry for her; but always winced when she thought of the disparity between Hilda and the dynamic sort of woman Philip ought to have.

Philip seemed uneasy in a way unnatural to him, as if simultaneously he wanted to tell Jeanne something of great importance, but for some reason couldn't—and he harbored some knowledge he hoped she would not be able to discern.

"Is something wrong, Philip?" Jeanne asked directly.

"Why, no," he answered too abruptly.

Then Jeanne saw the portrait, the painting Gordon Strand had done of her—centuries ago, it seemed. It was hanging prominently in the Pomeranz living room. "Oh, Philip!" Jeanne gasped.

Neither Philip nor Hilda responded.

"I think it looks just like you," Kevin said.

Jeanne's first reaction was one of pleasure simply at seeing it again. Her second emotion, and it became the dominant one, was one of embarrassment. Did Philip want this painting merely because he thought it beautiful? Was it because he admired the abstract image there (Never mind that Jeanne was the model) of a confident and glamorous woman? Or was it because the woman there *was* Jeanne Mason? Whatever the case, it did not belong here— *in Hilda's house*.

Jeanne couldn't look at Hilda. Even if there were no other consideration, an image like this could only have served to remind poor Hilda of how plain she was. Why didn't Philip see this?

Could the painting be behind Hilda's present uneasiness? Did Hilda know what the painting had to mean to Philip? What *did* the painting mean to Philip? Jeanne dared not ask. She did not know, in fact, what comment to make. Nor could she bring herself to turn back around and look at her hosts, until Philip said, almost in a whisper, "It's yours, if you want it."

"You bought it from Gordon?"

"In a manner of speaking. I thought . . . while you're getting settled, I'd hold onto it for a while. If you decide you don't want to keep it—and I can think of reasons why you might not want to—then perhaps . . . I'll keep it. I like it very much."

"So do I," Hilda lied. "And my guess is that it will fetch a pretty penny some day." Her uneasiness seemed to be dwindling. "Jeanne—I insist you stay for dinner; and I know you want time to catch up on what little Kevin's been up to. Let me get us something to drink while I'm getting Kevin's snack. Pitcher of martinis?"

"I think I'd rather not have anything that strong," Jeanne said. "Do you have some wine?"

"White, red, or purple?" Hilda bubbled as she headed toward the kitchen.

"White," Jeanne answered.

When Hilda was out of earshot, Philip said, "I think you've changed, Jeanne. Just in this short time."

"For the better?"

"Very much for the better. You're stronger."

"I'm just acting that way, I think. But I am growing, Philip."

Kevin asked tentatively, "Can I show you the model rockets Philip and I have been building?"

"I'd love to see them. Where are they?"

"In my room. Come on."

Philip indicated he would not join them. The maid came in with a tray of wine glasses, and Philip nodded toward the departing guest, suggesting that the maid follow her. He grabbed his own drink from the passing tray and downed the liquid in one gulp.

During dinner Jeanne sat with her back to the portrait, although she was constantly aware of it through Hilda's eyes. It was as if Hilda were trying to interpret the idealized woman on the wall by comparing her with the real Jeanne Mason. Jeanne wondered wildly if Hilda was trying to decide which of the Jeanne Masons her husband was in love with.

But that's insane, Jeanne argued silently with herself; if it's true, why haven't I guessed it before? Is Philip more careless about letting it show now that I'm no longer married? Is this why Philip seemed so unreasonably upset over losing my case? No! It can't be—not any of it! He just likes the painting and doesn't realize the implications of hanging it in his living room. That has to be it!

Hilda broke Jeanne's spell. "Would you like some more brussel sprouts, Jeanne, dear?"

Jeanne smiled. "Maybe a couple. The cheese sauce is delicious."

Philip reassured Jeanne about Kevin's situation, and Jeanne heard his key points—that the boy could stay here some time longer before Bill expected him back, that Hilda adored having him here, and so on. But Jeanne's mind was off on another tangent.

I've got to put a stop to this, Jeanne reasoned. Philip is a wonderful man, but whatever he has in his mind, it's not fair to Hilda, to me, or to himself. Why did this have to come up *now*? Why does everything keep hinging on what *I* do? I don't want the responsibility!

"Jeanne—you're a mile away," Philip commented.

Jeanne looked at him curiously for a minute then said in a very steady voice, "I just made one of those connections, you know, the why-didn't-I-think-of-that-before kind of things."

Philip looked worried and embarrassed; Jeanne came to his rescue:

"I suddenly realized that I am really not responsible for any lives other than mine and Kevin's, and that I am not the center of the universe."

Hilda laughed, as she often did at things she could not follow. It was a laugh that apologized in advance for her ignorance and her need to ask for assistance in understanding. "But Jeanne," she said, "whoever accused you of that?"

Jeanne smiled and relaxed. "I was accusing myself of it," she explained. Jeanne went on, addressing herself mainly to Philip. "I . . . am going to try to make myself happy. It's not that I don't care about other people—you or Hilda or

143

my parents or Alan. I do." Jeanne backed off a bit and said, "I hope you don't mind my telling you these things. It's part of . . . the thinking I've been doing."

"Please go on," Philip said with soft insistence. He knew she was talking to him, and he knew what she was talking about.

"I don't love anyone romantically," Jeanne said. "I hope I will some day. In fact, I hope I will someday soon. But among other things, this time around I've got to be sure there's really someone of substance up here." She tapped her forehead. "For another thing, until I'm sure about myself, I want to be able to enjoy life without anybody's help, for a change."

Philip nodded somberly and looked away.

Hilda said, "My dear! That sounds like such a lonely life!"

Jeanne said nothing for a time. She looked at Kevin as she considered whether to say more in front of his inexperienced ears. Finally she shrugged and told Hilda:

"I learned what loneliness was in another way altogether. During those last four years with Bill I was so lonely I thought I'd die of it."

Philip was looking openly at the portrait, not furtively as Hilda had done. He said, "Now I understand the painting. Strand was able to paint you in a way that emphasizes your self-assurance. It's beginning to show up more in your face Jeanne."

She laughed. "A sort of reverse Portrait of Dorian Gray?"

Hilda giggled and Philip smiled and nodded.

Philip asked, "Have you seen Adele and Gilbert yet?"

Jeanne shook her head. "I'm going to see them tomorrow afternoon. When I get back to the hotel tonight, I'm going to collapse and sleep the sleep of the dead. I've had a very tiring past few days. I'm going to sleep till noon, and then meet Alan at his theater for lunch. Then I'll face the Masons."

Kevin had missed a good many subtleties during dinner, but he had caught the gist of things. "They love you, Mother," he reassured her. "Grandpa sounds meaner than he is sometimes."

"Thank you, Kevin," she said.

"Want me to go with you tomorrow?" he asked eagerly.

"I'm afraid it would be better if I face the music alone."

Philip said, "I wonder what they'll think of the new Jeanne? I think she's quite a gal, if that means anything to you."

"It means a lot, Philip," Jeanne said. She could not meet Philip's eyes. She had just felt something startling; she had wondered: Could I love Philip some day?

nine

A few flood lights on the balcony rail threw stark white illumination onto the undressed stage. From high above, up in the "fly loft" where pipes and cables suspended various old pieces of scenery, another row of dusty work lights contributed an amber overhead glow.

Jeanne entered the theater from the rear of the auditorium carrying a bag of fat pastrami sandwiches and cartons of milk for herself and Alan. She was in the venerable and ornate Shubert Theater—the theater that perhaps more than any other meant "Broadway" to her. Alan's producer had obtained it for this day of auditions; and presumably it was filled with hopefuls, actors, and actresses responding to the "open call," where those without agents or managers were able to read for Broadway roles. But if there were throngs inside, Jeanne—her eyes not yet accustomed to the gloom—could not see them. She waited at the back until she was able to pick out rows of seats and dim silhouettes of the backs of heads.

Phenomenal, she reflected, that such a dingy unattractive stage is capable of such magic when a play is being presented.

She could see the brick wall at the back with

basement-like rows of piping and conduit and occaeional "legs" of old black drapery hanging from great heights; in the playing area there were battered tables and chairs arranged to simulate some kind of interior setting. There were three men and a woman close together standing at the edge of the stage. The woman, whose hair was bright red even in the dusky illumination, was Margaret Carlson, Alan's roommate.

The four separated, like football players leaving a huddle, and one of the four vaulted down off the stage, leaving three ready to play a scene. The vaulter was Andy Holloway, a friend of Alan's and the director of the play. Jeanne had met him before. One of the two actors took a chair, leaving Margaret and the other man facing each other center stage.

"Watch this guy," said a voice out of the darkness, right into Jeanne's ear. "He just read Pieter and now he's about to do one of Roy's scenes. He's damn good." The voice was Alan's.

"How did you know I was here?" Jeanne whispered to him.

"I smelled pastrami," her brother answered.

"Who's the actor?"

"His name's Mark Harris. British."

Good God, Jeanne thought, it *is* Mark Harris! This is the Broadway show he was talking about?

Jeanne and Alan took seats toward the uninhabited back of the orchestra section, removed their sandwiches with excruciating care not to rattle the paper bag, and watched the scene.

Alan had described *Conquerors and Candlelight* as a modern day swashbuckler, but that's all Jeanne knew about it.

"This scene," Alan whispered, intermittantly chewing on his lunch, "takes place in present-day Vienna at an Embassy Ball. You're looking at a gold-and-ivory-paneled anteroom where Pieter, sitting there under that splendid crystal chandelier on a gilded loveseat by that row of potted palms, is evesdropping —spying really—on his sister, Eva. Pieter's sort of a contemporary Scarlet Pimpernel. She's secretly on her brother's side—he didn' want her mixed up in this at all—but *he's* afraid she's aiding the enemy, Roy, who is actually nothing but the only true love of her life—whom she's on to. But she has no idea that the elderly statesman sitting back there is really Pieter in disguise; she thinks he's one of the villains in cahoots with Roy in a plot to murder the dictator of Albania. Now, in this scene, in order to help her brother expose the plot—and in so doing help thousands escape across the border—she's pretending to sympathize with her lover . . . who has to die in the end, of course."

Jeanne distilled all of that into a single interesting thought: It's a story about a love between a brother and sister, written by *my* brother. It had never occurred to Jeanne to wonder what she meant to Alan. I've got to read this play! she resolved. She hoped beyond reason that Mark Harris would not be cast in the role of the brother. That would be unbearable!

148

She determined that she would not let them give Mark a job!

Margaret's movements were quick and concise, appropriate for the light melodrama of the scene. She seemed for all the world like a nice girl trying to play a *femme fatale* in a deadly game that was over her head. Mark was, unfortunately, delightful as he bantered, cajoled, and tried to keep her from being serious when all he wanted to do was dance and make love. He even managed to suggest—even though the role was new to him and he had to read from the script he held as unobtrusively as possible in one hand—that there was a lie in his levity, and that underneath he was a treacherous and desperate man.

Jeanne heard a chuckle of delight rise from the front row. Well, she guessed, Andy likes him. Jeanne looked at her brother, whose attention was riveted to the stage. Alan was smiling and nodding.

Alan's words came from the actors and drifted with a bit of an echo over the mostly empty rows of seats:

" ' How can you talk of your brother at a time like this?' " said the amorous villainous Roy. " 'I'm talking of love.' "

" 'You're talking of sex and romance,' " said Eva. " 'I'm referring to another kind of love, a more enduring kind. But love him as I do, and always will, I'm not blind to his political leanings, and I'm not afraid to tell you he's dreadfully wrong about the ways of the world. He may be my bitterest enemy. Now stop that,

149

Roy; I'm trying to be serious. Roy!' ''

'' 'There's only one kind of seriousness I want from you, my dearest. And quite confidentially, I want it *now*. Women lose their attraction when they become revolutionaries. Have you noticed?' ''

'' 'When they become significant, you mean,' '' Eva said, with feigned indignation.

'' 'No, my darling,' '' he said sincerely, '' 'because you are more significant to me than . . . than all of those ways of the world you mentioned.' '' He drew her into his arms—she struggled just a bit—and kissed her passionately.

Andy jumped from his seat and leapt onto the stage. His action ended the scene and shattered the make-believe that even Jeanne had let herself fall into. "Alan!" Andy yelled out into the darkened theater.

"Hold this," Alan said handing Jeanne the crust of his sandwich. Since childhood he had eaten the centers out of sandwiches and left the crust—usually to nibble on the crust later until every crumb was gone.

Jeanne heard Andy ask Mark: "I assume you're available to begin rehearsals right away? Do you need to make arrangements with Equity for a work permit, or is that already taken care of? I mean, can we hire you with confidence that you won't be drummed out of the country by union regulations?"

Mark laughed. "Soon as I make a quick trip to the loo, I'm all yours. No conflicts, and I'm available as of yesterday."

Alan was up there with them now, and their voices dropped to an inaudible level.

Margaret looked out into the auditorium, shielding her eyes. "Jeanne?" she called out as quietly as she could.

"Here," Jeanne called back.

Soon Margaret was greedily digging into the lunch bag for her own pastrami and babbling to Jeanne excitedly about the progress of the play. Every few sentences she'd say, "I'm *dying* to hear about your trip!" But Jeanne had no chance to speak, until Margaret had her mouth full.

Jeanne asked, "Do you think Mark Harris will get the role?"

Margaret nodded vigorously. "Of Roy, not Pieter," she said, mumbling around the pastrami.

"There was no one else who auditioned who could do it?"

"Oh, there's always someone else. But Mark is absolutely perfect. Do you have something against him? Didn't you like his reading?"

Jeanne felt flattered that Margaret would ask her opinion on such a matter.

"I *did* like his reading, "Jeanne said. "I just don't like Mark Harris."

"Why not? You know him?"

"I met him, and learned to loathe him, in the Caribbean."

"You must tell me all about it, especially if he and I are to be working together. On second thought, perhaps you shouldn't. It's hard to make love to a loathsome man. I'm not *that* good an actress. How's Kevin?''

Trying to keep her situation from sounding pitiable, Jeanne sketched the current status of the legal and emotional problems surrounding Kevin, stressing that she was very glad Kevin was in Philip and Hilda's hands for now.

Margaret nodded from time to time and concluded, '' You know that if there's anything I can do—''

"I know," Jeanne said sincerely.

"Mark just got off a boat that ran aground," Margaret realized suddenly. "Some British liner. That wasn't *your* ship, was it?''

"The very same.''

"Ahah! I've simply *got* to stop eating bread.''

Alan returned and reported that unless a young unknown Laurence Olivier dropped by later in the day, Mark had the role of Roy. He said, "I forgot to tell you. Mother's expecting you for dinner at eight-thirty. Unless you want to go around earlier, you're welcome to stay here with me for a few more hours. It might be boring for you, but—''

"I'll stay," Jeanne said gratefully.

There was something almost hypnotizing to Jeanne about being in the mysterious theater watching the repetitious auditions. The afternoon was dramatic almost precisely because of its lack of drama—the same scenes over and over, seldom a voice with any distinction, the echoes of the gradually emptying hall, no sets or costumes, just concentration. Jeanne was watching a work of art being put together by men whose intensity rivaled that of brain surgeons, and she loved the fact that her brother was one of them—the main one, since it was his play.

Occasionally between readings he would turn and chat with Jeanne briefly.

"I have an idea," he announced once. "There's a job available with the play, a sort of secretarial general flunky. Why don't you take it?"

" Why the job offer? Do you know something I don't?

"You want a job, don't you?"

"How did you know?

"And, well, I've heard that Father is threatening to cut off your allowance for some stupid reason or another, unless you agree to . . . join a convent or something. I thought maybe you'd rather find a way to become self-sufficient. Tell him he can keep his bribes."

Tears came into Jeanne's eyes. "What would I do without you?" she said, a trifle too loudly.

After another reading—which showed Jeanne just how good Mark had been, by comparison—she said to Alan:

"I can't work with this company if Mark Harris is part of it."

"What do you know about Harris?"

"He was on my ship, and—"

"Of course; I should have wondered about that."

"You wouldn't hire him if he were a criminal, would you?"

"*Is* he a criminal?"

"Not exactly. May I tell you about him?"

"Sweetheart, unless he's wanted by the police, or Interpol or something, if he's the best actor for the part, we have to take him. Besides, Jeanne, it isn't all up to me. I have a very shaky veto power around here." He studied her face for a minute before saying, "We need to have a long talk, don't we?"

She nodded. "*Before* Mark Harris signs a contract."

"If possible. I barely have time to sleep."

"You're coming to dinner tonight, aren't you?"

"I thought I'd come around in case you need moral support." He smiled and studied her face once again. But I'm not sure you need it. You look terrific."

"Be there," she commanded threateningly.

"Confidentially, I have another motive for showing up. I'm going to ask Father to invest in the show."

"Tonight! Shouldn't you wait for a better—"

"It can't wait any longer," he said regretfully.

Jeanne was seeing things so much from Alan's point of view that it took her some time to realize that his plans interfered with her own. If the miserly Mr. Mason could be persuaded to invest in one doubtful enterprise, chances were nil that he could be persuaded to invest in two. It would come down to Alan's play or Jeanne's shop. Not both. And from what Jeanne had heard, her chances were close to rock bottom anyway.

Around five Jeanne leaned over and kissed

Alan on the cheek. 'I'm going ahead,'' she said. "I want to freshen up, and I think I'll walk."

"To Nintieth Street?'' he asked. "Do you have *that* much to think over?'' Without waiting for a reply, he advised, "You can think things through too much, you know, And everything *will* be all right."

* * *

Her father opened the door.

"Come in, Jeanne,'' he said, his voice businesslike and devoid of any trace of love, sympathy, relief, happiness, or even condemnation. "You have some explaining to do."

Jeanne stood there frozen. She had expected her father to be cool, angry perhaps, but not so impersonal. A tightness gripped her throat and her cheeks tingled as the color left her face—these sensations said to her: He has changed; this isn't the father I loved; he is an enemy.

Gilbert waited for his daughter to enter. The longer she procrastinated, the more smug his expression became. He seemed to be enjoying her evident fear.

In a flash Jeanne decided: He thinks I'm immoblized by feelings of shame! She closed her partially gaping mouth and let her father see an expression of condescension that was rather like his own. The expression arose so involuntarily that Jeanne did not grasp the insolence of it. The color returned bright and hot to her face.

"Jeanne dear?'' Adele called out, "Is that you?"

"Yes, Mother," she answered simply, walking past her father as if he'd been a bouncer insultingly placed at the entrance of a high-class establishment.

Adele hurried across the living room to embrace her daughter.

"We've been so . . . " Her voice quickly trailed off, her embrace slackened and, holding Jeanne at arm's length, she said, "What I was about to say isn't strictly true. I was not really terribly worried about you. I'm *very* glad you're back, but I honestly never feared much for your safety . . . or our sanity."

"Oh, Mother!" Jeanne said hoarsely, her tears wetting her mother's shoulder. "Thank you!"

Gilbert shut the door firmly.

Adele took a deep breath. "How was your trip, dear? Exciting? Was it good for you?"

Jeanne nodded, dabbing her eyes. "I was a mess for the first part of it, as I'm sure you can imagine, but there were times later when I . . . I don't think I've felt that adventurous since I was a child." Jeanne was not including her father in her answer.

"Adele," Gilbert suggested calmly, "Why don't you offer our guest a cocktail?"

Jeanne shot an astonished glance at him and said quietly, "Father, please don't keep hurting me in little ways. Please go on and tell me whatever it is you want me to hear."

Adele gasped. She had never heard her daughter address Gilbert this way.

"Sit down," Gilbert replied, his voice severe

156

and demanding—like that of a principal about to reprimand a recalcitrant pupil and hoping to shock the wrongdoer into obedience.

It worked, from all appearances. Jeanne sat gloomily in the nearest seat, a dining chair, which was a straight-backed and uncomfortable.

"Well?" Gilbert insisted.

Jeanne's look conveyed: Well, what?

Adele had not gone to prepare cocktails; she stood with her hand on her daughter's chair. Gilbert, oblivious to the fact that his wife was lending Jeanne support, said, "Adele, I can't reason with the child. Is she actually resisting me?"

Adele seemed to consider outright rebellion; instead, she lowered her head and her posture slumped somewhat. "Jeanne," she said, "your father wants to know why you took the trip, and why you didn't personally let us know when you were leaving and what you were up to. If there's anything you'd care. . . ." She stopped and stood a little taller. "If there's anything you would care to tell *me* about these things, please tell both of us now. It . . . it is time we all made an effort to understand one another."

Gilbert barked: "Adele, I will not be patronized! And I do not require your assistance and intervention on my behalf. You and I will discuss this later!"

Adele said slowly, choosing her words with utmost care, "No, Gilbert. Later there will be nothing to discuss. The three of us must see this through together. Or you and I must keep out of it and let Jeanne see to her own affairs."

Gilbert asked, with a touch of honest incredulity in his voice, "Are you defying me, Adele?"

"Oh, I hope not, Gilbert. I hope and pray that I am behaving as you would want me to."

Gilbert somehow realized that another tack was required of him. His manner softened and his facial muscles tightened. He said softly, "Sit down, Adele," as he pulled out a chair to help her. He abstractedly pulled out the captain's chair and sat facing, but not quite looking at, the two women in his life.

They sat before heirloom silver and crystal, handed down through generations of Masons, and fresh-cut roses amid candelabra. The hopelessness on their faces made the elegance ludicrous.

The maid pushed open the swinging door from the kitchen, saw their tableau, and returned having said not a word.

"Father," Jeanne said, holding in her mind an image of the Father she remembered with love and respect, "when the trial was over, I was confused. You *must* understand that I was confused. My whole world had been pulled out from under me. It was . . . like that old magician's trick of whipping off the tablecloth without disturbing anything that had been set upon it. Everything was still there after the trial, but nothing meant the same again. I had to . . . had to see where my values had landed after the foundation had been pulled out from under them. I had to figure out what was lost, what had been

158

broken, and what was still intact. I couldn't do it with all the pieces of my . . . my forner life crowding around me. I had to get away, alone.''

Gilbert seemed to be straining to conduct himself as Jeanne preferred. "Why—?"

"Why didn't I confide in you?"

He nodded once, regally.

Jeanne took a deep breath. "Because it was *you* that I had to get away from." She watched him carefully for a reaction. There was none. "Because I felt precious little respect for you at the time, and I had grown up thinking you were as fair and as solid as the Supreme Court. But you saw so little of what I was going through. You seemed to be making no effort at all to see things from my point of view. You condemned me without a hearing. Oh, you *heard* me when I testified at the hearing; but I said so little that it explained nothing. What's worse, you testified against me!''

"Now Jeanne," Gilbert said, taking this much too calmly. "There was no *prosecution* at that hearing, just an attempt to get at some very difficult and personal truths. I acted solely in your best interests. And I assumed that was clear to you.''

Jeanne was aghast. "How could you have assumed that? You sat there and told the judge you agreed with Bill that it might be best to take Kevin out of my care. You even acquiesced when he suggested I needed psychiatric care!''

"I thought you might. I thought your actions indicated that your grip on yourself, on reality, had slipped."

"I believe you, Father. I never thought you were *lying*." Then she added, in practically a whisper, "That's what hurt."

"And why have you behaved so disgracefully toward your mother?", he asked. He seemed to be allowing Jeanne to get it all out before he had his say.

"Mother," Jeanne said, taking her mother's hand, "I never felt that you had fully deserted me. You always smiled and tried to make me feel better. But all you were saying was that you would always love me—no matter what vile things I had done. That was horrible in the long run, don't you see, because what I needed—from both of you—was the idea that you knew me and trusted me. Not just that you loved me. I've never doubted that, and I don't doubt it now. But love isn't enough. In a way it's worse than nothing, because it makes me feel that you don't *know* me."

Adele nodded. "Yes," she said faintly.

"I know I made mistakes, Mother," Jeanne went on, not realizing she continued to ignore her father, "but I made them, well, cold-bloodedly. And I don't think now that I was wrong to want more from life than I had, and to start trying to find it. I don't care what the court made of it all. I want you to know that I was never dishonest with Bill. I kept nothing from him that he had any right to know. My . . . my affair with Gordon did not begin until *after* Bill struck me and I moved out. We were separated. I know the judge found that uninteresting, but to me it's everything."

Adele asked hopefully, "Jeanne, you didn't know beforehand, did you, that Gordon was homosexual?"

Jeanne thought out her answer. "I knew right from the start," she said. "He told me."

Gilbert made a groaning sound that said more eloquently than words that he was shocked and appalled.

Jeanne said sharply, "All right, Father. I never asked you to accept that; I merely asked you to believe that I had my reasons. I didn't care whether you liked what I was doing or whether you personally liked Gordon Strand. I just wanted you to show *some* sympathy for the difficulties I was going through!"

Jeanne's voice had not risen in tone or loudness, but each successive word had been more tense and rapidly spoken than the one before. As she finished, Gilbert grew red-faced and pulled himself to his feet.

Suddenly, Adele began to cry. It happened in such a way that both Jeanne and Gilbert realized she was not crying because of what was happening at the moment. She seemed unmindful of their presence, perhaps even unmindful that she was crying. It was a horribly lonely little sound, and the quiet misery of it jolted them both.

Gilbert sat down again. He watched his wife, his face registering something that might have been fear.

The maid, Lettie, who had served the Masons for many years, boldly stuck her head in from the kitchen. She caught Jeanne's eye and exaggeratedly said, "Dinner's ready."

Jeanne nodded. On an inspiration, she got to her feet and told Lettie, "Let me help you."

Lettie shrugged. She readily identified Jeanne's offer for what it was, a ploy to get herself away from the table.

Adele said, "No, Jeanne, I'll do it!"

Gilbert was no more deceived than Lettie was. Lettie was perfectly capable of serving by herself as usual. Detecting fear in his adversaries was a godsend to Gilbert; it meant to him that he had the upper hand. He therefore felt disposed to be generous, and this for a while calmed his nerves. As both women rose to hurry to the kitchen, Gilbert leaned back to take a pipe from the rack on the sideboard behind him. He lighted it, puffed luxuriantly, and came close to feeling relaxed.

In the kitchen Adele said, "Jeanne, can you ever forgive me?"

Jeanne was on the verge of saying she would, but it occurred to her to present a challenge instead. With a twinkle in her eye she replied, "Well, Mother, I'll always love you—no matter what."

"Don't worry," Adele said with dignity. "I'll prove it to you."

Dinner was almost comically civilized. It was as if the generals on both sides had called a truce to enjoy a good wine, a tasty bird, and the pretense that there was no war. Beneath the gloss, on both sides there was the hope that simple acts of civility would bring opponents closer together, that if the conflict could not be resolved through mutual understanding, it could at least be diminished by forgetfulness.

As usual, though, the opposite was achieved. To avoid volatile subjects, they had to keep them foremost in the mind. They had to prune, temper, delete, and dilute until only innocuous trivia came through—trivia that deceived no one.

"How was Kevin when you saw him, dear?"

"Fine, Mother. I saw Alan at the theater today. I thought he'd be here this evening."

"He'll be here. He called to ask us to start without him," Gilbert said. "Something he wanted to talk to me about."

Jeanne picked up and twirled her silver desert spoon. "Thank you for considering tonight's dinner special, Mother."

"So you enjoyed living the life of a sailor, did you?" her father asked.

"Yes, Father. You and Mother really ought to take a cruise again. You were in the Navy, weren't you Father?"

"Hardly the same," he said, his levity so like the old days that Jeanne felt she truly *had* lost touch with reality. "No caviar on a troop ship." He lifted the carafe. "Don't you like this wine, Jeanne? Care for some more?"

"No thank you."

Jeanne looked at her dish of strawberries. She felt more like staring at them than eating them. "Father," she said rather sternly, "what do you want of me?"

Gilbert put down his utensils with a clatter. He seemed annoyed at having his pleasant meal disrupted.

Lettie took away a number of spent dishes and asked, in her most deferential voice, "May I bring coffee?"

"If you please, Lettie," Adele said.

" Father," Jeanne prodded.

Gilbert said, "You are not in a position that allows you impatience. That at least ought to be obvious to you."

"Nothing is obvious to me. I don't know what position you think I'm in."

Gilbert looked to his wife. "Do you understand her attitude? Surely you don't condone her arrogance and self-righteousness."

Adele didn't say a word, and most people would have seen no changes on her face; but Gilbert saw his questions answered affirmatively even before he had finished asking them.

"Gilbert, dear," Adele said at last, "I think it would be best if you made yourself more specific. I understand Jeanne's point of view because she has told us what it is. You haven't."

"But surely—"

"Yes, dear, I can guess what you're thinking. But I honestly doubt that Jeanne can."

Gilbert studied both women, his expression accusing them of conspiracy. His anger was boiling up again. "I need not justify myself here. *I* am not the one under scrutiny! "

Jeanne asked, "You want me to justify myself? I don't see how I can, except to repeat—"

"Are you blind, girl? Have you lost all sense of ethics? Do you believe I can be taken in by your pretense at innocence. Don't you realize what consequences I can impose upon you if you force me to?"

"Father," Jeanne said resolutely, "I do consider myself innocent of all but a few foolish mistakes, minor things, things that hopefully won't happen again. I do not regret leaving Bill. I do not regret loving Gordon, not in any moral sense, anyway. I do not regret the trip I just took, nor the thinking I did while I was away. On the contrary, I feel proud of myself for it."

Gilbert was beyond anger; he had lapsed into the cold logical role of judge and executioner. Apparently he again felt nothing. "You want to divorce yourself from your family as you divorced yourself from your husband and child," he stated.

"No. You're the one who seems to be hinting at divorce." Jeanne was grateful that Alan had warned her to expect something like this.

"Hinting! There will be no more hints! I hoped you would beg our forbearance, ask us to overlook your moral lapses, ask us for another chance—which I would willingly have granted. But I resolved to suspend your income if you came to us in defiance. This is not a move made out of vengeance or pettiness or rigidity on our parts, but merely a step to demonstrate the seriousness of our disapproval. To make you more—"

"Obedient," Jeanne finished for him.

"You will move into this house at once. You will consult us—as you did as a teenager—concerning any men you wish to socialize with. You will—"

"Why would I agree to that?" Jeanne asked.

"Because you must. You'll have no other way to earn a livelihood," he said.

Jeanne was becoming giddy. None of this seemed to have any relevance to her. She said, "I could become a prostitute." Any hope of obtaining a loan to open the shop she thought about had vanished so long ago that there was no worry of jeopardizing the potential now.

Gilbert ignored her obscene suggestion and focussed merely on her flippancy. "Don't you know the *anguish* you have already caused this family? Don't you know that you have become *notorious*?

"Is that what bothers you, Father? The notoriety? The publicity?"

"You dismiss infidelity, child abandonment, cavorting about with perverts, and chronic disrespect for your parents. You dismiss them as 'minor things,' and then you accuse me of pettiness when I remind you of the stain you placed on our family name!"

"I didn't place the stain there. Other people did. *And you helped them do it!*" There was such constriction in her throat that she could barely be heard.

"Jeanne!" Adele exclaimed, shocked at the accusation.

Gilbert sought his wife's comfort and backing. He had risen from his chair.

Adele hurried to his side like an experienced nurse. "Please sit down," she said firmly, employing one of his own verbal devices. He obeyed. She said, "We must take it at a slower pace, mustn't we."

Jeanne, still feeling that none of this could really be happening, heard her mother and was reminded of the dulcet tones of the good witch in *The Wizard of Oz*. She had always associated her mother with that character.

Gilbert reached up and loosened his tie. To Jeanne, it was like seeing a fighter roll up his sleeves for the kill.

Adele said gently, "I do sympathize with our daughter. And I'm afraid I don't share your estimate of her situation. I never did, but I was too cowardly to say anything." She gathered more courage and added, "I believe this crisis, Gilbert, is more important than anything else in our lives. Anything." She could not look into his eyes when she said it.

Gilbert whispered, "Adele!" He had taken her remark to mean that she was capable of leaving him.

Jeanne interjected in the silence, "I'm planning to get a job and a small apartment. My things are in storage now, and—"

Adele shook her head. "No, dear. They're here—in the spare room."

"What's here?" Jeanne couldn't believe it.

It did not have to be repeated.

Jeanne got to her feet and walked, like one who has heard news of the end of the world, toward the front door. "I'll send for them," she said.

"Don't you walk out on me!" Gilbert screamed, leaping to his feet.

"I'll call you, Mother," Jeanne said as she opened the apartment door.

There was Alan, just reaching for the bell.

Gilbert yelled, "You're cut off without a red cent. And you'll need a court order to remove your things from this house!"

"Oh, my God," Alan said, gripping Jeanne firmly by the arms.

"I'm all right," she mumbled to him. "See if there's any good you can do for him. I've got to get out of here."

Gilbert pushed himself away from the table. It shook, and a fragile tea cup rolled off and exploded like a light bulb against the glassy hardwood floor. "No, Alan!" he yelled. "Don't offer her your sympathy!" He spoke wildly, as if he were on the verge of tears, or of losing his mind. He stumbled away from the captain's chair, tipping it over as he did so, and shuffled lamely toward Alan and Jeanne.

Alan rushed to catch his father, who had begun to topple over. He was unconscious as Alan lowered him to the floor.

"Mother, get an ambulance," Alan said, but Adele already had the phone in her hand. Jeanne had dropped her purse and was running to her mother's side.

ten

Donna Andersen hurried along East Fifth Street though it was near midnight, it was Friday, and there was an unofficial street festival on one of the blocks of Manhattan's Lower East Side. Since this was a particularly hot Friday night, everyone was out—leather-jacketed gangs, old men playing checkers on rickety card tables, women gossiping, and children running loose.

A siren sounded in the night and drew closer; Donna did not have to look far to find the reason for it: a gleeful band of urchins had set fire to the debris in a vacant lot. Fire trucks were on the way.

Donna was dressed in denims and a black sweatshirt; her hair was tied up under a black cowboy hat. She blended in rather well with her surroundings, as long as no one looked into her beautiful and frightened face.

One of the streetlights was out. She ran through its pool of darkness, not daring even to take time to look into the dark recesses of a building being demolished. She made it through and reached the next island of artificial daylight. Just one block more—the worst block.

During the day there was a row of shops,

second-hand stores, a hole-in-the-wall liquor store, a street vendor who sold produce, and a laundromat along that block. At night the stores were dark and protected by iron bars and locked accordion gates. It was a deserted block, a block ideal for muggings. There were even myriad nooks and crannies into which a victim might be dragged for robbery or rape or murder. Donna ran at top speed down the center of the street. Oddly, as is often the case in teeming Manhattan, the far intersection was well-lit and populated. A city bus thundered past just as she reached it, just as she reached comparative safety.

There was an open coffee shop there, and she entered it to catch her breath, and her courage.

I'm indestructible! she reasoned. My whole life is about to change, and I'm going to make it!

Jeanne was the cause of the optimism— Jeanne and the shop they might open.

She bought a pack of cigarettes and stepped out again into the noisy cluttered world. She made her way stealthily to an old board fence set at the entrance to what once was probably an alley. The fence had not been repaired— structures in this neighborhood seldom were—and the crack at a dark corner of it was right where it used to be, Donna was relieved to discover. She had been counting on it.

She slipped inside. She waited till the pit formed by crumbling buildings seemed not so dark, and then made her way cautiously into it.

The pit opened up into a world few would expect to find: courtyards with trees, barbecue

170

pits, picnic tables —private patios each separated from the other by fences erected more for privacy than security. The tall trees were of the sturdy variety written about in *A Tree Grows in Brooklyn*. The tree grew even here, where there was almost never direct sunlight.

Donna climbed over the first fence, and dropped onto the brick patio beyond. No one was at home, or else they were asleep, in the basement apartment to which the courtyard belonged. She tip-toed across to the next fence. She knew the occupants in the next apartment, the Colbs, an interracial couple. Nice people, hard-working. They apparently felt more comfortable down here, where society's elite could not look askance at them. They were at home. Donna could see lights coming from the kitchen and could hear the TV. The Colbs were watching a horror movie complete with blood-curdling screams. The hairs on Donna's neck bristled.

There was no other way through; she had to cross the Colb's courtyard. She sat down for a minute or two to see if she could hear their voices. Maybe they were about ready to turn out the lights and go to bed.

Jeanne is on top of the water, Donna thought. I wonder if she's ever been down under the way I have? No, Donna felt sure, she couldn't have been, not even with all the problems she's had.

For Donna, Jeanne Mason was some sort of ideal. Jeanne was a life-preserver—like the one Jeanne had tossed to her at sea—a marker-buoy drawing Donna upward by example, promising

171

to steady her, to keep her head above water. Donna vividly recalled those hours on the ocean—fighting away panic, watching the tiny lights of the far-off circling ship. That had nearly been the end for Donna—the bottom of the real sea and Donna's symbolic one, too. Jeanne had saved her from both.

Donna found an empty crate, dragged it as quietly as possible, and positioned it against the fence. The Colbs apparently had no intention of going to bed any time soon, and Donna was impatient.

Donna peered over. On the ground on the opposite side were rows of planter boxes to be avoided. The Colbs had strung Chinese lanterns in the tree limbs; luckily the lights were off.

She tried, but failed, to avoid splinters as she lifted herself up and over the fence of rotten redwood. She landed silently as her sneakers hit the soft earth just beyond the planter boxes.

She sprinted across the little lawn like a cat burglar and finally took a breath while leaning against her next obstacle. How would she make it over this side? She looked around for some kind of platform that could boost her over. Nothing. She could probably grab the top edge— she could reach it fairly easily—and just scramble over; but that would make a hell of a racket. Where was all that lawn furniture the Colbs used to have? Donna saw it stacked just inside their closed kitchen door. OK, scramble it had to be. The faster the better.

She gripped the top of the fence as tightly as possible and threw one leg up as high as she could while using the other to gain traction on the side of the fence itself. Not bad, she thought as she teetered on the top edge. Over she went—onto a stack of boxes and discarded folding chairs. Damn! she thought, I *knew* that stuff was there. The clatter sounded loud in the relative quiet of the area that was shielded from street noises.

The Colb's Chinese lanterns went on. "Who's there," Buster Colb demanded to know.

Donna lay still and tried not to breathe.

"Who's out there?" Colb repeated.

"Just a dog or a cat," his wife speculated.

"I don't think so."

"Well, let's *hope* it was a dog or a cat. Get back in here and lock that door."

The lanterns went out. There was a hair-raising scream from the distant TV set.

Donna looked around her. Dead plants, piles of trash, boxes of empty bottles—thank heavens she hadn't landed on those—a broken cabinet, what was left of a beaded curtain. This must be the place, Donna mused.

She extricated herself from the pile of chairs, rubbed sore spots on her arms, legs, and bottom, and hobbled through the clutter to the back door.

The tongue of the lock retracted easily, as she had known it would, when she inserted the blade of a pocket knife.

In the kitchen, the smell of burned grease blended with the heavy sweetness of stale incense and marijuana smoke. She made her way

173

around the scarred porcelain-topped kitchen table and into the living room. She clicked on the overhead lights—a wreath of small orange bulbs.

She was so confident that the apartment would be deserted at this time on a Friday night that she didn't think to wonder why the bedroom door was closed. The apartment was deadly quiet.

Her attention was suddenly distracted by a pile of hundred dollar bills on top of the record cabinet. It looked like several thousand dollars, at least!

On the cabinet with it there was a plastic pill box containing tiny sliver-thin transparent wafers. Donna knew "windowpane" when she saw it. Under its influence she had wrecked her car, had run away from her family, and had sunk farthest from the water-line that meant survival to her. She had the urge to flush the expensive wafers down the toilet, but she was stopped by a verdict: He deserves it; let him have them.

She took a suitcase from the front closet and stuffed a leather jacket into it. She left the suitcase open on the black vinyl couch. She tossed a silver ashtray, a small framed photograph, three books, and several record albums into it.

She opened the bedroom door.

Light streamed from behind her and touched the edges of a man and woman lying naked, stretched across the bed. But the man was snoring faintly.

Despite her fear of being caught, Donna had

to see the woman. She stepped into the bedroom to allow the light to hit her face. I've never seen her before, Donna realized; she's not very pretty. Her face is hard.

Donna could see to open and raid the drawers of the bedroom chest. Disgustedly, she estimated that in their condition an earthquake wouldn't wake the sleeping pair. She took a dress, a blouse, several undergarments, and two pairs of dungarees that had ended up in a pile in the corner. Donna wondered who owned the various other garments and items she stumbled across.

The man snorted, rolled over, then sat bolt upright in bed.

Donna crouched low against the chest.

He looked pale, almost blue in the harsh rusty light from the other room. His head was half bald; his face half obscured by a ragged beard; his chest and legs were practically hairless. His body looked as if it had once been muscular and had sagged. He looked like a consumptive college athlete onto whose body the head of a much older man had been grafted.

Donna's heart pounded. Richard Palermo! She felt as though she had been cut in half through the stomach. She had never wanted to see this man again. More important, she had never wanted him to see her again.

Palermo got out of bed and staggered to the door. He held onto the frame, apparently collecting his thoughts, trying to remember why the living-room light had been left on. Yawning, scratching his pubic hair, he clumped into the

175

living room and switched off the light. He did not return. There was no sound from in there.

Donna rose to a standing position in the dark. She wondered how she could get out without stumbling over him. She felt sure he had fallen asleep somewhere—on the floor, in a chair, or on the couch. But she hadn't heard him sit or fall.

She was about to steal a peek around the door frame when he crashed into the frame and nearly fell on top of her.

Donna frantically drew back out of the way as he tripped and fell headlong onto the bed, evidently on top of the woman. She woke up long enough to mutter, "Shit!" and then, as soon as the bed springs ceased to bounce from his landing, all was silent again. Donna imagined the heap of naked limbs she couldn't see in the blackness.

She waited a few moments more and slipped back into the living room, carrying her armload of clothing. She pulled the door quietly shut behind her.

Luckily, he had not seen the open suitcase on the couch. Donna switched on the light again and finished her packing.

The money.

He'll know I was here, Donna reasoned, when he sees that it's my clothes that are missing.

She picked up the loot, fanning out the stack of hundreds. What if he does know? she thought defiantly. What can he do about it? He can't very well call the police!

eleven

"I think it's time he gave serious thought to retiring," said Dr. Feldman.

"You don't understand, Max," Adele said wanly. "If we want him to avoid stress, then we mustn't ever allow him to retire. Nothing makes him more fretful than boredom."

The patient was sleeping easily amid the electronic paraphernalia surrounding his hospital bed. A monitor displayed the steady beat of his strained heart; a cardiograph made ticking sounds as it traced Gilbert's life second by second.

"In any case, you have the idea, Adele. Keep him quiet, particularly for the next few weeks; and then . . . at least get him to cut his business hours some."

Adele smiled and wiped away a tear.

When the doctor had gone, the room was breathlessly quiet except for the relentless ticking of the machinery.

Adele switched on the television set, selected a channel, and turned the volume to a barely audible level.

She watched two soap operas, with half her mind always registering the ticks of Gilbert's heartbeats, and then a game show that struck her as more than usually inane.

She checked her watch and selected the channel that carried the one serial she seldom missed. She had never before dared watch it in Gilbert's presence, or even to admit to him that she was a regular viewer. Gilbert would never have approved; he despised maudlin sentimentality, which he reckoned every daily serial to be based on, and he disapproved even more of this particular show's leading lady.

But Adele found the show rather true-to-life and appreciated its writers' apparent conviction that good things happen at least as often as bad. And the leading lady was Alan's mistress, Margaret Carlson.

I'm such a coward! Adele thought as Margaret's alert and lovely face appeared on the screen. That's my daughter-in-law!

Margaret played Julie Wayne, whose husband, presumed dead, had just resurfaced with amnesia (not *everything* about the story was true-to-life, not everyday life, anyway), and was married to another woman. The scene coming would pit the two women together in their first meeting after all the truth had come out. For a moment, eager to see the development, Adele forgot about her personal connection and was just watching Julie Wayne.

Julie smiled and said, "I hope we can be friends. We'll need to be." The other woman just gave her a suspicious look. Julie continued, "If John could love you, then you must be a wonderful person indeed, Enid, and it would be tragic if the two of us. . . ." Adele nodded.

Now she knew. Julie would handle the matter sensibly, as Adele would want to if she ever found herself in such a trying situation. It was rather like the way Jeanne had handled herself—when all those around her were tearing at her and losing their heads.

Adele suddenly realized that her own daughter was one of the most admirable women she had ever met! Her eyes clouded over, and the television picture dissolved into a smear of moving colors.

She repeated her accusation to herself: I've been such a coward, and such an old fool! The only way I could feel close to my daughter was by considering her still a child. The only way I could feel close to the woman Alan loved was like this—on TV! All because of Gilbert . . . not his fault, really, but because of him, nevertheless. Because of his stupid Victorian ideas, his stubbornness . . . and my willingness to let him go unchallenged.

Gilbert turned in the bed and awkwardly cleared his throat.

"Adele?" he said.

"I'm here," she said. Her instinct was to switch off the TV set so he wouldn't see Margaret; but she resisted it and merely lowered the sound.

"What are you watching?" he said—just to make conversation, she felt sure.

"A serial."

"Mindlessness," he muttered. "Am I going to be all right?"

"I think so."

"Have I slept long?"

"Yes, dear, fitfully, for nearly a day."

"Have you — ?"

"I've been here the whole time." Adele rose, as if she had read his mind, and poured water from a pale blue pitcher into a clear plastic cup.

Gilbert pushed himself onto an elbow and took the cup, careful not to disturb the electrodes attached to his chest. "I'm not to drink much of this, as I recall."

"Just wet your whistle," Adele said cheerily.

He watched the television screen for a moment and asked, " Isn't that — ?"

"It's Margaret Carlson," Adele said. "She's very good in this."

He made no comment.

She took his hand.

"When you leave, Adele, ask them not go give me any more tranquilizers. I hate feeling groggy like this."

"I suspect you need them for a while. They know best. You've had a mild heart attack, and they want you to lie still for a while."

In the quiet, Margaret Carlson's rich, feminine voice could faintly be heard.

Gilbert handed the cup back to Adele. He said, almost in a whisper, "I don't know what to do."

Adele turned away; she could not let him see her face. In all the years they had shared, he had never said those words to her.

Whatever happens, she resolved, I must never forget how desperately I love him.

The light that streamed through the glass wall

180

of the hospital lobby was bright and hot. Occasional noises and voices echoed in the gray marble entranceway. Adele stepped into one in a long row of telephone booths and dialed Alan's number.

"You have reached the friendly machine that serves Alan Mason and Margaret Carlson," said Margaret's voice. "If you'll leave a message when you hear our rude little beep, your call will be returned this evening."

Beep.

"Uh . . . hello, Margaret. This is Adele Mason. I thought that if it would be convenient, I would like to drop by this evening for a visit. Mr. Mason is doing well, but he will have to stay here at the hospital for a few more days. There's no reason for my wanting to visit, only that I thought I would enjoy seeing you both. I will call again to confirm—"

That was the end of the allotted message time. Adele considered ringing up again to finish her sentence but then realized that she had gotten her point across adequately. She inserted another dime and called Jeanne's hotel room.

"Hello?"

"Jeanne, it's—"

"Hi. How's Father?"

"He's going to be fine. He'll have to take it easy for a while. Maybe from now on."

"I'm relieved to hear it, Mother." From her manner, it was clear Jeanne had more to say. "Mother, I just can't go to see him. It surely wouldn't be good for him, anyway. But would you please let him know that I asked you about

181

him and that I'm glad he's all right?''

"Yes, dear. I'll do that. Let's hope he thinks things through while he's lying idle."

"I've never known him to think anything through. He has always known the answers immediately—or he *never* knows them."

Adele chuckled. "He just told me he didn't know what to do."

"*Father* said that?"

"It surprised me, too. It might be a good sign."

"Wouldn't you like to get away from the hospital for an evening? Donna Andersen, a friend from the cruise, is joining me for dinner. Wouldn't you like to come with us?"

"That's thoughtful of you, Jeanne. But I'm in the process of trying to wrangle an invitation from Alan and Margaret."

"That's wonderful! What do you mean *trying*? I'm sure Alan is turning handsprings at the idea!"

"He doesn't know it yet. I just left a message on his answering machine."

"Mother, I'm proud of you!"

* * *

Donna had entered Jeanne's room while Jeanne was talking to her mother. When the conversation was over, Donna asked, "Pardon me for being crass, but is there any news about the money?"

Jeanne shook her head. A look of sheer wonder came over her face. "You wouldn't believe all that's happened since I saw you last," she said. "I'll have to tell you about it over dinner. It looks like we'll have to go elsewhere for money for the shop. My father's out of the picture."

Donna looked crushed momentarily, then began to recover, "I—I have a little money. Not enough for the store, but more than enough to get us an apartment. Don't you want to reconsider that possibility?"

"We'll talk about it."

Donna smiled. "You don't look discouraged. How come?"

Jeanne laughed. "Don't ask me. I just feel optimistic, that's all. Let's go eat."

"I know a great place down in Chinatown. Let me take you. It's my treat tonight!"

The conversation picked up again and continued without serious interruption in the cab on the way down Second Avenue.

"We'll just have to arrange financing in a conventional way," Jeanne said. "A bank loan, for instance; or perhaps we can obtain backing from some investor—"

"With what for credit and collateral?" Donna asked, her tone implying that the situation looked hopeless. "How about your lawyer friend, Pomeranz?"

"I—I could ask him for business advice, I suppose, but not for money. I—I couldn't take advantage of him in that way."

"How about your ex-husband?"

"*What*?"

"I'm kidding. How about your ex-lover, Gordon What's-his-name. Is he rich? You don't talk about him enough to suit me.''

"I don't talk about him because there's nothing to say anymore. Except—''

"Except what?''

"I want to display his paintings in our shop. His work is beautiful and rather commercial, and it would be prestigious for us to offer his things.''

"Now you're talking. When do I get to meet Gordon?''

"Let's talk about shop hunting,'' Jeanne said, laughing lightly. ''You mentioned someone you used to know who handles Greenwich Village real estate. Have you contacted him?''

"OK, I'll mind my own business. No I haven't, yet.''

During dinner at a crowded little basement establishment called Wang Fat, which served delicious meaty and spicy Northern Chinese dishes, the burgeoning business partnership continued its development. They listed desirable merchandise on paper napkins and ransacked pockets and purses for scraps of paper on which to make further notes.

"Makes you think of all those mad scientists who invented atomic bombs and rocket ships on the backs of envelopes, doesn't it?'' Donna mused excitedly.

In fact, by the end of dinner both were so excited about their plans that neither had time to notice how excited they were.

They returned to the hotel and continued their communal daydream. By midnight it was understood that Donna would stay and occupy the room's spare bed. No end of the discussion was in sight.

"Some of these displays will have to come down," Jeanne said, indicating a scribble on a floor plan, "if we're to have room for the paintings."

"Why don't you ask him, for Christ's sake? See if he'll let us show them?"

Without thinking twice, or bothering to notice the late hour, Jeanne grabbed the phone from the bed table and dialed Gordon's number.

"Hello?" He didn't sound sleepy.

"Gordon, I was just—"

"Jeanne! Thank goodness you're not dead!"

She laughed contritely. "I—I'm sorry I haven't called. I did want to let you know that I was all right, but, well, I just didn't have much *else* to say."

"Sorry, I didn't mean to lay on the guilt. I'll confess. I knew you were doing fine; I've kept in touch with Philip."

To avoid a deadly pause, Jeanne rushed ahead to say, "I have a business proposition for you."

"I'll take it."

Jeanne laughed; it was getting easier. "Wait, you might not be so interested. I'm opening a shop, hopefully, sometime soon—"

"Terrific idea!"

"Gifts, jewelry, imports, art objects, minerals, that sort of merchandise; and I'd like very much to make one wall an exhibition of your work. For sale, of course."

"I'd be happy to do it! What commission do

185

you want?''

"Commission? I hadn't thought of that.''

"Thanks, love, but we'll have to speak of a commission. This is a business arrangement, remember?''

"Then we might get together next week sometime and have a bargaining session. I don't have any idea how you go about these things.''

He chuckled. "I can see that. I think I can help you some. When would you like to meet. Pick a time, any time.''

"Oh, how about, uh, Wednesday afternoon, around three.''

"Fine. Come to my studio. We'll brew a pot of my fresh-ground coffee, I'll show you what I have available, and we'll discuss a theme.''

"Theme?''

"Sure. An art exhibit ought to have a unifying idea behind it. I suspect your shop ought to have it's own overall theme, too. Have you given that any thought?''

"Not exactly. Gordon, I have a business partner, Donna Andersen. I'd like to bring her along.''

"Absolutely.''

The awkward silence finally came as both parties realized that the conversation was either at an end or was just about to begin.

"See you Wednesday, Jeanne,'' Gordon said at last.

Jeanne sighed, relieved. "Wednesday it is,'' she said. "Bye, Gordon.''

"Bye, old love. Glad to know you've come back to life!''

Jeanne's hand was hardly clear of the telephone when it rang. "Hello?" she said, not very happily.

"Jeanne, what are you doing next Tuesday night?"

It was Alan. "No plans I can think of. Why?"

"Margaret and I are going to play hookey from the hassles of show-biz and go to the Pops concert in Central Park. We're planning a super picnic dinner with wine, candlelight, and all. Care to join us?"

"That sounds marvelous! You don't suppose I could bring a friend?"

"Sure. You mean Donna, the girl you mentioned to me—from the cruise?"

"Un-huh, Donna Andersen. She's here; let me check with her." Donna heard the proposition and said, "Dynamite! I'm dying to meet them."

Alan asked, "She's in her mid-twenties, didn't you say?"

"Right. But what difference—?"

"Because I'm arranging blind dates for both of you. Don't argue! Incidentally, Mother's here and says hello. Bye now," he said. He hung up without allowing Jeanne an opportunity to protest the blind dates.

Donna liked the idea. She licked her lips lasciviously, raised an eyebrow, and said, "What have we got to lose?"

Jeanne shrugged and laughed. Life was getting better and better all the time. It seemed, that night, that it would be uphill all the way from then on.

"Now about our sharing an apartment," Donna injected.

Following a pause, a nod, and a smile, Jeanne agreed. "All right. We start looking tomorrow."

* * *

The following day was a hot, muggy July Sunday. Hilda Pomeranz winced as she stepped into it from inside her air-conditioned Long Island home. She still wore her pink quilted dressing gown, and her hair was disheveled and partly in rollers. She watched with profound disapproval as Kevin ran to greet his father. Bill was leaning against a sleek blindingly chromed racing car parked at the curb.

"Get a move on," Bill urged his son. "We've got a lot of territory to cover."

Kevin ran and climbed into the doorless, open projectile.

Hilda assumed that Kevin's enthusiasm was more for the car than for his father.

It was with unspoken disapproval that Hilda had agreed to Philip's bringing Kevin to their house. It was plain enough to Hilda that Kevin ought not to remain with his father, but she felt confident that other equally satisfactory arrangements could have been made for the boy. Hilda was not blind. She had seen it often in Philip's eyes—that inappropriate affection for Jeanne.

There was an awful, heartbreaking softness in his voice whenever he spoke to her, or even

188

referred to her when Jeanne wasn't around. Hilda used to wonder if Philip himself understood that he was in love with Jeanne—but not any more. With the sensitivity of a mystic, Hilda had picked up vibrations that told her he knew—almost from the instant it first occurred to Philip. Of course he'd loved Jeanne . . . Jeanne was beautiful and intelligent. Now, it seemed, Jeanne was strong and independent as well.

And here was Hilda caring for Jeanne's little boy. It wasn't fair to ask that of her. Hilda's only consolation lay in her suspicion that Jeanne did not return Philip's love. It was almost all right for Philip to love another woman, as long as he did not act on his desires. Almost.

Ironically, Hilda had come to adore little Kevin. The boy was a fine replacement for the children Hilda knew she could never have. That had been the start of it, Hilda recalled frequently, the start of her chronic terror that she would lose Philip—the day she had learned that she was infertile. She had always counted on children to act as the mortar that would bind Philip to her as she grew older and plainer, as she knew she would. Hilda harbored an irrational dream, a secret fantasy—that if she were to lose Philip to Jeanne, somehow God would give her Kevin to raise, as a consolation. She fed the fantasy even while knowing it was an absurd bubble that one day had to burst. If she lost Philip, she would lose Kevin, too. She would lose everything.

"Will you have him home by dinner?" Hilda

called out to Bill.

"How should I know?" Bill snapped back, as if to ask what business that could be of Hilda's.

Maybe I could have him arrested for making all that racket in a residential area, Hilda thought, half-seriously, as the racer sputtered to life, sounding like a fleet of motorcycles.

The racer zoomed away from the curb, and Hilda knew from the chill she felt that she was deeply concerned for Kevin's safety. She tried to remind herself that Bill was an expert driver, that he would be in conventional traffic until they reached their destination—a test track out near the tip of Long Island—and that Kevin would not be riding with his father on the track. But none of the reminders worked; they felt like evasions.

* * *

East Fifth Street was lined with police cars. It was an unnecessary show of force for the arrest of one fainthearted drug pusher, a man known as Troll to his college chums, as Pot Palermo to the police, and as Richard Michael Palermo III to his anxious parents back in New Hampshire.

Neighbors were hanging out their windows or sitting on fire escapes watching with dull interest as the alleged criminal was escorted out his front door and led to the nearest police car. He was behaving himself, which disappointed the onlookers, who began to return to their own affairs.

The bare-chested, half-bald young man

walked with a slouch that seemed to imply shame and defeat. He was handcuffed, and he obediently climbed into the back of the patrol car.

A plainclothesman ran down the block and climbed into the back seat with Palermo.

"Want to tell us where we can find your lady-friend?" asked the plainclothesman firmly but matter-of-factly. This was just a job to him, one that wasn't quite wrapped up.

"Don't I know you? Ben Sully, right?"

"Detective Sully to you. Yeah, we've met. Where's your girl?"

"Which girl?"

"We know you had a girl making drops for you."

"She gave you the slip?"

"Temporarily. We'll find her eventually, but it can't hurt you to cooperate."

"Listen, Sully, I don't have to tell you a fucking thing." This was not said vindictively; in fact, Palermo was almost friendly in his manner of setting the terms between them.

Sully waited; there was no need to repeat his request.

Palermo seemed to be considering his options. He suddenly smiled. It was not an attractive expression; it implied shrewdness. He said, "Tell me honestly, Sully, if you have her testify, will it make things worse for me?"

"I doubt it. I don't see how things could be much worse for you."

"Then go get her. You can hang her, for all I care. Her name's Donna Andersen. I don't

191

know where she is at the moment, but she's not far away. She snuck into my pad the other day and—hey, that's breaking and entering, isn't it?''

''You're up to something, Palermo. I can see it on your ugly face. You're being straight with me? The girl we want is named Donna—is that last name spelled with an *o* or an *e*?''

''Andersen with an *e*. And I'm being straight with you.'' He added sarcastically, ''Cross my heart and hope to die.''

twelve

Philip was completing a report of some kind and did not rise when Alan entered his office. "Sit down, Alan. Be with you in a minute," he said.

Alan said, "Don't hurry," and wandered to the window. He busied himself with the inspiring view from Philip's window on the seventy-ninth floor of the Empire State Building. He wished it were possible to capture that splendor of civilization in a stage setting.

Philip dropped his pen into a cork holder and said, "What is this little problem you called me about?"

Alan fell into the client's chair opposite Philip and said, "Nothing much. I have to raise $100,000 by a week from Thursday."

"Good Lord. What for?"

Alan said, with a shade of self-disgust in his voice, "I promised Wif Kist I'd try to get my father to invest that amount. I never was too hopeful, but now I won't even ask him. He's always considered Broadway riskier than the horses. He's just not a gambler."

"But your show is fully capitalized. Why the need for more?"

"They've decided to open it at the Manhattan, which might as well be Buckingham Palace when it comes to rental fees."

"The playwright shouldn't have to worry about this. That's what they have producers for."

"I don't *have* to. But it's one way to be sure they leave my title alone. Wif wants to change it to *Champagne and Caviar*." He grinned and added, "I'm learning the value of power, Philip."

"And you want to know if I have any suggestions?"

"Exactly."

Philip said, "Hmmm," and lapsed into thought. He pressed his intercom and asked his secretary, "Get me the list of backers from that Williams play we represented. Type 'em up for Alan, will you?" He suggested to Alan, "Match those against Wif's list of backers for your show, and go after any that aren't on there. I think you'll find some local millionaires who don't typically invest in shows. I really don't know whether this will help, but it's a place to start."

Alan looked on, admiring the business acumen of his lawyer and friend as Philip pulled a slip out of his desk drawer and scribbled hastily on it. He handed it to Alan. It was a check.

"Here's $10,000 more from me. Tell Wif to tack that onto my original ten."

"I'll be damned. You're a backer?" Alan quickly explained, "I don't want any favors, Philip, not this kind. As confident as I am that my play's tremendous, It's still a huge risk—"

"I'm just covering my bet. If the show never opens, or opens under-capitalized, I lose my *original* investment!"

* * *

Detective Ben Sully drummed his fingers against his desk. "Palermo says she spells it with an *e*. Are you sure you're not looking under Anderson with an *o*?" he asked the records clerk on the other end of the phone line.

"I checked both," the clerk said. "She has no record in narcotics. Have you checked the general files?"

"Yeah, nothing. According to Palermo, she went to Manchester University and hails from someplace in New Hampshire. Check out the school back for, oh, the last six years. And see if there are some parents in New Hampshire with a missing daughter."

"Will do."

Sully heard someone approaching the open door of his office cubicle. He glanced up at a familiar voluptuous brunette, short-skirted and wearing a big bouncing Libra sign on a chain around her neck. "Hi, Jude," he said. "Why the screwed-up face?"

"Because of my screwed-up mind, I guess," Judy Schwartz quipped sarcastically. "Being at the switchboard and having slow reflexes, I couldn't help overhearing that you're looking for a chick named Donna Andersen. I'm trying to remember the news item. This Donna Andersen was in her mid-twenties, I seem to remember.''

"So is *my* Donna Anderson. Let's have it."

"Remember when the *City of Liberty* ran aground?"

"Vaguely. Puerto Rico?"

"Virgin Islands, I think. There wasn't much about it—no damage or casualties—but this reporter dug up a human interest bit to beef up the story. A nut named Donna Andersen fell overboard. And get this; she had been a stowaway!"

"You mean she's dead?"

"No, they rescued her."

Ben grabbed his phone again. "Hey, who's minding the switchboard?"

"Patsy took over for me."

The switchboard answered. "Pats? Get me the New York office of the cruise ship *City of Liberty* . . . No, I don't know which line. Do you expect me to do all your work for you?"

* * *

The sun was down, leaving yellow and purple clouds in its wake, and a near-full moon floated in lavender twilight over the trees of Central Park. But it was the city itself that was taking possession of the night sky; it blazed a reddish twilight of its own from the lights of a million neon signs and a million windows.

The lighted skyscrapers towered majestically behind the outdoor orchestra shell where members of the New York Philharmonic were ambling in and idly warming up their instruments.

196

A jetliner coasted high overhead and caught the last rusty rays from the sun. A hundred thousand New Yorkers had spread their picnic blankets over the meadow and had scattered their own starlight across the ground in the form of flickering candles in colored glasses.

"Wake me before it starts, lover," Margaret said as she stretched out and rested her head on Alan's leg after playfully biting it first. Her knees were crooked around an immense wine bottle.

"You only have five minutes to snooze, unless you want to sleep through the New World Symphony," Alan said to her.

She ignored him blissfully, and Alan turned his attention to Jeanne and Donna and their dates. Not a matchmaker by inclination, Alan eyed his handiwork with amusement and some satisfaction.

Donna had been the unknown quantity. Alan had never met her and knew only from Jeanne's assurances that she was attractive and interesting. She and Barry Oster—a young actor from *Conquerors and Candlelight*, or whatever the play's title—were getting along splendidly, arguing some arcane point of politics.

"You're not thinking it through all the way," Barry was insisting. "Sure, all those government guarantees *sound* good, but—"

"Damn it," Donna spat out, "can't you take an idealistic point of view for once?"

That couple, Alan observed, was definitely a success. So was the other, in a vastly different way. Alan had asked Tom Chappell to come along as Jeanne's date. Tom was an associate producer of *Joy of Living*. He, too, had made a bust of a first marriage. He had a daughter who now lived with her mother, and Tom had found no other women to interest him in the last year and a half. Alan observed, with amusement and a touch of chagrin, that Tom and Jeanne were discussing the one subject he had expected them both to avoid: their first marriages.

"But *do* people really change," Jeanne was asking Tom. "I've about decided that they merely become more defined."

"They stay the same, only more so," Tom queried.

Jeanne laughed lightly. "Bill and I were essentially then what we are now. We just weren't clear to one another."

"Now you understand him better. But does he understand you?"

"I don't think so. I—I never wanted to stop growing. But he just wanted to . . . to solve the problem of survival, and then spend his time playing. That's not very well put, I'm afraid."

"Oh, I understand it. Why did it take you so long to discover the differences in your attitudes?"

Jeanne smiled wisely; she had thought a lot about this.

"He used to say, 'Don't analyze everything! Don't tell me *why* you love me, just show me that you do.' So we never analyzed."

"Neither did we." Tom hesitated, then confided what was really on his mind. "My wife wanted a child for the sheer experience of going through it. It meant some kind of fulfillment to her, but she never gave a moment's thought to the problem of bringing a new human being into the world. She didn't want a child; she just wanted to be a mother. She never *thought* about it. I don't mean to put all the blame on her; I was far from patient with her. And now I think she really cares for our little girl—but not the way I do, not as deeply. She doesn't know Cindy as a person."

"Bill seems to care for Kevin, too, but I honestly don't know how or why. Kevin doesn't even like his father, and I don't blame him a bit. Bill is rough and demanding and unreasoning. He just wants to mold Kevin into a standard American boy who likes only what everyone is supposed to like."

"He doesn't see Kevin as a young man with a mind of his own?"

"Exactly."

"Then that's the way Bill treated you, too, isn't it?"

"I don't understand what you mean."

"He expected you to be a standard American wife, who wants only what everyone else wants."

Jeanne's mouth dropped. "I never saw it that way—but yes, of course!"

"Did he . . . ever strike you?"

"Just once."

"Is that when you left him?"

"Yep."

"Good for you."

On stage an oboe sounded its A, and the orchestra tuned up, creating a vast dissonant chord that in turn tuned the audience's expectations.

"Have dinner with me sometime soon," Tom commanded abruptly.

"I'd love to," Jeanne said smiling.

The conductor tapped the podium for attention. Then the first ominous strains of Dvorak's masterpiece drifted out over the rolling plain of the meadow.

Donna leaned over and whispered into Jeanne's ear, "Well?"

"I like him," Jeanne whispered back. "How's yours."

"Interesting. If he were any more clean-cut, his skin would squeek when I touch him. But he has dreamy eyes."

* * *

On Wednesday morning Kevin happened to be looking out the front window when his father drove up unexpectedly in a car even more exotic than the last one. This looked like a speedboat—wedge-shaped and wicked-looking. There was a woman in the car with him. She had long blonde hair.

After he watched his father leap boyishly out of the car, Kevin hurriedly scrawled a note to Hilda, who had gone to the grocery store. "I went for a ride with Dad again," it said. He left it on the dining table and ran to answer the doorbell.

"Hi, sport," Bill said. "Grab your bathing

suit. We're driving down to the Jersey shore. And I want you to meet Margot."

* * *

"One problem solved, and a zillion to go," Donna said happily. She and Jeanne had just rented an apartment on East Eleventh Street, near the NYU campus. It was small, but if they could keep out of each other's way, it would do. "Prepare me. What's he like?"

She meant Gordon. The two were on their way, on foot, to his studio.

"I think it might be better if you just wait to find out for yourself," Jeanne said. It was clear that she was absorbed by thoughts of her own.

It was too early in the summer for the Greenwich Village Art Show, but some early aspirants had their wares hanging here and there from chain-link fences around parks and parking lots. The work was, for the most part, awful — particularly to Jeanne, who had Gordon's accomplished work firmly in mind.

Donna walked briskly along; Jeanne seemed to be holding back.

"Are you interested in all this garbage art?" Donna asked, "or are you dreading this visit. I think I have a right to know."

"I . . . neither, really. Well, maybe." Jeanne was reliving the past, as if she were setting a context for the meeting with Gordon. She saw the whole sequence, like a movie running at high speed. . . .

A cocktail party Alan had taken her to was last year, but it seemed like a generation ago.

The handsome blond man apart from the crowd, as if he didn't belong there. He was looking out at the serpentines of walk lights in Central Park just below. Her eyes met his. He smiled.

"Meet Gordon Strand," Alan invited her, "who creates beauty for a living."

"I've been watching you," Gordon said to Jeanne. "You don't like parties either."

Jeanne and Gordon stood together for the rest of the evening, looking out, talking.

Coffee after the party . . . lunch the next day . . . dinner two weeks later . . . opening night of Alan's *Night of the Bats* on Broadway . . . her first visit to Gordon's studio . . . Gordon's mysteriously angry young friend, Bobby. . . .

The night she left Bill. He had been drinking more than usually. Kevin was asleep. Bill wanted to have sex there on the living room floor, and he started tearing at Jeanne's clothes, demanding that she lie down, threatening to force her to take him orally, abusing her both physically and psychologically, calling her horrible names and laughing about it.

Jeanne couldn't believe he intended to hurt and humiliate her, and the only alternative seemed to be that he was playing out some masculine fantasy, finding fun in the pretense of using force to have his way with his own wife. At first, she tried to go along. But she couldn't. She felt demoralized and insulted—depersonalized, as if she could have been any woman to him at that time, any woman at all.

He pulled her to the carpet and stood naked over her. Laughing. He's crazy! she thought.

202

But she knew better; it was just that under excessive alcohol a new side of him was emerging. It was a side Jeanne found repulsive.

She turned away and tried to crawl from him. He grabbed her dress and tore it. He seemed to believe she was onto his fantasy and wanted to play it with him, wanted to play hard to get. He tugged at the front of her dress, trying to rip it off. She pushed him away so resolutely that he could have had no doubt that she was denying, rebuking, and rejecting him. She stood and faced him, breathing heavily. She was frightened.

He drew back and slapped her so hard she tumbled sideways into a floor lamp. Her ears rang and her cheek felt as if it has been burned with a hot iron.

Without thinking or planning, she ran. Out the door, into a cab, to Gordon's.

"My God, what happened?" Gordon whispered, taking her into his arms.

He put her to bed and took the couch for himself. They talked, practically shouting to one another, until nearly dawn, when he appeared at the bedroom door.

After she looked up at him and smiled, he said, "Move over."

They melted into each others arms. Their kisses were tender and never violent—they were reluctant kisses. He handled her body as if it were a wondrous discovery. She handled his as if it represented some only-dreamed-of ideal.

As if especially to defy Bill, she helped Gordon into the mutual oral position—and she found it unbearably sensual and thrilling. And daring. More than conventional intercourse, this granted a gift of intimate intimacy to Gordon and deprived Bill of it. Her emotions were like swarming bees. When her orgasm came—hours later, as she recalled it now—it was like deliverance, entry into a promised land that was to be the future. She didn't want him to remove himself; she wanted to feel his presence within her forever. His weight upon her seemed non-existent.

Later, when sunlight streamed in to warm and wake them, Gordon said, "Jeanne, I'm homosexual, or at least I thought I was. . . ."

It would have been easier if she had suspected it; but she hadn't. She said nothing in response. She got out of bed and found her legs were shaky, and she had a sinking feeling that was nearly nauseating. She wasn't running from him—or from the truth. She stood there near the bed, her eyes transfixed on a tall painting of the city. The image of it was burned into her memory so indelibly that even today she could have described every inch of it.

When it was clear that she had no questions or comments, Gordon continued, still lying there, his hands under his head. "I've been falling in love with you for months. I—I had a feeling this might happen someday. I hoped it would." She continued to examine the painting, her mind endeavoring to hear him and understand him. "I don't know everything about my feelings for you," he continued. "And I don't know what I can promise you in terms of the future. I'm sorry to inflict my problem on you . . . but I had to tell you. I've imagined just about everything you might have to say. I won't blame you, no matter what you decide about me.''

Her back was to him, but she felt, fleetingly, that she ought to cover her naked body. She thought of taking the sheet and draping it like a cape, but that would leave Gordon's body uncovered—and somehow that seemed just as improper. Her thoughts were not well connected to her emotions; nothing seemed relevant to anything. One way to cover herself would be to slip back under the covers with Gordon.

That's what she did. His side was warm and dry; she was aware of the contact of it from her shoulder to her toes. He made no aggressive move toward her, nor did he pull away.

They stared at the ceiling, where patterns of reflected sunlight were projected from the floor, tabletops, and shiny objects in the room. ''I'll try, Gordon,'' she said at last.

As she made no attempt to leave the bed, and neither did he, they became increasingly aware of the places where their bodies touched. They imperceptibly moved closer. It took a long time; it was a period of physical questioning and answering, with not a word spoken until they were again in each other's arms kissing more passionately, making love more insistently.

Jeanne couldn't bear to think of Bill after that. She took a furnished apartment for herself, and Kevin and moved out the things she and he would need.

Now, as she walked with Donna, not hurrying, toward Gordon's studio, Jeanne saw images of that temporary refuge she had made for herself . . . its mint-green drapery billowing at the open window . . . the view of the East River she had from the bedroom . . . Gordon with her there in her own bed . . . the happiness he brought to her . . . their harmless and amusing sexual games . . . Kevin and Gordon playing before supertime . . . the huge tropical plant Gordon had given her as a housewarming present . . . the night Bill had stormed in and taken Kevin away, the night Bill had. . . .

She yanked her mind away from that memory only to be reminded of another unpleasant one—when Bill's lawyer had asked Gordon, in court, if it was true that his previous lover had been a boy named Bobby Thaxton.

"A man," Gordon had corrected. "Yes, it's true." The look of defeat and humiliation on his face, Jeanne knew, was not so much from personal embarrassment as from awareness of the damage his admission was doing to Jeanne's case.

"And Jeanne was aware of this?" the lawyer persisted.

"I told her," said Gordon.

"Your honor, that's irrelevant to this situation," Philip objected indignantly.

"I find it quite relevant, Mr. Pomeranz," the judge declared, "as it reflects Mrs. Oliver's state of mind, her questionable judgment, and her expendable moral standards."

Donna grabbed Jeanne's arm, jolting her into

the present; "Hold it, oh fearless leader. Didn't we just pass Gordon's street?"

Jeanne looked around. "So we did. It's right back there." Jeanne checked her watch and was relieved to find that they weren't due for nearly ten minutes. "Let's have a cup of coffee," Jeanne suggested, indicating a little Italian street cafe across Bleecker street.

"Is anything the matter?" Donna asked.

"Not really. I just need . . . a few more minutes."

Donna placed the coffee order and was considerate enough not to speak, even so much as to ask for the cream.

The phrase from the courtroom that haunted Jeanne was, "irreparable psychological damage to the boy Kevin. . . ." The judge had been referring to Gordon's influence over the boy who, it was clear to everyone, liked Gordon more than his own father. Jeanne had been so infuriated when she heard the phrase that it later made her realize she didn't *know* whether there might be truth in it. Her reaction had been purely emotional. She knew only one person to ask.

"I honestly don't think so," Gordon said, "but I'm afraid I don't know much more about the *theory* of homosexuality than you do. I always just . . . took it for granted. You know I'd never do anything to influence Kevin. Not deliberately, anyway." He brightened considerably and added, "If anything, I might prejudice him *against* it. While I don't consider myself some kind of immoral monster for my past life,

I'm not proud of it either, and not terribly sympathetic toward homosexuality these days."

Jeanne visited a well-known doctor who told her, "Most psychologists and psychiatrists these days aren't worried about influences, certainly not about inadvertant ones such as Gordon might represent to your child."

Jeanne had a flash of violent anger directed at herself for not thinking to ask such a man as this to testify at the hearing.

"It is typically believed," he went on, "that homosexuality, a sympton of a disorder concerning sexual identity, is developed in childhood. Frankly, from what you tell me, I'd say your ex-husband's attitude is likely to be more instrumental in instilling the sort of self-doubt, and fear of unmanliness, that might sway a child toward homosexuality."

"Would you be willing to tell a judge that, on my behalf?"

He smiled. "Certainly, but I could only represent myself as a friend of the court and offer that as a general position. I don't know enough about you, Bill, Gordon, or Kevin to be able to apply it to your case. I would have to admit that Kevin might be perfectly strong enough and well-adjusted enough to withstand Bill's pressure. Uh, you tell me Kevin despises his father? That's healthy in this case—an indication of the boy's sense of identity. So you see, if they knew the right questions to ask, I might do you no good at all." He seemed to go off on a thoughtful tangent. Jeanne waited until he said:

"I think I ought to prepare you for a possibility, Jeanne. I've treated a great many homosexuals. Most have come asking me to make them more comfortable with their state; in many cases, I can succeed in doing that. Far fewer have come asking that I help them become heterosexual. In some of those cases, about half, I'd guess, we've succeeded—because of their strong motivation to change. I've never known a man to make the turnaround you say Gordon did—without the intensive guidance of a psychiatrist.''

''Are you saying—?''

''I'm not saying it's impossible, or that he's being dishonest with you. I'm merely saying: be aware of the possibility that his mental set might not last. He might find the subconscious urges and pressures too great to combat.''

''I shouldn't marry him if he asks me?''

''Are you morally comfortable being his lover?''

''I—I think so.''

''Then don't marry. Not for a while.''

''Should I tell him what we've talked about?''

''If he asks you, don't lie to him; but I'd say it might be a mistake to encourage him to doubt your confidence in him. Generally speaking, do you trust him?''

''Completely.''

''Then let him fight his own battle with this, help him when you can, and trust that he will confide in you . . . if it becomes necessary.''

It wasn't quite dark when Jeanne returned home that day, and she turned on every light in her apartment; but it still seemed dim and lifeless. In a way, she needed Gordon more than she had ever needed another human being. He was all she had. In another way, she knew that if she had to contend with one more difficulty, she would crack. She called Gordon and asked him not to come that evening. She would deal with tomorrow, tomorrow.

She believed she might be able to stand it if Gordon told her that his love for her wasn't growing, that it was all over. Or if he left her for another woman. But if Jeanne were to lose him to someone named Bobby Thaxton. . . .

The next day she told Gordon goodbye.

A week later she declined an invitation to her parent's. She was afraid she would throw something if she had to see her father face to face. A few days later she told Alan she could not meet him for lunch; she had a headache. After two more weeks of oppressive seclusion, of the feeling that the world was closing in and she had not yet figured out how to stop it, she booked passage on the first available ship leaving New York for anywhere.

There, Jeanne thought, gulping the last of the coffee she had allowed to cool, that's everything. What does that tell me about my true feelings toward Gordon Strand? Nothing; I'm feeling absolutely nothing.

"Ready?" Donna prodded.

Jeanne nodded. "Ready as I'll ever be."

* * *

Donna had not known what to expect, but

Gordon Strand exceeded her wildest expectations. He was beautiful! Tall, blond as a Californian, with a soft and sexy voice. And there was something worldly about him, something decadent that excited Donna more than all the rest.

He didn't hug Jeanne or embarrass her by being too forward; he just cupped her face in his hands and kissed her on the forehead. What an elegant understatement! Donna thought.

"Donna Andersen, I presume," he said to her, extending his hand.

" Don't I rate a kiss?" she asked.

He laughed. "My kisses have to be earned, pretty lady."

"How?"

He laughed again, "Through saintly thoughts and clean living."

"There had to be a catch," she muttered, amused.

Donna wasn't dense. She quickly registered the electricity in the air caused by the meeting of these two. They seemed unsure what to say. It was a sort of push-pull magnetic attraction.

He fled to the back, promising to return with the best coffee this side of Brazil—and he did.

"Do you have a sandbox?" she asked Gordon. He pointed, and she left Jeanne and Donna alone for a minute or two.

Donna returned to the room virtually certain that not a word had been spoken in her absence; they seemed to be waiting for her return to resume the talk.

"Tell me about this shop," he requested of

211

both women. "Let's see what would be best suited to it. Big landscapes? Little pen-and-ink drawings?"

They described an imaginary emporium that was small, quaint, filled with hanging plants, perhaps one wall of exposed old brick, display cases on the floor, and jewelry beneath a glass counter. Tiffany lamp shades, perhaps, both on the ceiling fixtures and for sale.

Gordon took a pencil and drawing pad and began furiously to set something down. By the time Donna and Jeanne had finished, he turned his drawing around and said, "Like this?"

There was their shop, an architect's sketch of the very interior they had been inventing. It looked so real! And against the wall opposite the brick (on which were hung heavy mirrors and antique pieces) were rows of small framed pieces of art.

" Drawings, I think," Gordon said, "and maybe a few small paintings. Let me show you what's hanging around already, and we'll think about, perhaps, a series of lithographs or woodcuts I could do exclusively for you."

Donna was awed. Gordon's offer was overwhelming. An exclusive series! But more, Donna was always astounded by the clear and positive evidence of *talent*. How could he do a drawing like that—pick it right out of her's and Jeanne's minds—and make it come to life?

How could Jeanne be indifferent to such a man? It was clear as Christmas to Donna that Gordon was so much in love with Jeanne that her presence was turning him inside out. He virtually never took his eyes from Jeanne—except to draw, or to see where he was going. When it seemed that there might be a lag in the proceedings, he whipped out an expensive plum wine and insisted that they open it. Jeanne had to be out of her mind!

The wine seemed to calm him a bit. They sat around a mosaic-topped coffee table and talked money, quite rationally. That part seemed easy for him. He showed her his books, in which other commissions had been recorded, as precedence. And they settled on a figure that seemed fair.

Then, from Donna's point of view, Gordon said the magic words, "Let me lend you some money for the enterprise."

"Oh, Gordon, no," Jeanne said unconvincingly. "I don't want—"

"To be indebted to me. I know; I can see that. I'm not talking about much; I don't have a bundle to spare."

Jeanne replied hesitantly, "I don't want to feel that I have to be helped. I need—"

"I understand," he said. "I'll charge as much interest as you want me to." He laughed, more at ease than he had been. "Just remember that the offer stands," he said.

When they left, Gordon did not insist that Jeanne call him. The two made no arrangements to meet again. Donna found the simplicity of their departure heartrending!

Once again on the street, where a strong afternoon breeze was bending the saplings planted along the sidewalk, Donna attacked. "I don't care," she said, "if that man is dying of leukemia and has just robbed Fort Knox; you're crazy if you don't run right back in there and pull his pants down! Who are you waiting for? Robert Redford? Billy Graham?"

Jeanne smiled helplessly. "I really don't know, Donna. There's a long story behind all that. I'll tell it to you some time."

"Do you feel all right? Seriously."

"I sure could use a drink."

"There's a cute little bar around the corner. Been here since the turn of the century."

"Fine."

"If you don't mind that it's a gay bar."

"No!" Jeanne said too vehemently.

"Prejudiced? A sophisticated woman like you? It's really nothing to be leary of. Most of them are perfectly nice. *All* of them are perfectly harmless."

"I've heard that theory," Jeanne said. "Let's have a glass of Chianti back at the little Italian place."

"Suit yourself."

Gilbert Mason was home from the hospital and obstinately trying to accomplish some work while technically obeying doctors' orders to stay away from his office. He was in pajamas and dressing gown, bent over a ledger filled with complex numbers under the light of the dining-room chandelier.

The phone rang.

Adele hurried to grab it so Gilbert would not be disturbed, and she kept her voice low.

"Adele? This is Philip. I . . . is Jeanne

214

there?''

"No, Philip, I haven't heard from her today."
Adele had already detected a wrong note in
Philip's voice and was instantly worried.
"What's wrong, Philip," she asked firmly.

"I have to reach Jeanne," he said weakly.

Adele detected the familiar hollow elec-
tronics of a long-distance connection. "Where
are you?"

"In New Jersey," Philip answered, then was
silent again.

"Philip, I'm a hardy woman. I can tell this is
terribly serious. What is it?"

After a pause, he answered, "There's been an
accident."

Adele would never be sure what made her
guess it so accurately and suddenly, but she was
a step ahead of Philip. "Kevin," she said quietly
and with certainty.

"Bill and Kevin and a woman. They went off
the road onto a shoulder of sand. It was one of
those two-seat racing cars. Kevin and the
woman were somehow trying to share a seat-
belt." He stopped.

Adele waited patiently; she had no questions.

"Bill is unconscious, in shock, but they say
he'll be all right. The woman is essentially un-
hurt."

Adele wanted to scream, *No, don't say it!* But
she knew the words had to be said, and she had
to hear them.

"Kevin was thrown out of the car. He . . . he
was killed instantly."

Adele walked into the bedroom, past where

Gilbert continued to work undisturbed, and fell onto the bed. A blinding anger and the desire to destroy Bill Oliver came and dissipated, but the horrible feeling remained that Gilbert was responsible for it all—because of his oblivious allegiance to Bill and his blindness to his own daughter's rightness.

Before she could bring herself even to tell Gilbert what had happened, Adele had to let some time pass. She cried as she had not cried in many many years.

thirteen

The Masons should be leaving the cemetery about now, Lettie thought as she caught a glimpse of the kitchen clock. She had prepared a light supper; the big coffee urn was filled; liquor was set out; dishes, silver, napkins, flowers. . . .

In her fifty-five years, Lettie, the Masons' maid, had developed an abundance of common sense. I've got to be strong, she reminded herself; today, that's what I'm getting paid for.

She sensed she had to be the touch of normalcy in the house, an indication that someday life would go on as before.

Satisfied that all the preparations were made, she picked up the wall phone in the kitchen and dialed her home number.

"Walter, honey," she said, "I'm going to stay here long's they need me . . . Yes, so far I'm just fine . . . Well, they're not doing so good. Poor Miss Jeanne walks around like a zombie. I can't bear to look at her . . . Yes, I went to the service, then I came on back while they went on to the burial. Mr. Bill Oliver was there for a time, and honey, I never seen nobody look so pitiful! He was drunk as a skunk and all red-faced, and everybody just glared at him like they wanted to pull him to pieces till he died . . . No, honest, Walter, I'm fine. . . .''

As she talked, she glanced up into a cabinet at a stack of eleven desert plates. There had been twelve, until one day when Kevin broke one helping Lettie load the dishwasher.

"I don't know what's to become of this family, Walter. You know what I think of them— that they are every one among God's chosen in this world, the best people I know. And Walter, they aren't consoling one another, helping one another. Nobody says anything. Everyone's suffering alone. It's frightful!

"Young Alan, he's about the only one with a head on his shoulders. He's kind and gentle and loving, but he doesn't say anything either. It's more like he was standing ready to toss on a bucket of water if a fuse gets lit. . . .''

Another cubicle in Lettie's mind suggested to her that she open the drapes in the living room to make it a little less gloomy. She felt instinctively that Alan would want it that way.

"Mr. Gilbert? He's bearing up. From his face you'd think he was on his way to the electric chair, but I think he'll come through. Right now I think he's blaming himself for Kevin's death; and Walter, that's the heaviest load a person can ever have to carry . . . No, he figures it would never have happened if he had seen to it that the boy was put in Jeanne's care; I heard him say it to Miss Adele. Why is it that folks always seem to make excuses for themselves when they're really to blame, and then go and take the blame for something they didn't do . . . ?''

218

Lettie remembered a picture of Kevin that was on the piano. She knew a way to leave it there, so its absence would not be conspicuous, and at the same time turn it so it wouldn't be seen.

"Listen, Walter, I got a few more things to see to before they get here. You get yourself a TV dinner, and I'll be home just as soon as I can get away. Bye honey; I love you . . . I just felt like saying it; maybe I don't say it often enough. Bye."

They came all in a group and entered like adults being careful not to wake a sleeping child.

Lettie tried to conceal the fact that she was avoiding their eyes.

Adele and Gilbert came in first—followed by Jeanne, Philip and Hilda Pomeranz, Adele's elder sister Rosanne, Donna Andersen, Adam and Sandy Caffrey, who had been Jeanne and Bill's neighbors for years, Margaret Carlson, the actress, whom Lettie recognized with a shameful touch of excitement, and finally, Alan, who pulled the door shut behind him.

Praise the Lord! Lettie thought, noting that Bill Oliver was not among them.

Adele noticed that the food and drink had been set out, registered Lettie's readiness to serve; then she stood, butler fashion, waiting for the others to find places to sit. When the room was still, Adele still could not bring herself to make a sound or move a muscle.

Alan put his arm around Lettie and led her to the coffee urn. "You're a jewel," he whispered to her. He turned to the assembly and asked on his mother's behalf, "Who would like coffee?

While Lettie served coffee, Alan prepared plates of chicken salad for himself and Margaret.

Gilbert was standing slumped at the piano staring at the back of the photograph he knew was of Kevin.

Lettie studied the guests in amazement. This just wasn't the way grieving people ought to act. There was no crying, although Hilda Pomeranz had the puffy red face of one who is cried out. No one spoke except Alan—and that was only to see to someone's needs or comfort.

The Caffreys rose awkwardly, made a few sorrowful remarks, and left. Lettie thought, They just couldn't stand it here!

Lettie found a common denomenator in some of the faces.

Gilbert, Adele, Jeanne, Hilda, Philip—they all displayed shades of anger and guilt. The actress's look of horror told Lettie that Margaret Carlson saw it too.

These people seemed to be here to receive, wordlessly, by some sort of ESP, the accusations they thought they deserved.

It was tragic that ESP did not work. If they could actually have read each other's minds, their burdens would have been lightened. They could then have held each other and let the tears, that were so excruciatingly held back, begin to flow.

Philip stared intently at Jeanne, who seemed hardly aware that he was in the same room with her. Oh, Jeanne! Forgive me, he projected futilely. Forgive me for failing you once again, for being unable to crush Bill before he could do something like this. Forgive me for loving you. I never wanted you to know! I've never felt so helpless. I need someone—someone like you. I can't go to Hilda. How could I expect her to understand?

Hilda sighed almost audibly and bit her lip. She felt that no one, least of all herself, should puncture the fragile silence that encased them all. She saw Philip looking at Jeanne. I'm sorry, Philip, Hilda said in the privacy of her thoughts. I'm sorry I'm not like Jeanne. I always wanted to be—for you. I don't blame you for loving her. Who could want a nobody like me? I wasn't even there when *Kevin* needed me; I let Bill carry him away and kill him. Oh, but he was such a lovely, honest little child. But I mustn't cry again! I mustn't!

Adele tried not to let Gilbert catch her looking at him but succeeded only in appearing furtive. My poor Gilbert, she thought; he must think I hate him for what he's done. I don't think this is the time to tell him I love him . . . he wouldn't believe me; he'd think it was only pity. We've never talked to each other as we should. I've never in all these years told him what things he does, and *is*, that make me adore him so. He was blind about Bill, but even so he only did what he thought was right.

Gilbert saw only the pattern of carpeting at his feet, and, on occasion, the back of Kevin's picture. He was thinking, perhaps I ought to take a hotel room. No, I can't leave. Adele would keep me here out of kindness, and to refuse her would hurt her sense of generosity. I am utterly defeated in the matter. Perhaps I should have died. Perhaps it is my punishment that I was allowed to live. Suicide would negate our insurance arrangements, but maybe my heart will just stop and make my decisions for me. If I were to pass away, they would all be better off. Even Alan. I don't know my own son, and I doubt that I ever shall. He surely despises me, too.

In Jeanne's mind there were two deep undercurrents of emotions making thought all but impossible: love for Kevin and hatred for Bill. Vivid pictures took the place of ideas: Kevin's coffin . . . mountains of flowers . . . Bill trying to speak to her at the funeral but losing his footing and falling back into a spray of lilies . . . Bill's car running off the road . . . the way it must have been . . . the terror on Kevin's face, the crash, Kevin's final flight through the air . . . Kevin as a newborn baby . . . Kevin running into her arms . . . Bill yelling at the boy and Kevin crying . . . Bill striking Jeanne . . . Kevin . . . Bill . . . Kevin . . . Bill . . . Kevin. . . .

fourteen

Bill Oliver was drunk almost to the point of passing out, and his telephone was ringing— endlessly it seemed.

Bill knew it was Margot trying to reach him again, as she had been for several days. She had even sent a telegram once; and besides, there was no one else in the world who could want to call him.

If Bill had been more perceptive, more adept at communicating with people, and less drunk, he might have answered the phone and explained.

Instead, he yanked the phone off its cradle and, after recognizing Margot's voice, growled, "Get lost! Don't bother me!" He pulled the phone cord out of the wall, wondering why he hadn't done it sooner.

He focussed his bleary eyes on the liquidation papers that glared back at him from under the hot light of the table lamp. Once those sheets were signed, witnessed, and delivered, Bill would no longer own his auto showroom. He felt that as soon as he lifted his pen after signing his name on the last dotted line, he would become transparent, then invisible, then would vanish from the earth.

But it had to be done. Bill could no longer stand the weight of being in debt to Jeanne's father. For the sake of his tenuous grip on life and sanity, he had to sever every remaining tie with the Mason family.

He sluggishly twirled his pen.

He glowered at his lawyer who was patiently waiting in a corner of the room, apparently embarrassed at seeing his client sloppy, drunk, unshaven, and half-dressed.

The lawyer's presence embarrassed Bill, too, and made him angry. Somehow, it made it seem that everything that had happened, and was going to happen, was the lawyer's fault.

The showroom was Bill's badge of membership in respectable society. It made him a man, a man with a business of his own, a man with his feet on the ground. Bill felt sure he could never have done it without Gilbert Mason, who not only pushed him into it, but provided the great sum of money needed to start.

Bill Oliver, the man, was crumbling; but there was a remnant of Bill Oliver, the adolescent, crouching in the back of his mind pleading, Sign it!

That youngster wanted to be a race driver more than anything in the world, but he also believed that it was childish. They'll laugh at me, the adolescent had feared fifteen years ago.

However, the cash remaining after this liquidation would be just about enough to allow Bill to buy his own racer. Why, the engine alone would cost nearly as much as a good year's income from the showroom!

Sign it! begged the young voice in Bill's head.

The remnant of youth won. Bill signed the papers.

Many days later Jeanne finally dressed and left her apartment. She even thought to wake Donna to say, "I'm going for a walk. Don't worry about me. Go back to sleep."

She was unaware of the cement beneath her feet and the aching muscles in her legs. She had walked for three hours, virtually alone in the streets of a city that slept through dawn on a Sunday morning.

The sky was clear and bright, but the oblique rays of the sun were stopped by all the tall buildings, and Jeanne walked in the chilled shadows, where a dry breeze hinted the end of summer.

A patrol car was parked near the on-ramp of the Willamsburg Bridge, and two policemen leaned against it and sipped steaming coffee from styrofoam containers. Their eyes followed Jeanne.

"Too much party?" one speculated.

"No," said the other. "She doesn't look drunk. Morning constitutional."

"She's asking for trouble. Think we should keep an eye on her?"

"Oh, it's daylight enough by now; she'll be all right. Or did you have another reason for wanting to keep an eye on her?"

"She's a looker, you gotta admit. I don't know. Somehow, I feel sorry for her."

It was in the way she walked. Her eyes were downcast, but her back was straight; her steps were slow but steady. She looked like a strong woman in trouble.

Jeanne half-registered the distant words of the patrol cops, but they were in another world somewhere.

She walked, not knowing where she was headed. She was aware at one point that the Wall Street district looked as it might after doomsday. No business on Sundays, no residents, no taxis, no strollers. The wind seemed colder here, and might actually have been, since the area was near the harbor. Sunlight was bouncing dazzlingly from building tops. One spire was goldplated and seemed to be on fire. The World Trade Center towers were too brilliant to gaze upon.

Jeanne heard music. It seemed unreal in the dead city. She let her ears lead her to it. From a room in a decaying office structure near the waterfront came the tinkling sound of ragtime piano. Probably some building guard listening to a portable radio. The melody was utterly carefree. It held Jeanne enraptured. It seemed to say, the world is not only alive and well, it is amused.

Jeanne sat on a bench at a corner bus stop and listened. At first she was delighted beyond all reason, then found herself sobbing uncontrollably, closing her ears to the sound of gaiety.

The music reminded her of Kevin. The connection was such a slight one—Kevin's new phonograph and his records. Jeanne was delighted that Kevin was developing a taste for music; he loved *The Nutcracker*. For an instant

Jeanne wondered if he would enjoy this piano rag as she was enjoying it; it would probably remind him of the music of an animated cartoon . . . but then she remembered that there was no Kevin.

The next sounds Jeanne was aware of were the outrageous *clunk* of her own coin falling into a turnstile box, and, as if triggered by it, the loud buzzing signal for boarding the next Staten Island Ferry.

Jeanne's world was like a jigsaw puzzle that had been repeatedly jostled. Just as pieces were falling into place, they were knocked loose again. Some pieces were lost forever. One has to look at the pieces and the gaps in order to reconstruct them; that was what Jeanne found too painful to do. Maybe it would always be too painful.

From her station on an observation deck of the ferry, as she watched the pinnacles of Wall Street recede, Jeanne reminisced only as far back as her hearing of the ragtime piano piece, as if hearing it had been the beginning of her life. That way, at least, her life had a future.

A layer of haze had yet to be burned off by the morning sun, and as the ferry drew farther away the city dissolved into the white of the sky.

A little boy about Kevin's age ran across the deck. As he passed Jeanne, she felt something akin to fear; but it diminished as he ran beyond her.

"Am I running away again?" Jeanne murmured aloud.

"I beg your pardon?" said a woman Jeanne

227

had not noticed standing near her.

" I didn't realize—"

The lady seemed light-hearted. "Staten Island isn't very far to run," she said. "I'm sorry; I didn't mean to interfere."

When Jeanne looked next, the woman was gone.

Jeanne got off the ferry, went into the Staten Island terminal, bought a cup of coffee, and boarded the next boat back to Manhattan, all without memory of her actions. She was momentarily disoriented when she looked toward the bank of white fog and saw the city appearing out of it, as if a theater curtain were being raised, and it was *larger* than when she had seen it last. Have we turned around? she wondered. Then she remembered.

Her eyes followed a seagull gliding effortlessly across the path of the ferry. The gull reminded her of Donna. What will happen to her, Jeanne wondered, when it becomes evident that there can be no Greenwich Village shop?

Jeanne thought of Donna, how considerate she had been through the recent days, or was it weeks? And how important to her well-being that shop would be. Could Donna do it alone? Jeanne doubted it. If Jeanne abandoned the project, Donna would also have to abandon it. Perhaps Jeanne could offer help now and then. Right now, even that was unlikely.

The only course that seemed open to Jeanne, her only logical future plan, was to move into her parent's home, as they wished her to, and live her life their way.

Their way.

* * *

The cast of *Conquerors and Candlelight* had just completed the first run-through "off the book" without sets, lighting, or costumes. It was the first performance of the play in any sense, the first time even Alan had seen whether it worked dramatically or not, and the first time the director had a chance to ponder his handiwork as a whole.

"What do you think?" the director, grinning, asked the playwright.

Alan chuckled. "It overwhelms me! You people have gotten more out of my play than I ever dreamed you could. Is Margaret as good as I think she is?"

"Stupendous. But please don't tell her I said so until after we open. And don't breathe this to a soul, but I can't remember being so satisfied after the first run-through of any play. Alan, you have written, as the oldsters are wont to say, a truly well-made play. I'd have trouble ruining it."

They were in a large rehearsal hall that was "air-conditioned" with exhaust fans in the windows, and illuminated by the kind of ceiling lights one finds in gymnasiums. Only strips of masking tape on the floor separated the "stage" from the "audience," but that magic line seemed to hold even after the imaginary curtain had fallen. Mark Harris stepped to where the footlights would have been but no farther, as if

229

he wanted to avoid tumbling into a non-existent orchestra pit. He said, "Author! author!"

He triggered a response from the large cast, most of whom were huddled off stage where the wings would be. They cheered. "Marvelous play!" Mark shouted above the din.

"And," director Andy Holloway said to Alan, "Mark Harris is a dream; he's perfect in that snake-in-the-grass part."

"Apparently it's typecasting," Alan muttered as he got to his feet to approach and speak to the actors.

"What's the matter?" Andy persisted. "Is he after Margaret?"

Alan raised his hands to stop the applause and said, "The play looked awfully good to me just now. It's *I* who have to congratulate *you*. You're bringing it to life for me. And you're doing it right!"

Holloway interrupted their second burst of enthusiasm. "If you guys can shake off your orgiastic pride long enough, I have *reams* of notes to give you. It's pretty good for this stage of development, but it's light-years from being perfect. Take ten minutes, then meet me in the green room."

Margaret threw Alan a kiss as she left the rehearsal hall with the rest of the cast.

When the exodus was over, Wif Kist ambled gloomily into the hall, as if he had been waiting outside so as not to have to swim like a salmon upstream. "How does it look?" he asked Alan Mason and Andy Holloway.

After hearing their enthusiastic report, Wif

said, "I suppose you realize it's *got* to be a hit. If it doesn't get practically unanimous raves, from Bill Warner and every other executioner in town, we close on the second night."

Andy, still high on the adrenalin of expected success, nudged Alan and said, "See that little man there; he just made a noise like a producer."

"I kid you not," said Wif. "If we don't fill the barn up from the very beginning, we won't have enough capital to keep it going till it can build from advertising and word of mouth. Ever played Russian Roulette before, gentlemen?"

Alan said, "I hope that analogy holds true. With Russian Roulette you have five chances out of six for survival. Pretty good odds for Broadway."

"Take me seriously," Wif advised. "I attacked that list you got me from Pomeranz," he said to Alan, "and so far not a single nibble. We have Philip's ten and another fifteen from about eight timid people, most of whom were investors already who just upped their ante by a grand or two. I'm afraid you're a bust as a fund-raiser, Alan, my boy. Daddy said no, huh?"

"I can't ask him, Wif."

The producer nodded and shrugged, attempting to be understanding. "Your sister, again?" he asked nosily.

Alan said, "And other things."

"How is she?" Wif asked. "Holding up?"

"I'm worried about her, but I think she'll . . . I think she'll pull through."

"I'm sorry," Wif commiserated. "Tell me,

Alan—I can keep a confidence—how much is your character, Eve, based on Jeanne? I have this funny feeling that I know and love your sister, even though we've only barely met. I'm convinced you're Pieter; is Jeanne Eve?''

Alan smiled. ''They're not dissimilar. I guess Eve acts the way I'd think Jeanne would if she found herself embroiled in an espionage plot with me. She's the only sister I know, after all.''

''Can't you get Jeanne to go in for spying? Put her in the CIA or something? It might save her everlasting soul,'' Wif suggested, half-seriously. ''Has Jeanne read the play?''

''I don't think so. She has a copy, but I don't think she's been in the mood to do much reading lately.''

''Bring her to the next run-through,'' Andy suggested.

''Incidentally,'' Wif said, in a magnanimous mood, ''I've decided that, even though you failed as a financial wizard, Alan, I'll let you keep your title, *Conquerors and Candlelight*. I kid you not.''

''Yeah, Wif,'' Andy said, ''You're not kidding anybody. You wouldn't use the title unless you were finally convinced it was better than yours.''

Wif shrugged, feigning innocence.

''Say,'' Alan said brightly, ''why don't we invite all the present investors to the next run-through?''

Wif said, ''See if we can squeeze a little more blood out of those turnips? Maybe. But what if the next time through is a disaster? You know

232

how these things go. On-again, off-again.''

"What have we got to lose?" Andy asked. "They can't ask for their original investments back, can they?"

"They probably can. You guys have no idea how legally complicated it is to juggle the books at this late date. Asking for more money now alters the value of the percentage points the investors think they have." Wif lapsed into thoughtfulness and mused,"Maybe we ought to cancel the opening-night shindig at Sullivan's and buy a few costumes with that money."

Andy reflected, "Interesting about theatrical Russian Roulette. You can have a celebration after you've pulled the trigger, and still not know whether you're dead or not."

* * *

Ben Sully answered the buzz of his office phone, "Yeah, Jude?"

"Ready on your call to England, Ben, but Captain Martinson's not there. Want to speak to his wife?"

"Put her on."

"Yes? This is Mrs. Martinson."

"Sorry to disturb you, Mrs. Martinson, but I'm trying to locate your husband, and the New York office of the steamship company said he was on vacation."

"He's out of the country. May I ask the nature of your business with him?"

"I'm a police officer in New York City. We need to locate a passenger from one of the Captain's recent Caribbean cruises, and—"

"But surely the New York office has the passenger records."

"Yes, but this is an unusual circumstance. The passenger was a stowaway who was not listed on the original manifest, and now there's nothing there but her name. Another passenger paid her fare, and it's that other passenger we're trying to identify."

"You must be talking about the Andersen girl. The one who jumped overboard."

"Jumped? We heard she fell."

"I think it was my husband's impression that she jumped. Is this a terribly serious matter?"

"We think so. A narcotics case."

"Dear me. How dreadful. My husband did tell me about it. The benefactor was a woman, and I'm sure he mentioned her name. It seems to me it was a name not terribly unlike Martinson, as a matter of fact, but not Martinson precisely."

"Can you tell me where I can reach the Captain?"

"That's difficult. He's taken our children on holiday to the game parks in Kenya." She was silent for a moment, then said, "He'll call me in the morning. Why not let me have him contact you. I'm sure he'd be happy to."

"Fine, Mrs. Martinson. I'll get our switchboard girl to give you the particulars for calling back. You've been very helpful."

"Wait a minute! I remember now. The woman's name was Mason. Jeanne Mason."

234

fifteen

Jeanne sat alone with a photo album.

She had been the main family photographer, so there were very few pictures of her; most were of Kevin or Bill. She flipped through the pages. She was exempt from the limitations of time, as if all the moments of her life were crowded into one day. Kevin was a baby, he cut his first tooth, said his first word, made a Christmas present for his mother, learned to ice skate, and won the second-grade Young Scientists Award —all just yesterday.

Bill looked handsome, carefree, and exciting. So incredibly young, like a teenager. He laughed and smiled. Lines appeared around his eyes—laughter lines; and around his mouth, lines of anger and tension. In the last few pictures, he wasn't smiling. But Bill never changed, because all of those years happened in a single instant—yesterday.

A tear fell onto a photograph of Kevin. Horrified, Jeanne blotted it with the sleeve of her blouse. That photograph had always meant something special to her. The three of them had gone camping at Bear Mountain one weekend. Kevin wandered off to go exploring, and Jeanne happened to catch sight of him as he was running back to their campsite with a dead lizard clinched in his fist. She snapped the picture just as he leapt over a stump, his arms flung wide for balance.

The door buzzer sounded.

Could Donna have forgotten her keys? Jeanne wondered.

Donna had gone out with Barry Oster. They were going first to scout out an advertised location in the Village, a place that might be right for the shop; then they were going to a disco. Donna shouldn't be home so early, Jeanne reasoned, unless Barry was irritating her even more than expected. After their meeting at the Central Park concert, Donna had ranted for hours about how infuriatingly precise Barry was, and how uncomfortable she felt with him. Barry's phone call had interrupted that very tirade, and Donna had accepted his invitation to dinner without thinking twice. They had seen each other several times since, and after each time, Donna complained about him even more.

Jeanne opened the door.

It was her father, alone.

Jeanne felt her cheeks flush and knew that her mouth was hanging open.

"Hello, Jeanne," he said uncertainly. He was thinner than when she'd seen him last; he was clearly not in good health.

"Come in, father," she said, having no idea why he had come or how she ought to handle this meeting. "Sit down. I—would you like something? I have some decaffeinated coffee."

"I think that would be fine."

Jeanne scooped up her photo album and spirited it away to the kitchen with her. She put water on to boil in the whistling kettle.

She returned to find him looking her apartment over; she felt a moment of embarrassment seeing it through his eyes. The supplied furnishings had seen a lot of wear, and the walls needed painting.

"Are you all right, Jeanne? Is there anything I can do?" His voice was perfunctory, as if he expected her to doubt his sincerity.

"I'm fine, father," she said, indicating that she had no difficulties she wanted to confide to him.

"Your mother and I will be going to see the opening of Alan's play on Wednesday. I—your mother insists that I go. Will you go with us?"

Jeanne was suddenly angry. "Did mother ask you to come here?"

"No, it's a matter of business really."

Jeanne said vindictively, "Well I'm sure Alan will be pleased that you wanted to attend the most important night of his life." She instantly regretted putting it that way. Her father was evidently trying, with great difficulty, to make some kind of amends. She added more graciously, "I don't know how I'll feel on Wednesday."

Gilbert Mason shook his head, as if to clear the slate and begin again. "Let me tell you the proposal I have for you. First, I must say that I was wrong in the way I abused you that night. Your income and inheritance are still yours."

Jeanne felt morally tempted to refuse them

237

both. She felt it might be liberating to break financial ties with her father, but yet she believed that the money was rightfully hers, as long as he offered it willingly. Her anger increased with the realization that what he really *owed* was an apology for attempting to rule her life.

He continued haltingly, "Your mother has told me about the shop you want to open. I thought . . . if you would like to borrow a sum against your inheritance, perhaps that would help."

The kettle whistled insistently, and Jeanne fled from the room. She turned the stove off and practically ran back into the living room, tears flooding down, her brow unwrinkled.

"Father! I'm so happy," she blubbered. "Not because of the money, but because you . . . you approve of my project! Do you mean . . . I really have your blessing?"

Her emotional outburst gave him strength. He took her in his arms as he had not been able to do in nearly a year. "Of course, you have my blessing," he whispered, finding it difficult to speak. He then destroyed with a single sentence the edifice of understanding they had just created. "I hope you will want to offer me a consideration in return."

Jeanne pulled away. "What is it?"

"Wouldn't you find living at home more economical, until you are financially more independent? Please consider that. And I want you to . . ." He took a deep breath, recognizing the nature of the request he was about to make. "To see Bill. To offer him another chance. At least let him know you forgive him."

Jeanne was too astonished to feel outrage. She almost laughed. "No," she said simply.

"I saw Bill the other day; he—"

"Don't say another word about Bill."

"Will you at least come home, Jeanne?"

"No."

"You're an intelligent woman. Surely you can sympathize with my position. You must know how your behavior looks to people."

"I *don't* know. Tell me."

"After the scandalous affair of the divorce, the publicity, and now you're sharing a shabby apartment with a woman: I mean, everyone knows homosexuality has touched your life once—"

"Father!" Jeanne was alarmed, but she did not really think her father was expressing his own suspicions or beliefs. She found herself intrigued to learn a bit more about the way his mind worked. "What has any of that to do with you?"

"My dear Jeanne, you truly do not understand?" He seemed as intrigued by her position as she was by his.

Jeanne felt she was on the verge of learning something about her father that she did not want to know. She also felt that it was too late: she had already learned it.

"I am a prominent man," he said, choosing his words meticulously. "Consequently, you are in the public eye. I, for better or worse, placed you there."

Jeanne nodded. So far, so good. "And when members of your company file into the Board room and ask, 'How is your little girl doing these days?' you imagine they disapprove of me. Do you *know* they disapprove of me? And what if they do? I'm not running the company; you are."

"I must maintain their respect for me."

"And my actions affect that?"

"Certainly."

"Why don't you just make it clear to them that you disapprove of my life style? Wouldn't that get you off the hook?"

"No! Surely I don't have to explain—"

"You'll feel better if you can tell them I'm back under your thumb."

"Can't you compromise for me just this once?" His voice was almost a whine; but he was perplexed, not angry.

Jeanne calmed herself and pronounced: "The worst thing is that you want me to pay you homage as interest on a loan."

Jeanne stepped coolly to the door and opened it. "I can't accept the money, Father. Not any of it. Keep my income, my inheritance, too, if you wish."

The next move was up to him. He could have started over again and withdrawn his compromising request. He rose. "Thank you for seeing me," he said to her, a feeling of defeat evident in his voice.

She closed the door gently behind him.

Without saying so, she had also told him that she would not be moving back home. Without deliberating, without even deciding, she had also committed herself to a renewed interest in paving her own way, and in seeing the shop through . . . perhaps to the end. Gilbert Mason had boosted his daughter's morale, but not at all in the way he had planned.

* * *

When the time came, Jeanne begged out of attending Alan's opening night. She had by then read the play. Just *reading* it she had cried all the way through; and she was afraid she would be devastated if she saw it performed. She saw lots of herself in Eva, and would have liked to believe that she, Jeanne, was the marvelous character Alan apparently saw her to be. But she did not believe it. She felt a little embarrassed at his overestimation of her. But the brother-sister love depicted throughout was a marvel to Jeanne; it was this more than anything that made her sob from first page to last. In addition, Jeanne felt unprepared for the ordeal of sitting with her family, and Donna, watching a play starring Mark Harris.

Jeanne's ticket, consequently, went to Barry Oster. Donna sat fourth-row-center in the first-night audience of a major Broadway play between squeeky-clean and sexy Barry and the playwright himself.

She surveyed the opulent new theater, the bejeweled audience, and stared at the mysterious expanse of gold velour before her that would soon rise on a play the world had never seen before.

The house lights dimmed, and the curtain rose to the strains of a wierd and dissonant waltz to reveal a stunning ballroom setting. The audience applauded enthusiastically, and from that moment on, Donna was lost, unconscious even that Jeanne was the prototype for Eva, swept away by the fiction, until Mark Harris made his entrance toward the end of the first scene.

Donna squirmed. She was back on the *Liberty*, seeing Mark for the first time. He had been so handsome and civilized, not at all like the cynical misfits she had run with in college, the people who seemed bent on making themselves unsavory and unattractive. But never had Mark looked as handsome as he did here on stage!

Donna felt her worship of Mark turning to hatred again. She couldn't stand to hear his voice!

She was startled when she felt Alan's hand on hers. He leaned over and whispered, "Don't be put off by his heroic manner; he turns out to be the villain."

Donna realized at once that Alan knew everything and was trying to make things easier for her. She clapped her hand over her mouth to keep from laughing aloud.

From then on, Mark Harris was merely a character in a play.

* * *

Sullivan's Skytop, perched on one of the new skyscrapers in the Times Square area, was fast becoming the favored spot for Broadway opening night parties. The management, consequently, had seen fit to invest in equipment that allowed partygoers to view each of the television reviews following a Broadway opening.

Dragging Barry by the hand, Donna followed a small group which was heading for the big TV projector in a rather isolated corner. She and Barry were squeezed in among members of the cast and crew who crowded in to see and hear.

"I saw a disturbing play this evening," said a reviewer. "Disturbing because it's a new play, not a revival of some museum piece. *Conquerors and Candlelight* is as trivial as its title, but I suspect it will have an appeal for a certain type of audience—"

Someone near Donna said, "He means an audience of morons with no taste."

The reviewer went on. "It's sort of a contemporary swashbuckler, set in a decaying little country, and has to do with love and freedom and brotherhood and apple pie and rocket ships and knavery and bravery."

"Is that all he saw in it?" someone wailed.

" . . . in an era when so many *serious* playwrights are delving into the dark heart of human nature, into the dehumanizing aspects of our age, into the futility of our lives—"

Andy Holloway said, "Speak for yourself, crybaby."

" . . . seems a waste of money and talent to produce strictly escapist theater. The acting, however, is good, and the direction is skilled. Special mention must go to Margaret Carlson, who pulled off the poise of the old movie stars, and newcomer Mark Harris, who had one of those meaty roles and made the most of it.''

"We're done for," said Jo Savalon, "if the rest of them are like that.''

Barry excused himself from Donna and went to talk to a friend of his in the *Conquerors and Candlelight* cast; and Donna found herself staring at Mark Harris. He was across the room, a drink in his hand, standing alone. So, thought Donna, nobody else likes him, either!

He caught sight of Donna staring at him. He smiled, bowed slightly, and raised his glass to her.

"Incredible," Donna said aloud. She was feeling good, and free of his influence, and she thought, he didn't *push* me overboard. I can at least tell him I liked the play.

But something, maybe innate common sense, held her back.

On her way, she saw Adele and Gilbert Mason. They were sitting together on a loveseat by a potted palm. They were holding hands and seemed to be enjoying the milling party crowd. Donna waved. Adele smiled and waved back. Donna hadn't seen them since their one meeting, at Kevin's funeral, but she instinctively liked them both. She envied Jeanne having such lovable parents, parents so evidently in love with each other.

She looked for Mark Harris again. He wasn't where he had been standing. She saw him with a woman, out on a balcony.

As Donna crept nearer, she saw Mark try to

kiss the woman, who gently pushed him away. Donna froze. The woman was Margaret Carlson!

Realizing that neither Mark nor Margaret could have seen her approaching, she slipped as inconspicuously as possible into a niche in the wall that would hide her and allow her to hear.

"If you need someone to tell you, Mark. You're handsome and a splendid actor."

"Well, then?"

"Meaning, why don't I take off my clothes?"

"At least consider it, m'love."

"I'm sorry."

"Can it be that you're underestimating me?"

She laughed. "You go on thinking that, if it suits you."

"I beg your pardon?"

"You're barking up entirely the wrong tree, Mark. I suppose I'm flattered, but frankly I'm not interested."

"I've seen affection in your eyes. Off stage as well as on."

"No, you've seen appreciation."

"Appreciation, then. We're adults. Can't we find ways of expressing our mutual regard more intimately than through glances and handshakes?"

"Look, Mark, God and *The New York Times* willing, we could be acting together for some time. We have to have an understanding. I've watched you flit from one woman in the company to another. That assistant stage manager first, then Bev Malory, then your abortive attempt on the dignity of Jo Savalon. Three utterly different kinds of women—except that they all had the right kind of body. And there's that poor little girl on the ship—"

"I wondered if you knew about that."

"Alan told me."

"He didn't tell you my side of it, did he?"

"You seduced the girl merely to get closer to Jeanne?"

"Certainly not. How crass do you think I am?"

"Well, the only alternative is that you did what you did simply in order to seduce them *both*. Am I to consider that more refined?"

"Let me tell you the story as I recall—"

"No, Mark, I have no desire to hear it. I wouldn't be interested in you no matter what happened on that ship. No, don't leave yet; let me finish."

"It isn't necessary. I have grasped the essentials."

"Oh, there's more. You've known all along that I am seriously involved with Alan. Now you're gleefully ignoring the fact or just testing to see if you can take Alan's woman away from him. Disgusting either way. Your line is as adolescent as your motives are transparent. I want you to know I see it that way. Honestly, I'd rather this conversation had never been necessary, but you forced me into it. I still hope we can have a civilized working relationship, but if not . . . then not."

Mark brushed past Donna without noticing her and hurried toward the safety of crowds and television sets.

"Did you hear that?" Margaret was at Donna's shoulder. Donna nodded sheepishly.

"Don't be embarrassed. I'd have evesdropped if I'd been you. Think he deserved the demolition job I did on him?"

Donna answered with amazement, "How did you do it? How did you learn so much about men?"

Margaret steered Donna into a chair and took one opposite her. "It isn't just men, I suspect," she said. "It's my attitude toward people in general. Maybe it's from a hardening of the artistic arteries. You have to be resistant and resilient in my business. You have to have some formula for ignoring rejection." She flagged down a waiter passing with a tray of champagne. "Have one?"

"Love it," said Donna.

After taking a sip, Margaret said, "If you don't mind hearing wise old sayings from women ten years older than you are, I'll tell you the secret of life."

Donna chuckled. "Shoot."

"Try to be concerned with what *you* think of other people, not with what *they* think of you."

Donna nodded. "I can see how nice it would be to operate that way."

"Oh, I had to work at it, but it's fairly automatic now," Margaret said, smiling. She passed her hand in front of Donna's face and said, in the voice of a wise old mystic, "A whole new world will open to you."

A tumultuous cheer rose from the TV area.

"One of the stations must have given us a

rave review," said Margaret.

"Aren't you dying to hear them? How can you be so calm?" Donna questioned.

"I'm not exactly calm, Donna, but I *try* to be patient, at least until more returns are in. Don't ask me why, but the papers count for more than the TV reviewers anyway, and the papers won't be out until the wee hours. You're with Barry?"

"When I can find him," Donna said.

"Why don't the two of you come over to our place after the party thins out. Alan will invite a bunch, and I will, and we'll get quietly drunk waiting for the *Times*. I'll make sure Mark Harris *isn't* on the roster." She leaned forward, evidently about to move on. "I think I'll go speak to the Masons. See you later."

* * *

Donna returned to her apartment at nine the next morning.

"I hope you weren't worried," she said to Jeanne. "After the party, Barry and I went to Alan and Margaret's with a fantastic group of people to wait for the remaining reviews. Have you seen your brother's videotape equipment? He had the reviews of every single station on tape, recorded automatically while everyone was gone!

She was eager to talk about the evening and rambled on, even though Jeanne tried to get a word in here and there.

"You have the most wonderful brother in the world, Jeanne. And Margaret is the greatest

248

human being I've met since I found you!"
Donna kept talking as she shed the coat she had
borrowed from Jeanne. "The reviews were like
a suspenseful election! Mr. Kist can't decide
whether the show got enough good reviews or
not, so they don't know."

Donna noticed two things at once: Jeanne's
somber expression and the man standing in the
living room, watching.

"What's wrong?" Donna asked.

"This is detective Sully, Donna. He's with
the New York police."

Ben Sully gave her the rest of his credentials.
"Narcotics Division, Miss Andersen."

"What do you want?" Donna asked sharply.
"I don't feel like being very friendly. I've never
gotten along very well with cops."

Sully scratched the back of his head, betraying frustration. "Do you know Richard
Palermo?"

"He's finally in trouble? Whatever it is, he's
guilty."

"We have him on a charge of pushing
marijuana and a whole rainbow of hallucino-
gens. We've connected him to the death of one
teenager who died from the stuff; so there's
second-degree murder in there, too, more than
likely. What do you know about it? No—wait,
I'd better warn you that anything you say—"

"Can be used against me. Yeah, I know. I've
heard that before."

"You don't have a police record."

"No, but back in college I must have been at a
dozen parties that got busted. I was hauled in

249

several times, but never booked. Also, for a little while there, I was in one of those political groups the cops like to persecute."

"Miss Mason tells me she's never known you to use drugs except alcohol. Care to expand on that?"

Donna directed her answer to Jeanne, feeling that she had a right to know. "When I was in college, I tried every pill in the pill box, and I have never met anybody from my age group who hasn't smoked grass. But I was never addicted to anything. That's one of the things I had to get away from when I . . . headed out to sea. I wasn't addicted to drugs—just to those awful people."

"When did you last see Palermo?" Sully asked.

"About three or four months ago. Except . . ."

He waited for her to go on.

"Except one night a month or so ago. I broke into his pad to get some clothes I had left there. I saw him, but he didn't see me." She saw no reason to mention the money.

"You haven't been working for him, making drops?"

Donna glared at him contemptuously. "Of course not!"

Sully scratched his neck again, leaving pink streaks. "He has implicated you in his statement."

"Oh, damn!" Donna yelled. She realized at once that this was Palermo's method of revenge. She also realized that if they dug deeply enough, they would find witnesses against her.

Sully pulled an envelope from his jacket pocket. "I have a warrant for your arrest, Miss Anderson. I'm sorry. I'll have to take you in."

Donna quickly changed into jeans and sweatshirt, as if she thought that's the way the cops would want her to look, and grabbed the leather jacket she had retrieved from Palermo's. On the way out, she said to Jeanne, in order to make Detective Sully uncomfortable, "I wanted to tell you about Barry. We finally made it last night at his house after leaving Alan's. Barry has the cutest little peter. . . ."

Sully just shook his head to let her know her hostile ploy hadn't phased him. He said, "Interested in anatomy, are you?"

"I'll call Philip," Jeanne said at the door. "Is there anything else I can do?"

"Yes," Donna said defiantly, with her eyes overflowing with tears. "Don't let this affect the shop. Go on with it until I get back. *Please*!"

* * *

"Good morning, Philip Pomeranz' office."

"Morning, Angela, This is Jeanne Mason. Is Philip in?"

"Yes, Jeanne. Just a minute." She pressed the intercom button and said, "Jeanne Mason on two-four." There is very little a perceptive secretary does not know about her boss. Angela watched the flashing light until, at last, Philip picked up the extension.

Before answering the call, Philip had stared

251

momentarily at the doodlings on his pad by the phone. He was like a schoolboy in love with his teacher or an old man in love with a memory. His was a love unreasonable to hope for. It had been incomparably easier when Jeanne had no inkling of the way he felt about her. He sighed audibly and reached for the phone. "Hello, Jeanne," he said like an eager friend.

"Philip, I'm sorry to do this to you, but I'm in trouble again, and I don't know who else to turn to."

"What can I do?"

"Donna Andersen, my roommate, has been arrested on a charge of handling drugs. I'm sure she had nothing to do with it, but . . . will you help?"

"Of course, I'll help. Has she been arraigned?"

"I'm not sure what that means. They've just taken her to jail. There was a warrant for her arrest."

"I'm going to put you on hold, Jeanne. I'll be right back." He asked his secretary to call City Hall on the other line and find out Donna's disposition.

Angela buzzed in shortly with the information, and Philip was back on the line with Jeanne.

"She's being detained until nine in the morning. She'll go before a judge then, and bail will be set. I'll be there, and I think you also might want to be there. I'd better warn you, Jeanne. If she's guilty, there will be little I can do. New York State has the toughest drug laws in the country."

"I know you'll do your best, Philip. I'm not worried."

Philip mumbled an assurance and then hung up. The only thing wrong with Jeanne, he thought, is her indiscriminate choice in lawyers. When a lawyer fails you once, you're supposed to look for a better one.

He signaled his secretary. "Angela, postpone all my appointments till day after tomorrow. I'm taking a drug case for Donna Andersen, and I've got to get onto it right away. I'm on my way down to the jail to learn her side of it now. I'd appreciate it if you'd get out copies of all the extant drug regulations and criminal definitions. I'll need them tonight."

"Right, chief. The hearing's tomorrow morning?"

"Wouldn't you know. Just when I need time, the court decides not to drag its feet!"

sixteen

Why do I draw trouble like a magnet? Jeanne wondered. How is it that I deserve to be sitting here, waiting to testify, to further influence the course of someone's life?

She was in a chamber just outside the main courtroom. There were guards scattered here and there, and other witnesses were being brought through, one of whom was obviously "Troll" Palermo. A guard had brought in a cardboard tray of coffee and doughnuts. Jeanne helped herself.

Jeanne wondered, Is it some sort of divine punishment for moral crimes I have committed? Lies I have told? People I have wronged?

Alan thinks for himself. Yet he seems to bring only positive things into the lives of those around him. Father may disapprove of Margaret, Jeanne realized, but Alan never devastated him the way I did. Is it merely because Alan is a man and I'm a woman? Are the ways of the world to blame after all?

Perhaps it's because Alan has a one-track mind, an overriding goal—to write plays. He produces, and I merely react. Maybe I'm not so unlike Donna's puppet-woman after all. She handed other people her strings. I just let the strings lie there, expecting them to operate on their own, with no help from anyone, me included.

"Independence of spirit, whatever that is." Donna had said in their pledge. Jeanne was beginning to feel that she had some idea of what it was. The shop. Everything always came back to that. The shop—and Donna.

It was no mystery why she felt so close to the high-spirited and misdirected young woman. Donna was like a little sister, only friend, and co-explorer in life, all rolled into one. It seemed insignificant that they had arrived at such similar stages of life by such utterly different routes. Donna's past was her own concern; Jeanne's was hers. It was only their present and future that were tied emotionally and by design.

The shop. Everything pointed to the shop. A shop on paper and growing in imagination. Jeanne had recently wondered if Donna could do it on her own. Now she wondered if she could go on without Donna.

* * *

The courtroom was a modern one, with walls of walnut paneling and a ceiling of white acoustical tile. It looked like the neat interior of a brand new packing crate.

Judge Malcomb Byrnie sat on an elevated dais flanked by the flags of New York and the United States. In a depressed pit before him, which had a brown and white checkerboard floor, Philip and Donna sat at a table on the judge's right; the district attorney and an assistant were on the left. The jury box, against a side wall and elevated to the judge's level, was empty. The only two occupants of spectators' chairs were James and Flo Andersen, Donna's parents.

Uniformed policemen stood wearily at the doors to the courtroom, beyond which was the room where Jeanne waited to be brought in.

The atmosphere in the courtroom was one of solitude and forbidding cold—intensified by an overactive cooling system that kept the room chilly.

The clerk announced that the next case concerned a Donna Andersen, accused of complicity in a drug-peddling ring.

It was established that her plea was to be not-guilty. Then the judge nodded disinterestedly to the prosecution table.

The district attorney, a disheveled man ludicrously misnamed Regal, outlined his case against Donna without once raising his voice. He projected a lazy boredom that indicated that these proceedings were an annoying formality, since his evidence was so incontestable.

The prosecution's first witness was brought in through the side door. Richard "Troll" Palermo took the witness chair and was sworn in.

"Don't let him upset you," Philip whispered to Donna. "We know he's going to implicate you. Don't react if he lies. I'm going to trip him up on dates. That's all we need to do."

"Your honor," Regal began, "Palermo has

been arraigned and awaits trial. The defendant, Donna Andersen, was, we contend, his accomplice. He has been led to understand that his free testimony here will be taken into account at his own trial."

"See that the record so states," the judge instructed the stenographer.

"Now Mr. Palermo," Regal drawled, "Please tell us simply what your relationship was to the defendant."

Palermo looked down at Donna indifferently and shrugged. "Simply? We were bed buddies, and she gave me a hand with the business."

"What do you mean by 'gave you a hand with the business'?"

"What I said. Sometimes she helped me pack the stuff, grass mostly. Sometimes she'd make deliveries for me. Cocaine once. And some angel dust."

Regal turned to Philip and said, "Your witness," daring Philip by his smirk to gain any advantage from cross-examination.

Philip rose but stood by his table, his hand on Donna's chair.

"Mr. Palermo, you were arrested last July twentieth. Is that right?"

"So they tell me."

"And when did you first begin your operations in New York City?"

"Middle of May."

"And you claim that Miss Andersen was your companion and business partner all during that time?"

"More or less."

"Which—more, or less?"

"I don't get you."

"Well, when was the last time you saw Donna Anderson?"

"She cut out on me. Middle of July, I guess."

"Middle of July. And what did she take with her when she cut out?"

"Her clothes and things."

"And a stack of bills amounting to more than $3,000?

"What if she did? That just makes her a thief as well as a pusher, right?"

The judge leaned forward. "No remarks, Mr. Palermo. Just answer the questions."

Palermo shrugged. "Yeah, she took it."

Regal's eyebrows went up, showing his first touch of curiosity about the case.

Philip said, "I have no further questions at this time."

Again, Judge Byrnie's perfunctory nod gave the floor to the prosecution.

"Next," said Regal, pushing himself back to his feet, "I'd like to submit as evidence this sworn deposition to the effect that a young woman identified from a photograph and who presented herself at the time as Donna Andersen, did deliver a package of marijuana, cocaine, PCP, and the hallucinogen known as windowpane, to one William Pierce on May twenty-six of this year. The deposition is signed by William Pierce, who cannot readily appear in court. He currently resides in the intensive care ward of a state drug rehabilitation center."

Philip looked to Donna for some sign of confirmation or denial.

She whispered, "I took a package. I had no idea all that stuff was in there. It must have been worth a fortune!"

Judge Byrnie handed the document to the court clerk.

"Accepted conditionally, considering the source. Let's see what remains of the Prosecution's evidence."

"Please call Martha Dandreau to the stand."

Donna mumbled, "Oh, shit."

Martha Dandreau was a pretty wisp of a girl with dusty-blonde hair that hung like a spiderweb down to her waist. Her voice, as she was sworn in, was high-pitched.

"Miss Dandreau," Regal began, "are you acquainted with the defendant, Donna Andersen?"

"I am," she said meekly.

"Would you kindly tell us how you came to know her, and in what circumstances you had dealings with her?"

The arresting officer, Ben Sully, quietly entered the courtroom. He took a seat toward the rear to remain unobtrusive, but made sure he could watch Donna's face.

"Donna and I were roommates at college for two years, up until she left last March."

"Was Miss Andersen, to your first-hand knowledge, acquainted with Richard Palermo?"

"Yes. They were lovers."

"How can you be so sure of that. Perhaps they were platonic friends?"

259

The witness hesitated; her cheeks turned visible pink. "They did it once in the dean's outer office."

"I'm afraid we'll have to ask you to be a little more specific."

"They . . . had sexual intercourse. In front of lots of people. At least, they sure wanted it to look like that was what they were doing. See, Dean Jenkins was about to expel Palermo for breaking into our room, Donna's and mine. We were in a restricted all girl's dorm, cause that's the only room we could find. So they did . . . that . . . in the dean's office to protest the bureaucratic attempt to break up their love life. Lots of people at school thought what they did was terrific. Palermo was always doing things like that."

Philip interrupted. "I object to this line of questioning, your honor, for perfectly obvious reasons."

"Where *is* this getting us, Mr. Regal?" the judge asked, with a side glance at his watch.

"I mean to establish that from her relationship with Palermo, one might logically expect Miss Andersen to engage in the sort of activity she has been accused of."

"To my way of thinking," the judge said pointedly, "you're on the wrong track. The defendant is not here on a morals charge."

Regal cleared his throat. "All right, Miss Dandreau, tell us about the drug parties you attended with Miss Andersen."

The diminutive witness betrayed an indignant anger that made her squeaky voice rise notches

260

in both pitch and volume. "They weren't *drug parties*! Just get-togethers. And sometimes, we might . . . try things."

"You were present on one occasion, were you not, when Miss Andersen—what's the expression—dropped acid?"

"Yes."

"And another time when she took window-pane?"

"Yes."

"Tell us about the event that transpired following the session in which she took window-pane."

"She wrecked her car. It was a Ferrari that Palermo gave her. He had *lots* of money that year. Donna banged it into a tree. On purpose, she told me. Then we all got out of the bashed-in car, and Palermo suggested we roll it over a cliff to see if it would explode. So we did. It didn't explode. It just bounced down and fell into the water."

"And she continued to see Palermo after that?"

"I don't think she blamed him for anything."

"What do you mean by that?"

"Well, she swore she'd never take any drugs again."

"And did she stick to that?"

"I don't know."

"To your knowledge, did either Palermo or Donna Andersen sell drugs on campus?"

"Well, *he* did; and she knew about it. I always assumed she—"

"Objection," Philip said. "Calling for a conclusion."

"Sustained," the judge agreed.

"I have no further questions," said Regal.

"Mr. Pomeranz?" the judge signaled.

Donna was whispering to him. "Ask her anything you can think of. She'll tell the truth. She always does."

Philip whispered back, "You mean—"

"Everything she said was true."

"Mr. Pomeranz?" the judge prodded again.

"I'm ready, your honor." He left his table this time and stepped forward to rest his arm on the witness chair. He was hardly seeing Martha Dandreau; he was reviewing in his mind the damaging testimony the prosecutor had drawn out of her. Morally damaging, Philip thought, but *legally*, there's only one point, . . .

"Miss Dandreau," he said slowly, "on those occasions when you saw Donna trying one or another of those drugs, did you try them also?"

Regal waved his hand for attention and said, "I object, your honor. That's irrelevant, and for her to answer affirmatively, the witness would have to incriminate herself."

Judge Byrnie nodded, seemed to have a second thought, but said, "All right—sustained." He had perked up and clearly had gained interest in the hearing.

"What was *your* relationship with Palermo?" Philip asked her.

"Objection," Regal said.

"I'm going to overrule that one," Judge Byrnie said. "Go on Mr. Pomeranz."

"It's a little more than just part of his group,

isn't it?'' Philip prodded.

Her eyes glistened. "I love him," she said faintly.

"Did he ask you to testify here today?"

"Yes. But I haven't said anything wrong."

Philip hesitated. Ordinarily, this would have been a cue for him to break the witness down and discredit her objectivity.

But he remembered Donna's saying, "She always tells the truth," and had doubts that in this case he'd succeed. "Miss Dandreau," he said, "the night that Donna entered Palermo's apartment and took her clothes and the money, there was a woman in bed with Palermo. Was that you?"

"No. It was Jenni Hammond."

"Wasn't it Jenni Hammond and not Donna Anderson who worked with Palermo and made deliveries for him?"

"I—I don't know. I'm pretty sure that Donna—"

"From what you know first hand, isn't it possible it was Jenni Hammond and not Donna Andersen? Did you ever know Jenni Hammond to make a delivery?"

"Yeah. She did. If you're working up to also accusing *me* of making deliveries, I swear I never did."

"Somehow, I didn't think you did. I suspect he asked you to testify precisely because you were not all that close to his operations. Thank you, Miss Dandreau. That's all."

Regal got halfway to his feet to say, "This witness concludes the State's preliminary case,

263

your honor."

"Then let's have the first witness for the defense," the judge said.

"Please call Jeanne Mason to the stand," Philip requested.

Jeanne entered solemnly and stood at attention while the oath was being administered. Unconsciously, Philip heaved a nervous sigh. To look at them, one might think it was Philip about to be questioned and Jeanne about to do the questioning.

"Miss Mason," Philip began ever so gently, "I want you to tell the court two things. I want you to tell us when you first met Donna Andersen, and to what extent you can account for her whereabouts. And, as a character witness, please reveal to the court Miss Andersen's general behavior since you have known her, in particular as it relates to actions you have taken together."

"Certainly," said Jeanne. "I first met Donna on May thirtieth aboard the cruise ship *City of Liberty*. That ship left New York on the morning of the twenty-ninth. We became friendly during the trip, which lasted until June twelfth. I cannot account for her movements during the three days following the cruise; she told me she had affairs to settle. We lived under the same roof from then on, however; we now share an apartment. I can readily swear that I never saw her in possession of any drugs whatsoever, and even her consumption of alcohol was very occasional. Neither of us has been employed, so we have spent quite a bit of time together."

"Has she seen any men?"

"One, an actor, Barry Oster."

"What do you know about Richard Palermo."

"Almost nothing. I had never heard of him until yesterday, and saw him for the first time as he was marched through here a few minutes ago."

"What, principally, have you and Donna been doing with your time?"

"We've been working on plans to open a gift shop together. This has involved long hours of figuring and scanning catalogs of merchandise and looking for locations."

"When did you discover that Miss Andersen might have had some involvement with illegal drugs?"

"Yesterday. I—"

"Go ahead, tell us."

"I was not shocked by the discovery, really. Donna has always seemed to me a little ashamed of her past. And knowing something of present-day college life I had an idea where her adventurous philosophy might have taken her."

Regal half raised his hand to object to the witness' expressing an opinion, but he shrugged and let it go.

"Palermo claimed," Philip continued, "that Donna worked for him off and on from the middle of May to the middle of July. Is that consistent with your knowledge?"

"Not at all. I honestly don't see how she could have spent any time with the man from May twenty-ninth to the present—except for those few days just after the cruise. During that time, I believe, she broke into his apartment to get her clothes. She'd surely not have to resort to breaking in if she were seeing him openly —"

Regal shot his hand up. "I object!"

"Sustained."

But Philip smiled because Jeanne had made her point—and a damn good point it was, too. "Your witness, Mr. Regal."

"Miss Mason," the prosecutor began, "you and I seem to be discussing two different Donna Andersens. You've painted a conventional portrait of an industrious, moral, and innocent young thing; but I can't help thinking you haven't told us all we need to know. We admit that Miss Andersen was on the ship when you say she was, but isn't it true that she was a stowaway? That, in fact, she planned to rob the steamship company to the tune of more than $900, the price of passage?"

"That's true."

"And she got you to pay her passage when she was apprehended?"

"No, I paid her fare as a loan; but she never asked or even hinted that I should."

"Apprehending her . . . that was something of a drama, wasn't it? Did she not, in fact, jump overboard, causing further financial losses to the company and the delaying of the progress of the ship's paying passengers?"

"That's true."

"And are you telling us that a woman of Miss Andersen's reputation *never* spent a night away from home, while you've been sharing accomodations?''

"Only one that I can recall. Two nights ago she went to a party with Barry Oster, then to an extension of that party at my brother's apartment.''

"But can you be *certain* she never had a rendezvous with Palermo during all that time?''

"I'd have known it if she were keeping anything from me deliberately.''

"That's an astonishing interpretation of the facts, Miss Mason. But again, can you prove to us that she did *not* see Palermo?''

"Of course not, but that's unnecessary. You have to establish that she *did*.''

"Yes, well, that's all, Miss Mason.''

Philip winked at Jeanne and motioned for her to join him and Donna at the defense table. "Our only other witness, your honor, is the defendant, Donna Andersen.''

After the oath was administered, the judge leaned forward and sluggishly raised his right index finger. That tiny gesture effectively stopped the process of the hearing. "Before you start in, Mr. Pomeranz,'' he said, "let me see if I can cut this short. Miss Andersen,'' the judge asked, "did you ever involve yourself knowingly in Mr. Palermo's drug operations?''

Donna opened her mouth, closed it again, then said, "Yes.''

"Did you make that delivery sworn to by Mr. Pierce? Just yes or not, please.''

"Yes.''

"Did you once live with Palermo as his common-law wife?''

"Yes."

"Did you take the sum of money from his apartment without his knowledge or permission?"

"Yes."

"And are you indebted to Miss Mason for the kindnesses brought out in her testimony?"

"Yes."

"Is the testimony of Martha Dandreau substantially correct?"

"Yes."

"Whose idea was the gift shop? Yours or Miss Mason's?"

"We thought of it together."

"To be financed with Miss Mason's money?"

"Not necessarily. We're hoping to borrow the money we need."

"Again, Miss Mason's connections and her generosity would have bailed you out of a financial hole, wouldn't it?"

Donna turned to face the judge directly. Her lips were drawn thin and her brow was low and menacing. "What you're implying simply isn't true," she said, holding her voice steady. "I've kept a careful record of every penny I owe Jeanne. Yes, I did hope her money might be a help in getting the shop started, but my first reason for wanting to go in with her was so I could make enough money to pay her back!"

Judge Byrnie opened his eyes wider and nodded, apparently pleased that he had elicited an angry response from the defendant. "Your witness, counselor," he said to Philip.

Philip said, dismayed, "There's so much I

have to undo! Donna, *when* did you act as Palermo's courier?''

''A few times at college, and once right after we got to New York.''

''Was that once to this Pierce fellow?''

''Yes.''

''Did you know what you were delivering?''

''No, but I'd have to be even stupider than I was not to have some idea.''

''When did you leave Palermo?''

''The night I made that delivery to Pierce. I had to get out of there. Pierce was just one of our group from college, by the way.''

''Why did you leave Palermo?''

''Isn't it obvious? The son of a bitch was ruining my life. I hated him by that time.''

Philip hesitated, perhaps to let the sincerity of her words impress the judge, perhaps to choose his next question with exquisite care. In the short space of time Donna's mind was evidently flooded with memories of hell, thoughts, Jeanne imagined, of ''bad trips'' with dangerous drugs, and thoughtless, mindless actions. She was recalling with horror a Donna who no longer existed. Jeanne saw transfixed upon Donna's face an expression she had seen once before—at the Voodoo ceremony, when Donna had screamed, when Mark had said, ''The natives would say you've been possessed by a *loa. . . .*''

The expression fled with Philip's next question, and Donna was her composed self again.

''What about that stack of hundreds you took from him.''

"He owed me that much and more. And I knew it was the only chance I'd ever have to get it back. That car—he put it in my name because he wanted to conceal the fact that he had so much money. In fact, he blew every cent he had in ways like that. I had to support him for a while at college. I even paid his train fare to New York and set up the apartment. Then we were both broke—until Palermo started to get his operation going in the city."

"Where did you go after leaving Palermo. Where did you live?"

"No place. I slept in Washington Square Park for a week—till the cops ran me out. I barely had enough money for a hot dog now and then. I begged my folks for some money, and Mother sent me $50. When that was gone, I—"

"Why didn't you go home to your parents?"

"They told me they never wanted to see me again after . . . after the mess at college. They were within their rights, I guess. I don't blame them much."

"Why stow away on a ship?"

"I had taken a cruise once before, and I knew I could find a nice corner or deck chair to sleep on, and all the free food I wanted."

"Didn't you feel that stowing away was criminal?"

"No. You don't know what can happen at college—to a person's head. Maybe it's better now, but back then a humanities major at that school was taught—indirectly—to figure a steamship company was just another big business, and since they could exist only by exploiting workers, they were fair game. I would only be stealing from an even bigger thief. It takes a lot of fear and hatred to hang onto an idea like that. I don't think like that now.''

"What changed your mind?"

"I'm not sure I ever really bought it; it was just a handy rationalization to let me do what I wanted to do. But working with Jeanne on the shop sure drove it home. We were estimating one night how much shoplifting we had to take into account; and I got roaring angry at the thought that there were people who would dare take something from me that I had worked hard for.''

"What do you think of Jeanne Mason now?"

"She's the only real friend I've ever had.''

Philip stood there reflecting for a moment, then said, "I think that's all. Your witness, Mr. Regal.''

"Mr. Regal," the judge asked, "any cross-examination?''

"I think not. Your honor did my work for me.''

Judge Byrnie turned to Donna without a moment's deliberation. "Young woman, for what it's worth, I tend to believe you. I do have some sympathy for your situation, since you do seem to be working to improve it.'' He noticed a shocked expression on Regal's face and merely smiled.

The judge continued. "A few months ago I might have gone so far as to dismiss this case with only a stern warning and a recommendation of a fine. But new laws are in effect now that require me to be unmerciful. I'm afraid you are clearly guilty, by your own admission, in the Palermo affair. This court has no choice but to order that you be held for trial in Superior Court, and charged with complicity in the Palermo affair. Bail is set at $5000."

"I have the money," said a gruff voice from the spectators' gallery. It was Donna's father.

Mr. and Mrs. Andersen, their faces grim with determination, passed Donna without so much as a smile. The clerk handed them papers and directed them to a payment window elsewhere in the building.

Mrs. Andersen turned to Donna and said timidly, "Will you come with us? You will have to sign some papers."

Donna said to Jeanne, "Wait for me?"

"Certainly. In the lobby downstairs."

* * *

The court house lobby was a glassed-in colonnade of black granite. Jeanne's and Philip's voices rang in the emptiness as they waited for Donna to join them.

"I was sure the judge was against us," Jeanne commented.

Philip laughed. "I wasn't even sure he was paying attention. His decision was fair, under the circumstances. There were some surprises—for all of us."

Ben Sully walked up to them. "Good morning, Miss Mason. Mr. Pomeranz, I'm Ben Sully, the detective who tracked down the dangerous

272

Miss Andersen. I just wanted to warn you about that new drug code. In a case I saw last week, the defendant, who was no more involved than Donna, got five years and a stiff fine. The judge told me afterward that the defense attorney had made a mistake by having his client plead guilty in the hope of leniency. He said it should have been a not-guilty plea. I'm not suggesting you would make the same mistake, but, well, I thought you ought to know."

"That *is* helpful. Thank you Mr. Sully."

Ultimately, Donna emerged from a nearby elevator and joined the group.

"Morning, Dick Tracy," she said to Sully. "You saw my performance. I spotted you at the back."

"Wouldn't have missed it."

"Did you believe me?"

"Had to. You confessed to everything."

"You want to take me to lunch, don't you?"

Ben laughed. "Yes, I'd like to take you to lunch. How did you know?"

"Well, the look on your face said you wanted to do *something* with me, and lunch seems as likely as anything."

Philip said, "I was going to ask Jeanne. Should the four of us—"

An unenthusiastic reaction parted the pairs; Donna and Ben went one direction, Jeanne and Philip another.

* * *

As they stepped into the refreshing early-autumn air, Ben said to Donna, "I thought you were a confirmed cop-hater."

"Oh . . . not today," she said. "Don't ask me why, but for some reason, even with prison hanging up there in the air, I feel damned good about myself right now. And that makes me like everybody—even cops!"

* * *

Jeanne and Philip topped off a gourmet luncheon at the Lawyers Club by ordering coffee and cordials. Their discussion of Donna's case at an end, Philip said, "Jeanne, you're overwhelmingly lovely when you're happy."

She smiled. "If you're asking me why I feel so good, I don't know. Something in court."

It is often easy to sense when a person is about to say, "I love you." And as Philip began softly, "Jeanne. . . ."

She interrupted. "Philip, do you remember the day we first met?"

"Vividly."

"Father invited you to the house. You worked for a new law firm his company had engaged, and he told us all how impressed he was with you. Remember? Well, I was far more impressed than he was. You were tall and handsome and brilliant. To a seventeen-year-old girl, you were like a knight on a white charger.

"I used to dream about you. About loving you, living with you, having sex with you. Some girls my age were nuts over rock singers and movie stars. I had my mysterious defender of

274

truth and justice. I——I cried myself to sleep the night I learned you were going to be married."

"Jeanne, I almost didn't marry because of you. I was afraid the marriage might not work because Hilda didn't measure up to you. Jeanne—it *hasn't* worked."

Jeanne continued as if she had not heard what he said. "But I got over my crying that night and learned what it was to have you as a dear friend. I never envied Hilda again, Philip, because I realized I could never have married you, because that was not the kind of love I felt for you.

"Philip, I have deep affection for you, and feelings of gratitude, and the most profound hope that you will be happy. But I——I'm not enough of a psychologist to explain it clearly, but you were too much a part of my growing up. I can't think of you romantically. I could never marry my . . . my favorite uncle."

Philip looked pale, even in the dull amber of the restaurant lighting. He muttered, "Your favorite uncle."

The waiter brought the check, and when he was gone, Philip said, "I think I understand, my love."

When Jeanne had left, Philip stood by the door of the club for a time, lost in thought. An acquaintance jostled his elbow and said, in a suggestive tone of voice, "She was lovely, Philip."

He nodded abstractedly and said, "My niece."

* * *

Jeanne felt like running as she made her way through Wall Street from the Lawyers Club to the Staten Island Ferry. She had to get away again to think, but this time it was not because she was troubled; it was because she was excited.

Hurrying to catch the departing boat, she saw a tall blond man. A second glance told her it was not Gordon Strand.

She stood on the aft deck watching the city of monuments recede. She thought of Donna on the witness stand, and suddenly an answer came.

Donna had acted proudly up there. Not because she was innocent, but because she had been guilty, and she knew the guilt was all in the past! Jeanne had seen the new Donna, the Donna with nothing to hide. With that realization, Jeanne admired her young friend more than ever before.

That's the way *I* must be from now on, Jeanne determined. A woman with a future, who's past belongs to an older and less able version of myself!

It was all true, what I told Philip, but I didn't know it myself, until I was saying it! Now that's settled, too. Out of my hands.

What if Donna goes to prison?

But *I* want the shop. And if necessary, I can do it alone, eventually.

A wondrous flock of gulls descended—there had to have been hundreds of them, incandescent in the sunlight—and they hovered over the ferry's wake.

Jeanne thought, *I am free*!

Only halfway to Staten Island Jeanne was already impatient for the ferry to return her to that towering city of promises. The city made her think of Alan's play. She felt a little ashamed for missing his opening night. She resolved: Not another day goes by! I'm going to see it tonight!

She looked around again, hoping as in a fantasy to see Gordon. Perhaps he had come for her at the courthouse and followed her here. Perhaps he could step up now and say something cheerful like, ''What's new?''

But there was only the cry of gulls and the whisper of the wind and the rumble of the ferry motors.

It was Gordon she wanted to see, to explain things to, to share her discoveries with.

A clearing of her head brought a disturbing realization:

Who knows that love is anymore? But the closest thing to it I can feel . . . is what I still feel for Gordon Strand!

Jeanne knew that the problem had not yet been dealt with honestly and openly. She would have to see Gordon again. Soon. Even though his past was more clouded than Donna's or her own. With this thought came still another realization, one that freed her spirit further. She realized that, for her at least, life did not hold pat answers, till-death-do-us-part solutions . . . and that she was strong enough, adverturous enough, to survive uncertainty.

She laughed and thought: Maybe I've finally discovered the secret of life! And what a lot of uncertainties there are!

seventeen

"May I speak to Phil Pomeranz? Wif Kist calling."

"Oh, yes, Mr. Kist. Mr. Pomeranz isn't in today; he's in Sacramento till the end of the week."

"I must talk to him today. Do you have a number where he can be reached."

"I can have him contact you. May I tell him the nature of your business?"

"Nature? Hell, yes. You can tell him *exactly* what it is. My play has just received an anonymous cash endowment of $100,000, and—now don't laugh—I don't know what on God's green earth to do with it! I have to make sure I'm legally in the right to spend it. Have the old boy ring me up at my office or at my home—you have both numbers there—*immediately!* We've posted a closing notice backstage—a *one-week* notice. And this just might save our necks. Is there anything more I can say to impress you with the urgency of this thing?"

"I understand completely, Mr. Kist—"

"Call me Wif."

"Uh, I'll try. Is the theater really so empty? I heard tickets were selling well."

"What's your name again? Andrea?"

"Angela."

"Angela, if that was a hint for complimentary tickets, it was handled like a pro. How about tomorrow night? Two be enough?"

* * *

"Good morning. Metropolitan National. May I help you?"

"Mr. Fallon, please. Jeanne Mason calling."

"One moment, please."

A flashing button politely signaled the transfer of Jeanne's call to a cathedral-tall reception area of the alabaster bank. A svelte woman who looked like a spinster librarian lifted the receiver. Her voice was muted and musical. "Mr. Fallon's office."

"May I speak to him, please? This is Jeanne Mason calling."

The secretary caught sight of her employer making his way through the sanctuary of tellers and clerks, smiling his good-mornings to those he passed as he approached his office. "Would you mind holding for just a minute, Miss Mason? He's just coming in."

"Yes, I'll hold."

"Mr. Fallon," the secretary called out. "I have Jeanne Mason for you on line one—"

"Who?"

"Jeanne Mason. You received a letter this morning that I couldn't help seeing. It concerns her. I thought you might like to read it before taking the call." She handed him the letter, which had been opened and paper-clipped to its envelope.

Mr. Fallon read:

My dear Oswald,

I have a delicate favor to ask of you.

My daughter, Jeanne Mason—until recently Jeanne Mason Oliver—is planning a business venture for which she will require a fairly substantial sum. I wish to help her in her affairs without her knowledge. Consequently, I wish to underwrite her credit reputation, which, on her own is practically non-existent. Will it be possible for you to grant her request for a loan without letting her know my guarantee stands behind her request?

I am assuming—as you may surmise—that she will come to you, at least in the long run, because your establishment presently sees to her checking and savings needs, and your association with my family and my company goes back a good many years.

I am at your disposal.

Cordially,

Gilbert Mason.

Fallon mused, "I wonder how many New York bankers he sent one of these to?" He picked up the phone on his secretary's desk. He nodded, and the secretary punched the line-one button. "Miss Mason? This Oswald Fallon. What may I do for you?"

eighteen

Jeanne's mother had a sense of history and society that few knew to commend her for. Adele thought her interest just a hobby, and a sentimental one at that. But there was great utility in it, and it had confirmed—in Adele's mind at least—the significance of the individual.

Her first entry was a press clipping about Sergeant Mason's decision that led to the capture of an Italian farmhouse which would have remained in the hands of the Nazis, if not for him. She could still recall pasting it in on a rainy spring day as she waited for her true love to come back from the war.

Her original intention had been merely to follow Gilbert's career, but she expanded her scope by beginning to register her own influences with a clipping titled, "Citizen's Committee Backs Teacher's Higher-Pay Crusade." Adele had been the chairwoman.

Alan's first public notice came with his winning of a creative writing contest in junior high school. And "Twelve-year-olds To give Piano Recital" marked the start of Jeanne's coverage.

Four volumes later, Adele faced a crisis of journalistic integrity when she was confronted by the first of numerous items concerning Jeanne's divorce—"Heiress Loses Son in Tawdry Divorce Contest." Should Adele include the bad as well as the good? She included it. Adele wanted to document Jeanne's recovery and her new start in life. She wanted to show her rising above all this!

But when Bill Oliver became the instrument of Kevin's death, Adele could not bring herself to paste those items in. But she kept them, her impulses telling her that in time she could read them again.

She also kept the bad reviews of *Conquerors and Candlelight*, along with the good ones. She kept the pieces from the Mason Enterprises newsletter that documented Gilbert's heart attack and recovery and return to work. She even had, in that stack of unentered clippings, the single *New York Herald* bit about Donna's rescue at sea, since Jeanne had been instrumental in it. A recent clipping told of Donna's arrest for drug trafficking, with a mention of Jeanne's testimony on her behalf.

On the day before Christmas eve, an ad, splendidly rendered in art-noveau style, announced the forthcoming mid-January opening of "Discoveries," a new shop offering gifts, paintings, and *objets d'art* in Greenwich Village. Jeanne and Donna's shop. Adele knew without having to ask that the stunning advertisement had been designed by Gordon Strand. It was the appearance of this ad that had prompted Adele to take out her scrapbooks, get out the glue, and catch up on neglected entries.

In the same issue of *The Village Voice* which contained the ad was another in the seemingly unending series of articles and editorials on the saga of "Pot" or "Troll" Palermo and his retinue of wicked ladies, who were being persecuted by a cruel law that stemmed "from the Dark Ages." This editorial mentioned that the trial would take place in January, on the first working day following the winter recess.

Adele located last Wednesday's *Variety*, which she had saved intact until she could attack it with scissors and glue, and extracted the paragraphs which claimed that *Conquerors and Candlelight* had done a rousing box-office business in its thirteenth week.

Her paraphernalia was spread over the dining table and adjacent chairs. A classical FM station was on, and Adele was humming along with a familiar Tchaikovsky piano solo, when Gilbert returned home from work.

"I didn't expect you so early," she said, hardly looking up. A page was drying. "I wanted to have all of this put away before you came back. Is everything all right at the office?"

"Everything is fine," he said absently. He stood by the fireplace smiling faintly. "Don't hurry with your scrapbooks. I like seeing you busy."

Adele noticed that he carried a folded newspaper. She wondered if he had noticed something there she had missed. Something about one of his children? She knew his interest in their activities had soared now that he had taken an active, albeit secretive part in them. Adele hated being sworn to secrecy, simply because she felt they deserved to know that Gilbert had at last offered them support without qualification or bribery.

"Gilbert, I've asked Jeanne and Alan to have Christmas luncheon with us."

"Are they coming alone?"

"That has to be decided. I hoped you would let me invite—"

"I'm sorry. Can't we have an uncomplicated Christmas day? I want to see the two of them—very much, really. But not if they have their . . . lovers along. I don't think I would enjoy that."

Adele looked at him sadly. "We'd better call if off. It would embarrass me too much to tell them to come alone."

"I'm sorry," he said again.

"I know," she said quietly. She meant it.

Gilbert left the fireplace and pulled up one of the few dining chairs not covered with papers. "I'll tell you something, Adele. Alan's woman, Margaret—I like her. It's Alan who exasperates me when I see the two of them together. Why in heaven's name won't he marry ner? I have never yet felt comfortable around the two of them. But I suppose it's none of my business."

Adele chuckled. "I suppose not." She felt a warmth akin to a blush. It was nothing more than an awareness of the love she felt for Gilbert. His simple act of pulling up a chair and inviting conversation was an act of intimacy and trust he had not performed in ages.

He went on. "Now Strand is another matter. I doubt that I will ever be able to accept that . . . man. I just don't want him in this house."

"I know, dear. But have you ever considered his point of view? The anguish he has gone through to have left such a central part of his life behind him?" She looked up from her pasting, smiled mischievously, and asked him, "Are the other men at work as Victorian as you are?"

"They sympathize with me, but I'm coming to suspect that they don't really care much. Frankly, only a few of them seem to have principles of *any* kind."

"I love you for having principles, Gilbert. But there are a couple of them I wish you would reconsider."

"I have. A man does not enter into a complex business arrangement without a contract, does he? He defines his responsibilities and accepts them legally, which protects both himself and his partner. Why should other relationships be immune from recognized responsibility?"

Adele said, "Before endorsing a business contract, don't you explore all the possibilities, perhaps even test the relationship under a gentleman's agreement beforehand?"

"One might, in certain cases."

"I rest my case. Would you give me a hand collecting these things so Lettie can set up for dinner?"

"I wonder," said Gilbert, reaching for the newspaper he had brought in with him, "if you would like to include this." He unfolded the paper to the sports page.

Adele read the opening paragraph of a piece titled, "New Yorker Wins Argentine Primary." It said, "BUENOS AIRES. Prior to the Argentine 500, a tryout was run to eliminate all but the best contenders. Yesterday a newcomer, William Oliver of New York City, won top honors driving an Autorite 2800. . . ." Adele said firmly, "No, Gilbert. Kevin's death will be Bill's final entry. He could become President of the United States, and I still would not be tempted to continue thinking of him as part of this family!"

Adele's native sense of history would soon cause her to change her mind. She had not yet made Bill Oliver's final entry.

* * *

On the evening of January tenth, the mercury dropped to seven below. The streets of New York glistened with a layer of powdery snow.

A few taxis inched through the treacherous ice. The only sensible place to be was at home, in bed, and not alone.

They were at Jeanne's. Donna had left a note: "I'm staying at Ben's tonight. We'll go straight to the courthouse in the morning. Why don't you and Gordon stay at our place for a change?"

"I have a quaint idea," Gordon said, "How about some hot chocolate?"

Jeanne was delighted. "I've even got some marshmallows! Tell you what. While you're making the chocolate, I'll pop some corn. Any decent late movies on TV?"

"Let's play Monopoly. I know it's not as much fun with just two playing, but we could cheat." He added, "If you lose, you have to marry me."

"That old whine again," she teased.

"I'm not insisting, you understand; it just seems like a novel idea."

She turned and put her arm on his chest. She ran a finger along his far side, down past his hips, and up again. "Who needs the piece of paper?" she asked. She stopped the movement of her hand. "Okay," she said, "let's get serious for a minute. Gordon, it's homosexuality that scares me. And I'm not sure what you could say to set my mind at rest. Call it a prejudice, if you want."

"I don't blame you. And I'll keep living with you in sin as long as it takes for me to prove that as long as I have you—"

"Why did you have to tell me about it? I don't think I'd ever have known."

"Sure you would have. Bill knew. The judge knew to ask me about it. I *had* to tell you from the beginning."

"Why did you tell Bill?"

"I didn't. Bill came bursting in looking for you that night. You weren't here, but an old friend of mine was. A very obvious and effeminate fellow, who went into a tizzy and picked up the phone to call the police. Bill could see what he was without asking. Bill yanked the phone out of his hand and called him a faggot. I opened the door and told Bill to leave. I said, rather self-righteously, that he was not to insult my friends. That's all there was to it. I saw by the expression on Bill's face that he was putting two and two together. Then he slugged me and left."

Jeanne rubbed Gordon's bare stomach, as if she were soothing a wound, and said, "My poor darling." She had one more serious suggestion. "Let's take our time making plans."

"Okay," he said, "but not making hot chocolate." He tossed back the covers and bounded out of bed. He reached for his trousers.

"Don't put yor clothes on," she said in a sultry voice. "I want to be able to look at any part of you any time I feel like it."

He laughed. "Okay," he said, padding barefooted into the kitchen, "but if you expect us to get through a whole game of Monopoly with getting sidetracked repeatedly, *you'd* better slip into something. Something dowdy and unattractive!"

Jeanne was reaching for a dressing gown when the doorbell sounded. Not the bell downstairs, the one right at her door. "Just a minute," she called.

She saw Gordon reaching for his trousers again. "It must be the building superintendent," she told him, "probably coming to tell me the pipes are frozen again and there'll be no hot water in the morning. Just stay out of sight till I get rid of him."

She opened the door, leaving the chain latch connected, and peered through the crack into the bleary, unshaven face of Bill Oliver.

"Please let me in," he said hoarsely.

nineteen

"It's Bill, isn't it?" said Gordon. "You might as well let him in."

In a daze, Jeanne slipped the chain off its hook and opened the door.

"Maybe it's the worst thing yet," Bill muttered, "but I have to see you. I have to be sure that—" Then he saw Gordon stepping toward him, buttoning his shirt.

Bill's reaction was the last one Jeanne would have predicted. The words caught in his throat, but Bill merely said, "Hello, Strand," almost as if he were relieved to find him here with Jeanne.

The two men eyed each other with stern expressions. Then Gordon said, "I'll get you a drink."

Bill's nod had the effect of breaking Jeanne's spell of suspended animation, for the moment at least.

"Sit down," she invited Bill, her voice as expressionless as a robot's. Her mind was clearing. He looked like Kevin. She had never been so aware of how much father had looked like son. It was a cruel coincidence, but it somewhat softened her toward Bill, but only for a moment. Then all the realities rushed against her, and she grew dizzy from the desire to kill him. "What do you want?'' she demanded coldly.

Bill did not flinch, as if her animosity made him more comfortable.

Gordon handed Bill a brandy. Bill took it and, without looking up, answered Jeanne's question. "To say I'm sorry." He mumbled the word again, like an echo. "Sorry."

Jeanne and Gordon looked down at him dumbly. Bill had not said what he was sorry for. It seemed that he was saying he was sorry for having lived.

"At the door," Gordon reminded him, "you said you came here to be sure of something." Gordon's tones struck Jeanne as oddly sympathetic. "Have you found out what you wanted to know?"

"I suppose so," Bill said. He downed his drink and rose to his feet.

Jeanne had assumed that Bill was drunk. She saw now that he was perfectly sober. She surprised herself by saying, "Do you want to rest before you go? You look terrible."

"No," he said, "my plane leaves in a couple of hours, if it can take off in this weather. I'd better get back to the airport."

"Back?" Jeanne questioned.

When Bill offered no explanation, Gordon said, "You're racing down in South America Saturday, aren't you?"

Bill nodded. "I won the preliminary," he said, then appeared to regret saying it.

"I read about it," Gordon said.

Jeanne wondered if Gordon was trying to keep Bill from leaving.

Gordon continued, "You're doing what you want to do now, aren't you?"

"Yes."

"I'm glad. I hope you do well on Saturday."

Bill was not expecting generosity. Tears welled in his eyes as he fumbled for words. "It's my . . . happiness that's killing me. I just can't . . . it's that I know it's Kevin giving this to me . . . that if it weren't for . . . oh, God!" That was the last he could say. He started to sob as he hurried out the door and slammed it shut behind him. Jeanne and Gordon heard him running down the stairs.

When it was quiet again, Gordon said, his voice deep and quiet, "I think I'd rather see people dying of terminal illness than see anyone in Bill's condition." He closed his arms around Jeanne. "Still want hot chocolate? You're trembling."

"Can you put brandy in hot chocolate? Lots of it?"

* * *

The Sunday *News* carried a story Adele felt obliged to include in her Mason family chronicles. It was a story from the running of the Argentine National Cup race.

" . . . Oliver lagged behind until his approach to the final stretch, when he managed to get up a screaming burst of power. He careened around the dangerous final turn on two wheels, and then skidded toward the barricades. He had the spectators gasping to their feet."

"Experts said they had never seen driving to match it for audacity. Out of the turn, Oliver's 2500 cc, 1000 hp, $30,000 Autorite 2800 bounced down onto its balloon tires with such impact that the car was tossed up completely off the speedway track. Miraculously, he never lost control. He landed with a wail of rubber that could be heard even above the thunder of the race, and then he rocketed into the final straight-away."

"He passed his only three competitors— Nikosan, the Japanese entry, the Canadian Apollo 500, and Sparky, another U.S. contender, and crossed the finish line still accelerating at a terrific rate."

"The tumult of the cheering crowd fell suddenly as it became apparent that Oliver was unable to stop. The voice of the crowd rose again as a ghastly scream just before the powerful car plowed into the outer barricade at well over 200 miles per hour. A billow of fire streaked out like the stream from a flame thrower, and fragments of metal rained far out into the lake beyond the barrier. The magnitude of the tragedy needed no confirmation. The horrified spectators knew at once that no one could have survived such a crash.

"The nature of his trouble has so far not been determined. An expert on the scene told this reporter that, 'the chances of a racer losing both his brakes and his accelerator control are one in a billion.' "

Gilbert had read the story over and over before handing it to Adele.

"I'm so sorry," Adele muttered futilely.

* * *

The trial of "Pot" Palermo and his gang was becoming interminable. On the seventh day of it, with a dozen witnesses yet to be called, Donna told Jeanne, "Open the shop without me!"

"Not on your life," said Jeanne. "We'll think of something."

They were sitting on a long slab bench outside the courtroom during a brief recess. Donna took a cigarette from her handbag. Her movements were jerky and compulsive.

From the long hours Donna had put in readying the shop, and from her amazing strength during the first days of the trial, when Jeanne had offered her brief testimony, Jeanne had decided that Donna's energies were limitless. Now she could tell they were not.

Day after day Donna had watched her past life dissected in public—the seedy people, the dangerous ideas, the memories that meant nothing but pain from years Donna wanted only to forget.

Philip had enter her plea as not-guilty, since she had never profited from Palermo's drug sales, had not organized the business with him, and had "split" the first chance she got. Under the law, her most vulnerable spot was that she had known of the illegal operation and had not reported it to the authorities. But since Donna had been living with Palermo as his common-law wife, Philip hoped the judge and jury would see this in the light of a wife's not being required to testify against her husband. It was a risky technicality on which to hang a claim of innocence, and Donna could ruin it all if she in any way lost the sympathy of the court.

Palermo was already sunk. From confirmed evidence and his own admissions, Philip estimated that he would get from ten to twenty-five years. And it was not unlikely that many of his co-defendants would go down with him.

"I'm going to cancel my Chicago trip," Jeanne said.

"The hell you are," Donna barked. "We need more stuff! Listen, I'm going to be sitting here for days, and I'd *rather* you were off doing something productive."

After thinking it over, Jeanne finally agreed. "I'll make the trip, but I'm going to postpone our opening till the trial is over."

"And let the shop just sit there? We'll lose a fortune!"

"It won't just sit there. We'll keep working on it and have an even bigger and better opening—when the time comes. Who knows? In a couple of more days, our Japanese shipment might arrive."

The next morning, Jeanne flew off to the Chicago Gift Mart.

That afternoon Gordon taped a decorative sign he had just made to the front door of the little shop on Jane Street. It just said: OPENING SOON.

"No specific date?" asked a bearded young man who had watched Gordon attach the sign.

"Within a few days," Gordon said.

"You're waiting until after the trial, then?"

Gordon admitted that that was right, and the young man, a reporter, called in the story to his editor.

The editor, who put out a growing "area" newspaper serving Manhattan from Murray Hill through Greenwich Village and SoHo down to the "new village" on the upper fringes of Wall Street, wrote what he thought of as a human interest editorial about the oppressive drug laws and the inhuman injustices of the legal establishment. It was all about this poor little girl about to lose her shirt when the government sent her up the river because she once came close enough to smell cocaine.

The *Voice*, oddly conservative by comparison, dredged up police records concerning the social damage Palermo had done during his brief but flashy career as a subtle killer, and called for punishment for him and all his confererates. At the same time, the *Voice* editorial made an empassioned plea for drug liberalization.

The *Herald* picked up the story, too. Their story, on page three, sobbed over the life-destroying power of hard drugs, called for more stringent drug laws, and named Donna as a prime example of the innocent victims who get sucked into drug cultures by the wish to "belong." It was the *Herald* that found out who Donna's partner was, and tied the "left-wing college revolutionary" to a prominent heiress

295

with a checkered past.

Within five days millions knew Donna's story. Of those, some were typically sympathetic to the underdog, or were advocates of greater civil liberties, and a few were actually collectors of antiques and art pieces. A modest little gift shop could never have purchased such publicity.

But no opening date could be disclosed, and it still was not known whether the shop would have one proprietress or two.

* * *

"Gordon Strand? This is Ben Sully. You don't know me, but—"

"I know who you are. What can I do for you?"

"Donna has been keeping me pretty much up to date about things, and the other day she told me about an idea you had for some sort of arched cubicle for one corner of the shop. She said they had run out of money and time, but still hoped to build it sometime in the future. I have a little money, maybe enough, and I wondered if you'd be willing to use me as your construction assistant. I'm pretty handy with woodwork. We could sneak in tomorrow while Jeanne is still in Chicago. You have a key don't you?"

"Un-huh. Go on. I like the way you're thinking. Can you work all day and all night Saturday and Sunday?"

"At your service."

"How about going half and half with me. I

suspect it will cost no more than, oh, around $600."

"Got yourself a deal. Tell me, what is this thing for?"

"They're setting up a small department for imported toys, which they want to set apart from the other merchandise. I'd better get off the phone and place a lumber order, fast. What's your number? I'll call you back when they tell me the delivery time."

* * *

FINAL WITNESS FOR PALERMO DEFENSE HEARD THIS MORNING, ran one of the headlines.

That afternoon, while Gordon and Ben were putting finishing touches on the toy department gazebo and waiting for Jeanne to arrive from the airport, a delivery truck pulled up at the front door of the shop. The jet-streak lettering on the side of the van said, Atlantic Air Express.

Gordon, in paint-splotched work clothes, opened the shop door.

"I got a zillion cartons out here," the driver announced. "Give me a hand with them?"

"What are they?" Ben asked as the three men formed a brigade to carry the cartons inside.

Gordon stopped to look at a box. "Tiffany lamp shades, if we can trust the scrawling on the side of the boxes.

"All of 'em?"

"Jeanne must have found that irresistable item she's been looking for to put on sale for the opening. They're from Chicago.''

The phone rang while Ben was signing the shipper's invoice. Gordon ran back to the closet of a business office.

"Hello?'' he answered breathlessly.

It was Jeanne. "Gordon? What on earth are you doing there? You weren't at home, so I—''

"Are you at the airport?''

"On my way in.''

"Fifty Tiffany lamp shades just arrived. How many do you want unpacked?''

"Good heavens! They arrived before I did. Oh, unpack a dozen, I guess. Is there any place to put the crated ones?''

"We'll find a place. I talked to Donna at lunchtime. She thinks they'll reach a verdict this afternoon.''

"Thank God. Will you be at the shop for a while? I need to go home and clean up before I come down. I'm pooped.''

"Hey Gordon,'' Ben yelled, "there's another shipment pulling up.''

"Is that Ben? Is he there, too?''

"My love, your shop is in very capable hands. Are you expecting another delivery?''

"Not that I . . . well, maybe the hand-made dolls from Japan. Listen, come to think of it, don't wait for me there. I'll go directly to the courthouse.''

"Get off the phone, love. We're too busy to just stand here gabbing.''

"It's just flowers,'' Ben called out. He stood at the office door with a gigantic spray of ferns as Gordon was hanging up the phone.

"Right-hand corner of the far window," Gordon instructed.

"Who sent them?"

"Jeanne's mother. That tree by the door is from her father. Funny they didn't send something together."

Gordon smiled. "I think I understand why they didn't."

Someone was banging on the door. Ben couldn't see through the fern he was carrying, and Gordon had to wait for Ben to clear the aisle. "Just a minute," Gordon shouted.

"Liquor Store!" The delivery man yelled.

"Who ordered liquor?" Gordon wondered aloud.

The driver handed him a delivery order and, at a glance, Gordon saw that it came from Alan Mason. "He sent a whole case?" Gordon asked, watching the man lift one from the rear of his truck.

"Look again, buddy," the man said.

Gordon studied the order more closely. "Five cases champagne, 200 champagne shells," it said.

Another load of flowers arrived, and among them was a pot plant with a good-luck card from Barry Oster.

Ben frowned at the card. "Who the hell is Barry Oster?" he asked.

"Don't know. But he's not very imaginative," Gordon said, chuckling, indicating the foil-wrapped geranium. "Before the day is over, this place is going to look like a florist's! Want to give me a hand with the track lights? They're no longer focussed on my pictures; we've knocked them all out of whack.''

"Sure. Then I'd better hustle my ass down to the courthouse.'' He noticed that Gordon had suddenly grown pensive. "What's up?''

"Oh, nothing. I was just thinking. It occurred to me that all the toys Jeanne ordered for the gazebo are for girls.''

"I can't see Donna being so sexist,'' Ben said, laughing.

"I think . . . there is nothing there that might excite a boy like Kevin.''

* * *

Outside the courtroom film crews of various TV news teams chatted boisterously with other reporters. This was really none of their affair, after all.

Inside there was a subdued hum of conversations.

Jeanne easily made her way to the defense tables and sat with Philip and Donna. Donna smiled genuinely enough, but her lips were obviously dry, and her eyes were opened wide, unblinking.

"How do you feel?'' Jeanne asked her.

"I've been praying to God, Buddha, Zeus, the planets, and any passing aliens in UFO's. I'm petrified, but otherwise I'm fine.''

Philip smiled. "She did very well on the stand. We have a fair chance, I think. And even if we lose this one, I've got a few cards up my sleeve for an appeal. How are things at the shop?"

"Gordon and Ben are puttering around down there, getting things ready."

"Ben's there?" Donna asked, a grin turning up the corners of her mouth.

"They just accepted our shipment of fifty Tiffany lamp shades."

"Our what?!"

"I found them in Chicago. Wait till you see them! They'll make us famous—until we run out of them."

The judge approached the bench; the clerk banged a gavel.

The sound made Donna jump, as if she'd heard a gunshot.

"Court attention. All rise," said the bailiff.

The jury filed in somberly and stood at their places in the jury box.

"Have you reached a verdict?" the judge asked the foreman, an intense young woman who looked almost as haggard as Donna.

"We have, your honor," she said.

"And was your verdict a unanimous one?"

"Yes, your honor."

"What is your verdict?"

She read from a slip of paper: "We find the defendants Richard Palermo, William Pierce, Jennifer Hammond, Dawn Cartrand, and Elmo Clifford guilty as charged." She took a deep breath and continued, "We find James Hathaway, Donna Andersen, and Martha Dandreau not guilty."

Jeanne could feel relief down to her very toes; she felt almost like cheering along with the others, but she wasn't the type. She saw an odd stillness come over Donna, who was looking across at the other defendants, particularly at the bowed figure of Jenni Hammond, whose shoulders sank lower with each convulsive sob of her body.

Donna watched steely-eyed while the verdicts were being handed down. She heard that Jennifer Hammond faced a term of ten years in prison. Donna did not break her angry stare until court was adjourned.

"Let's get the fuck out of here," she said to Jeanne.

Five microphones were suddenly thrust under Donna's nose.

"Congratulations, Miss Andersen," said the local CBS reporter. "Do you consider the verdicts fair?"

"No," said Donna bluntly. "If Jenni Hammond had had my lawyer, she'd be free as a bird. She's no more guilty than I am."

The girl from Eyewitness News asked, "You agree with the judgement against Palermo?"

"He was guilty as charged," Donna said, "but he's still a victim of unjust laws."

"Are you going ahead with plans to open your shop?" asked the NBC man.

Donna brightened instantly. "Certainly!"

Eyewitness News asked, "When will you open?"

"I'm so glad you asked!" Donna beamed. "Tonight! We'll be open from seven till midnight, and the whole city is invited!"

The ABC woman asked the obligatory silly

question: "How do you feel now that it's all over, Donna?"

"Actually," she said confidentially, "I'm dying to go to the bathroom."

There was a hearty laugh from nearby, and Ben Sully rescued Donna and pulled her into his arms. The cameras kept running, and someone asked Ben, "Aren't you the police detective who arrested Miss Andersen in the first place?"

"Yep," he said, leading Donna away.

* * *

Gordon and Ben were inside the shop chilling champagne in galvanized tubs of ice. Several cameramen, a handful of individuals who had "reporter" written all over them, and a fast-gathering crowd waited on the sidewalk. Jeanne and Donna had been sent home from the courthouse and were instructed to arrive at seven on the dot and open the shop from the outside.

Gordon had brought a cassette deck and enough tapes to last several hours. Lush violin music swirled through the romantically illuminated shop. Tiny lights outlined the gazebo that Gordon and Ben had built, which now housed an array of exotic dolls and toys. Gordon's art work seemed to be glowing just from the sunlight drawn or painted into them. Flecks of gold, green, and violet splattered from the row of Tiffany shades which Gordon had managed not only to display but to light from within.

"That's quite a mob out there," Ben commented.

"Why don't you make me an honorary detective for the night? Teach me how to spot a shoplifter," Gordon suggested.

"Who'll serve the champagne?"

"He will," Gordon said, indicating Alan Mason, who had just arrived at the front door with Margaret Carlson. The famous actress had acted as a trigger, causing all the reporters and cameramen to move at once.

Gordon opened the door to let only Alan and Margaret enter.

A few minutes later Jeanne's parents knocked gently on the window and were admitted. Another middle-aged couple Ben recognized as Donna's parents arrived and were sneaked in shortly thereafter.

Jeanne and Donna stepped out of a taxi and stood across the street gaping at the crowd. They looked fresh and beautiful in their new outfits bought for the occasion—diaphanous silky blouses and chic dress slacks. They looked different but complementary.

"It sure pays to advertise," Donna mumbled, astounded at the mob. "Just think of how many we'd have gotten if I'd been convicted!"

Jeanne felt giddy with excitement. She looked across the snow-covered street, which sparkled under the streetlights, to her future, a life she was eager to begin living.

"Come on," she said, taking Donna's arm. "Let's go unlock the door!'